1114conspiracy
64,300 words/4/15/15

Conspiracy!

Hazards of an Author's Book Tour

A mystery by

Harley L. Sachs

Harley L. Sachs

ISBN-10- 193938110x

ISBN 13- 978-1-939381-10-1

Author's Note:
Originally published by Electric Umbrella in 2002 which went defunct, *Conspiracy!* was later re-released in 2009 by Zumaya Publications. This is the fourth edition.

Acknowledgements:
Thanks to Debi deSantis for the use of her original cover art.

Books by Harley L. Sachs:

Novels

Queer Company
Never Trust a Talking Horse
The Gold Chromosome
Murder by Mail (Scratch—out!)!
Ben Zakkai's Coffin
The Search for Jesse Bram
The Mystery Club Solves a Murder
The Mystery Club and the Dead Doctor
The Mystery Club and the Hidden Witness
The Mystery Club and the Serial Widow
Conspiracy!
Murder in the Keweenaw
The Lollipop Murder
Betrayal
Retribution
Burnt Out
White Slave
Sam in Love
StopRape.com
The Accidental Courier

Collections of short fiction

Ahoy! Quarterdeck! (Irma Quarterdeck Reports)
Anna-Lena's Troll and other stories
Threads of the Covenant: The Jews of Red Jacket
Misplaced Persons

Non-Fiction

Freelance Non-Fiction Articles
The Misadventures of Cpl. Sachs
The 1957 Sachs Arctic Expedition
From Tent to Castle: Memoir of a Year-Long Honeymoon
IS
Chilly-Chilly BANG! How We Freelanced Through Europe's Coldest
    Winter in a VW with a Kid
Essays and Columns: 1992-2011
The Writing Life

Cartoons

Hunting the Mail Buoy and other hazards to navigation

Prologue: Portland

Jake Friedman didn't believe in ghosts or clairvoyance, but he did have foreboding. When he opened the office door and switched on the light he felt a presence in the room that made him pause. There was no one there. Everything appeared to be the way he had left it: recycled metal desk and office chair, garage sale fax machine. Only the filing cabinet and the computer monitor were new. What could be the cause of his uneasiness?

Smoke, Jake decided. Someone had been smoking. He told himself it might have been the janitor, except there was no janitor, and Jake was the only one who had keys to the new lock.

If someone had picked the lock and let themselves in, they'd be disappointed. The computer monitor was just a screen he plugged into the laptop he carried with him. There was nothing in the filing cabinet but some correspondence, stock contracts, and authors' manuscripts. Maybe some disgruntled author with second thoughts had somehow gotten in to search for her manuscript. Who could do that?

There was no telling. The slush box behind the desk was full of unsolicited and unread manuscripts, a pile that grew faster than he could chip away at them. The world was full of authors and they were all determined to impose their attempts on him.

Authors could be weird. They could mail in a bundle of yellow pages typed single spaced in a godawful italic face, swear in the cover letter that the story was all true, and demand an immediate contract for a million bucks. Jake had seen more than enough of those kooks when he worked at the Meridian Agency in New York. Now, thank God, he had made the leap, put the whole continent between him and Sol Meredith at Meridian to set up his own agency in the Pacific Northwest.

Sol had been a con artist who had found it easier to extract fees from authors than to actually place their work with a publisher. Sol's ads in the writers' magazines had lured wannabe authors so he could collect reading fees, consultation fees, editing fees, and charges for spurious expenses. Occasionally Sol had actually placed a book, but none had ever earned back the advance on royalties.

Meridian was a racket and working for Sol was degrading. Jake had needed his own space, and not have anyone tell him that he had to read that single spaced italic junk because the alleged author could pay the reading fee. That was why he got out.

His agency was legit. His own name in gold letters was on the door. He decided himself what books had hope of publication, even though it was a struggle. Mergers and conglomerates in the mega entertainment industry had turned what had been a stable business into quicksand. Relationships developed with editors over years of lunches in Manhattan evaporated overnight when the accountants' computers ferreted out the editors whose choices had not reaped the high return demanded by greed. There was no tenure for editors.

Considering market volatility, Jake's hit with the Godot book, Conspiracy! had been a coup. The agent's cut of the hefty advance from Nile publishing had put him in the black. It also made it possible to move the business out of his home. His house was a worn out duplex off Everett Avenue, what the real estate agents coyly called a fixer-upper, a euphemism for gut the place and rebuild from the inside out. You couldn't meet an author in all that plaster dust. The plan was that once the other half was fixed and rented it would pay the mortgage.

Moving into a real office on the third floor of a run down building in the Pearl District with its galleries and studios was an improvement over having to rendezvous with authors at a table at Starbucks. Thank you co-authors Harold Stevenson, Tom Godot, Nile publishing, and the luck of seeing Conspiracy! make the best seller list.

Jake went to the one window in the office that wasn't painted shut and threw it open. Some fresh air would get rid of that mysterious smell of tobacco smoke, wherever it had come from.

1. Minneapolis

Someone was hammering on his head. The light was too bright. Tom Godot turned painfully in the bed and tried to open his eyes. What time was it? Where was he? He put his feet on the floor and tried to sit up. It was a hotel room. Before he had opened his eyes he had a fantasy that he was waking up beside that redheaded, braless assistant manager at the book store in Madison, Wisconsin. Dreams of glory.

He tried to focus. He was not in Madison, Wisconsin or Rochester, Minnesota with its audience of medicos and the relatives of patients who bought books and read while awaiting the final verdict on the latest biopsies.

Minneapolis. If this is Thursday I must be in Minneapolis. If it's... oh, shit! nine o'clock, I'm supposed to be at Minnesota Public Radio's studio for an interview. Tonight's reading would be at the Mystery Lover's book store in Saint Paul.

Normally he would be in San Jose in his cubicle editing technical documentation for MOM. Now, thanks to a series of events he could never had predicted he was three weeks into a book tour as co-author of a hit. Except for the many months of work that had gone into the collaboration, it was like winning the Publishers Clearing House sweepstakes.

It was good fortune Tom Godot sometimes felt guilty about. He had given up aspirations for being a writer of anything but mundane manuals. His luck in placing a couple of short stories as an undergraduate he had to dismiss as the machinations of his writing instructor, Professor Wilensky.

Those abortive dreams of glory had faded pretty quickly after graduation as he settled into the mundane repetitious work of editing bad writing on a LAN, a local area network of MOM writers, editors, and programmers.

Originally Machino Office Machines, the company was later renamed MOM when it went into specialized computer chips and micro circuits for military hardware. Instead of duplicating machines anyone could buy, MOM was linked to the government and everyone needed a security clearance. The confinement behind secure doors and surveillance cameras had made Tom Godot uncomfortable. He felt like a prisoner at MOM. It wasn't Big Brother, but Big Momma watching you.

Bored with life in a cubicle and stressed by the pressure of editing three pages a minute, Tom was thinking of quitting when Ivar Hansen, the founder of MOM, invited him to ghost write a family memoir.

The ghost writing job of the Hansen family memoir was a welcome escape from the stifling demands of editing. It also afforded him some status, akin to being Ivar Hansen's personal secretary. Instead of a mere cipher, he had acquired importance: authorized by Ivar Hansen to probe into family history.

He had been freed from his cubicle and began with a long talk ("Hold all my calls, Sally") with Ivar Hansen.

Ivar Hansen was a tall, energetic man with a shock of unruly blonde hair that was always falling into his eyes. He had acquired a mannerism of pushing his hair out of his face, but kept it long. Even if he was a Californian, at fifty, Hansen was too old to tie his hair into a pony tail. That might have been acceptable in southern California, but this was San Jose, not LA or even San Francisco.

Tom soon learned that though Ivar Hansen might come to work in an old sweat shirt he kept a business suit and sport jacket in his office closet for the appropriate occasion.

Tom started with dictated notes, but Hansen wanted the whole family in his memoir. He had a brother and a sister. The brother, Jon Hansen, was married, the sister, Kirsten Streicher, divorced. There were several nieces and one nephew. Researching the memoir required interviews with members of the family, some travel at company expense, even a few family dinners. Tom had almost been treated as a member of the Hansen clan.

Tom was not part of such an extended family. He was an only child and his father had taken early retirement to be what was called a full timer, a gypsy in an RV who roamed the national parks and had mail forwarded from an address in Texas where it was cheap to register recreation vehicles.

Tom seldom heard from his own family. Adopting the Hansens, even as their mere chronicler, made him feel at home more than he did with his own absentee parents. Certainly he knew more about the Hansens than some of their own relatives. He had been privy to intimate secrets that had to be left out of the official memoir.

Like any dynasty, the Hansens had their family intrigues and scandals. Ivar Hansen's father had been in the OSS during World War II. Ivar's mother had been in the French resistance. They had never been permitted to tell their war stories. Ivar Hansen had inherited his parents' penchant for things clandestine. He liked schemes and his business deals hadn't been strictly kosher.

One family intrigue Tom stumbled on was a falling out with Hansen's ex-brother-in-law. If every family had a black sheep, Erik Streicher was one of them-- if Ivar Hansen's version could be believed. Other family members had a different point of view, but whatever had caused the rift, whether it was about Streicher's suitability to marry Hansen's sister Kirsten or Streicher's brief period of employment at MOM, Tom couldn't find out. Just the mention of Erik Streicher could cut short an otherwise pleasant interview. He was left out of the memoir entirely.

Tom did know there was some connection between the shunned Erik Streicher and Ivar's favorite niece, Sylvia Hansen, but he didn't know what.

Interviewing Ivar Hansen's niece Sylvia was a definite fringe benefit. Sylvia was a petite blonde who would need to wear heels to reach five foot five if she wore them. Her taste ran to Sorrel hiking boots. Sylvia was a grad student in the MBA program at the University of California.

She shared an apartment with another grad student. Tom had met the roommate and was surprised that short, shy Sylvia was friends with an outspoken, tall, beefy brunette who smoked little cigars and swore.

Sylvia's Uncle Ivar had promised her a job when she graduated. Sylvia's rock climbing hobby explained her surprising strength for someone so small.

Tom had used the memoir job as an excuse to interview Sylvia several times before his boss's book was printed. She knew that Tom already had enough information about her for his memoir and that "interview" was an excuse to get to know her better.

Sylvia was an enigma. On the one hand she was diminutive and fragile; on the other she climbed cliffs. He wondered what drove her to take such risks. Tom couldn't imagine himself climbing a cliff or a mountain. Climbing a high ladder gave him the willies. As a kid he had once gotten stuck on the roof when he went up to rescue his kite. The fire department had to be called to get him down. When he asked Sylvia why she climbed, she said it gave her confidence. "Confidence?" What vulnerability was she trying to overcome, to compensate for by scaling cliffs? She wouldn't-- or couldn't say. She liked the challenge, she said. Climbing helped her overcome her fears. She put on a front that said she had succeeded, but Tom sensed that it was a facade, that she was vulnerable. Sensing that made him want to protect her.

One evening when Tom brought her home after a dinner at the Olive Garden, parked in front of her apartment building, Sylvia acted strangely. When he put his arm around her and kissed her she froze, started trembling all over. "Sylvia, what's the matter?"

She couldn't answer. He sat there, holding her gently, trying to calm her down. "It's all right, Sylvia. It's all right." He helped her out of the car and led her to the front door. By then she had recovered, apologized, and as if to repay him for his kindness, kissed him full on the mouth before rushing inside.

The next day he had sent her flowers. She phoned him at the office and agreed to another date. There was no further necessity to pretend it was an interview for Uncle Ivar's memoir. Tom couldn't understand what had upset her, but he wanted to know her better. Was it more than curiosity? Why did he care about her so much?

Because the memoir was family business, the manuscript had been headquartered at the MOM central computers where Ivar Hansen could log on and lurk while the writing proceeded. Tom never knew how close a watch his boss kept on the progress of the memoir, but from time to time he'd see a comment or get a call of encouragement or a caution to leave something out.

Once the memoir was complete, however, he was back in his cubicle, suffering a combination of boredom and stress, boredom at the repetitive nature of the job, stress at the pace he had to maintain. It was a comedown from the heady atmosphere and prestige he had experienced while moving amidst the Hansen family. He was about to quit the editing job when he got another surprise opportunity.

Ivar Hansen not only paid Tom Godot generously for writing the family memoir, but talked him up among his influential friends and business contacts. Then one day Tom got e-mail from someone called Harold Stevenson. Stevenson had a book idea and a draft manuscript that needed revision. You never knew where a writing assignment could lead. That was how Tom Godot found himself the co-author of Conspiracy!

Tom had never met his co-author. All he knew was that Stevenson sometimes contradicted himself in the comments he would add to the text as they worked on it. He had mood swings. It was almost as if Stevenson had two personalities, or was really two people working under the same name. Who was Stevenson? Tom imagined he was some shady friend of Ivar Hansen who had inside information but was using the book as a mechanism to avoid the red tape of a security clearance.

Like most of the workers at MOM, Tom and Harold Stevenson communicated by computer. Used to the arrangement with the Hansen family memoir, Tom worked through MOM's server. The Grand Poobah in charge of the system set up a firewall so Stevenson had a password to access the novel manuscript, but not get beyond it into the classified areas of the plant.

Unlike the memoir, however, Tom had to do the writing on his own time. When he logged on at six in the morning, Stevenson would already be at work. Either he was also an early riser, or was in another time zone. If Stevenson was in New York it was already nine A.M.

They had spoken on the phone twice. He didn't have Stevenson's phone number, only an e-mail address, HLSteven@Falcon.com. The web server called Falcon could be in Washington, New York, Europe or on the moon. It was a strange way to write a book.

There were other strange ways to write books. Professor Wilensky had once told his creative writing class about the best seller, Naked Came the Stranger, a pot boiler cooked up by an agent and his wife who had done the plot outline and farmed out each of the twenty four chapters to free lance writers. Each thought he was competing for the job of ghost writing the whole book only to learn that it was a spoof and each contributor was to share in the royalties. Sheer hype had done the rest. Naked Came the Stranger had exposed some of the shenanigans of the publishing world.

Conspiracy! had only Stevenson and Godot on the title page, not twenty-four ghost writers. Half of the author's royalty for a best seller was a helluva lot better than a flat fee for ghost writing a family memoir, even if he did have to do all the readings and signings himself. Stevenson wouldn't take part in the book tour.

Being a celebrity of sorts was a role Tom was not used to. He admitted to himself that the success of the book was a fluke. As a writer he was nothing special, nor was Stevenson with that wooden, technical prose. To Tom Godot the machinations of the publishing world were unknown territory. Publicity worked. Enough ballyhoo and people bought books.

That was how he found himself in Minneapolis with a hangover. There was just so much wine and cheese you could take. Switching to bourbon had been a bad idea. How was he going to get through that radio interview?

Nine o'clock already. Where was that map of the Twin Cities? He'd call the MPR studio and tell them he had taken the wrong exit off the freeway and was miles out of his way. At least for radio he didn't have to dress up. This was the Midwest, not New York.

Tom Godot steeled himself for the shock and forced his head under the cold shower, fumbled with the little bar of hotel soap, rinsed and leaped out again. The cold water helped even though he nearly choked on his scrotum. He rubbed down hard with the bath towel and looked in the mirror.

Tom needed a haircut. His black hair wanted to stand up straight like the coxcomb on an English punk kid in chains and leather. His dark eyes looked sunken into his head like an apparition. God, he looked awful. At thirty he already had the beginnings of a paunch, a harbinger of what middle age would bring if he didn't cut out the telephone ordered pizzas delivered to motel rooms. In spite of the grueling schedule of the book tour he was putting on weight. His normally gaunt face was filling out, and his heavy beard did not conceal an unhealthy pallor.

The book tour had disrupted the normal patterns of his life. In San Jose when he wasn't working on the book he would jog before breakfast To do that on the road he would have to wake up a lot earlier than nine o'clock.

The schedule in the Twin Cities made it possible for him to stay two nights. Tom made sure he had several copies of his press kit in his briefcase along with a copy of Conspiracy! For a change he didn't have to pack up everything before looking for his Budget rental car in the lot. It was a white Dodge Neon.

There was no time for breakfast, not even an egg Macmuffin at a drive through. Besides the press kit and a copy of the book his briefcase had a stash of herbal tea bags. If he was lucky someone at MPR would give him a cup of hot water and a donut.

2. Minnesota Public Radio

Minnesota Public Radio was in a low, brick building on the St. Paul side of the Mississippi not far from the AMTRAK station in a non-descript neighborhood. Tom waited by the receptionist's desk until a tall, fading blonde in her forties came out to escort him to the studio.

She had passed that brief couple of years when she would have been stunning. She wore a beige blouse that looked like silk and no jewelry, not even a ring. Her nails on the hand she extended in greeting were neatly trimmed, the fingers hard and bony, the grip perfunctory. "Tom Godot," she said with a forced smile. "I'm Inge Olsen. Sorry you got lost. We'll go right into the studio if that's all right."

"Sure." Tom handed her his press kit. "My editor prepared some typical questions in case you haven't already got some. Not everyone has time to read the book."

Inge Olsen shrugged. "We interview a lot of authors but I've skimmed yours. One soon learns how to pick out the key passages. In here, please." She led him into a cramped studio with a big sound proof window across one wall, stacks of tape decks everywhere, two worn swivel chairs, and a pair of microphones. "Would you like some coffee?"

Tom took an herbal tea bag out of his briefcase and held it up. "Could I drown this?"

Inge Olsen smiled. "Sure." She slipped out the door and came back a minute or two later with a Styrofoam cup of scalding water. Her own mug had the MPR logo, coffee stains that indicated it was rinsed, not washed, and a stuck on label, "Olsen."

"Sorry I can't offer you a Danish to go with that, but if you eat something sweet it tends to muddy your voice for the recording."

He'd have to find some breakfast later. That's what he got for sleeping late and waking up with a hangover.

While Tom's tea steeped she put on headphones, did a voice level check, studied his list of suggested questions, put a cassette in the recorder and they were off.

"I have here in the studio today Mr. Tom Godot, co-author of the best seller, Conspiracy! Tom, I've read Conspiracy! and was frankly disturbed by it. It seems to me that some terrorist groups could use your book as a blueprint. Don't you feel that writing a book like that is unethical?"

The question was not on Tom's list. "I, well, ah... no. I see the book as a warning to the public, not a blueprint. If someone wants to make bombs, for instance, they can find that out on the internet."

"Yes, but what you and Harold Stevenson describe is far more disruptive than bombing a building. You make Timothy McVeigh look like prankster with a couple of fire crackers. Won't you feel responsible if someone tries what you describe in your book?"

"We don't tell anyone they should actually carry out what the book describes."

"Where did you get the idea?"

Tom took a deep breath. This was more familiar ground. "Harold Stevenson is the expert. If someone knowledgeable had the first draft of the book they might take what Stevenson provided and try to use the information for something horrendous. I pointed that out, and what finally appears in the story is fictionalized. It can't work as published. You don't have to worry about that." Tom tried to sip his tea and burned his mouth.

"Tell me about the mysterious Harold Stevenson."

Tom realized he had moved away from the microphone and reached up to adjust it, but Inge Olsen quickly grabbed his hand and shook her head. Embarrassed, he moved back. Touching a live mike would make a sound she would have to edit out or start over.

"I've never met him."

"Really? Never met your co-author? That explains why your picture is on the dust jacket but the space for his is just a blank box."

"I think the publisher is trying to make the book more enticing, an advertising trick."

"But the substance of your book, Conspiracy! is no trick."

"Oh, no."

She was making it sound like he was a fake, that his book was a publicity stunt. Tom hadn't expected a hostile interviewer. Now he dreaded the result of the broadcast.

Inge Olsen shifted her attention to the note he had added to the interview questions. "Tom Godot, co-author of Conspiracy! will be reading and signing books in St. Paul this evening at the Mystery Lovers' Book Shop."

"At seven o'clock," Tom interrupted.

"Yes," Olsen said. Odd how her face could show irritation but her radio voice was unchanged.

"Refreshments will be served," Tom added.

"I must be sure to come and see you in action." Inge Olsen switched off the recorder.

The tea was still too hot to drink. All that hassle for no more than three minutes on the air.

"When will this be broadcast?" Tom asked.

"After the noon news." Inge Olsen was sticking a label on the cassette.

"Thanks for the opportunity to be on your show," Tom said. He hoped she wouldn't edit out his reference to refreshments. People were like dogs; they had to be rewarded with treats.

"So what do you do until seven o'clock?" Inge Olsen asked as she led him out of the studio.

"For starters I'm going to find myself some breakfast. Then I'll check in at the book store. The usual thing."

"Good luck," Inge Olsen said, but she had turned her back to walk away before he said good-bye.

3. Mystery Lovers'

At 6:30 when Tom returned to Mystery Lovers' book store a few people had already gathered, reserving their places on the gray metal folding chairs set up in the aisle near the front of the store. There was room for hardly more than twenty chairs. Latecomers would have to stand.

Better to have too few chairs and a standing room crowd than too many in case nobody showed up. You never knew. In Oshkosh, Wisconsin Tom had done his reading for an audience of one, a drunk who had wandered in out of the rain and fallen asleep.

The store manager, a narrow chested, broad bottomed Lotte Schmidt, had set a tray of cubed cheddar and quartered bagels on the crowded counter. She did have wine, a couple of bottles of what Tom called tanker truck red because it was shipped from the wineries in tanker trucks and bottled like lineament. His head still had a residue of the hangover. This time he would pass on the wine.

The Mystery Lovers' was a small but successful independent near the science museum in downtown St. Paul. If he hadn't already done several readings in such specialty shops Tom would have been surprised at the number of mysteries on the market. Considering the competition it was a miracle that Conspiracy! had risen above the pack onto the best seller list. Of course it wasn't a miracle. It was lots of advertising by the aggressive marketers at Nile publishing.

"Is the microphone OK for you?" Lotte Schmid's clerk asked.

In accordance with name tag protocol which didn't reveal last names the clerks was called Trish. She was about eighteen with dyed, short black hair and eye makeup in the now out of fashion drug addict style. She wore a black tank top that showed the white straps of her bra. Besides having her ears pierced for three earrings she had her nose pierced as well. A tattoo of some sort of insect peeped out from under the tank top on her left breast. Tom wondered what the rest of it looked like.

"It's OK, Trish. Is that short for Patricia?"

"No. My name is Trish." The voice was more pleasant than her appearance suggested.

Tom prepared for his performance. How many of these had he done? He hardly needed notes. He put his briefcase behind the battered lectern and set his copy of the book on top. He would decide which passage to read when he saw the audience.

"I think your book is wonderful," Trish gushed.

"Thanks."

"I'm going to be a writer myself some day."

"Really. What have you written?"

"I had some poems published in our high school paper."

Tom almost groaned. Another one. The world was full of people who wanted to be novelists or poets or screen writers but never would be because they lacked the essential ingredient: they only thought about writing. They didn't actually apply butt to chair and pen to paper.

"I'd like to show you some of my stuff, if you'd like, after..."

Was this kid coming on to him? She was hardly more than jail bait. "I have to get back to Minneapolis tonight."

He was afraid she might say she lived in Minneapolis and ask where he was staying, but he was rescued by Lotte Schmidt. It was time. Tom stood quietly aside and waited for her to do the introduction.

Lotte Schmidt wiped the palms of her hands on her hips and picked up Tom's copy of his book. She turned it over and improvised her introduction from the brief bio on the dust jacket. Holding it up for the audience to see she commented, "Tom Godot is the co-author of Conspiracy! along with Harold Stevenson who you can see by his picture is invisible. Now that's a mystery in itself. Here's Tom Godot."

A decent crowd had gathered. Tom decided to read from a passage that was entirely his, not one that Stevenson had originated and Tom had worked over several times. Stevenson's style was wooden and pedantic, obviously not a person with an ear for the rhythms of language. This was a passage Tom had performed many times. He had even begun to add a little body English and gestures to make it more of a one man show than a dull reading.

As he neared the end of the passage he noticed that someone was standing at the back with a camcorder. It hid the face of the photographer. Who could that be? Why would anyone want to record him? Should he insist that there be no photographs or videos of his reading? He had been so distracted by Trish of the pierced nose and tittie tattoo that Tom had forgotten to mention a ban on photography.

"If you have any questions, I'd be glad to answer," Tom said as he finished the passage.

The camera person had put down the camcorder. It was a man, a burly guy with a receding hairline, beefy shoulders and wearing a faded denim jacket. What would he want with a tape of this? Some people were weird.

A red haired, good looking woman in the third row had her hand up. "What inspired you to write your book?"

Tom hesitated. He had been asked that before and each time he tried to invent a plausible answer. "Communication has always intrigued me. All human problems except disease are communication problems. I felt that terrorists like the ones who tried to blow up the world trade center or the federal building in Oklahoma City were way off base. Finding a way to disrupt communications would be a better way."

"A better way?" The red haired woman was being sarcastic. "A better way to disrupt society?"

"You could say that."

Now it was the man with the cam corder who had a question. "Do you see yourself as a communications terrorist, Mr. Godot?"

"Oh, no, certainly not."

"But your book could be a manual for terrorists."

Tom shook his head. Had the man heard the MPR interview with Inge Olsen? "No. Certainly not. In fact, I had to persuade Harold Stevenson to change the plotters' methods so nobody could use them as described."

Trish had joined the audience. "Is Mr. Stevenson a terrorist?"

Tom smiled. "If he is, I should think he wouldn't want to expose himself or his plans. Not to the general reading public."

The red haired woman didn't raise her hand this time. "But his picture's not on the cover. Why not?"

Tom had to field this question before. He had decided to create a persona for Harold Stevenson just to satisfy people's curiosity. "He's shy about his looks. He can't do a reading himself because he has a speech impediment." It was a lie, of course. The two times Tom had actually spoken to Harold Stevenson there was no hint of a stammer. Stevenson, like his writing style, tended to simple sentences broken by long pauses as if everything he said had to first be approved by a committee. Whoever Tom had spoken with had been educated, vaguely Eastern, probably Ivy League. If he was willing to make a public appearance, Stevenson was more qualified than Tom was. It was odd, but Nile publishing had specified in the book deal that Tom Godot alone would do the tour. Maybe Stevenson was confined to his house by a disease. He might add that to his explanation the next time someone asked.

Lotte Schmidt invited people to have their books signed and Tom was occupied for a few minutes at the lectern. Seven people wanted signatures, and he was careful to get the spellings of the names correct. He used a marking pen that didn't bleed through the title page but stood out. Seven copies. What was his half of the royalty for those, minus the ten percent for Jake Friedman in Portland? Hardly enough to justify the tab for the hotel room and the rental car. But Mystery Lovers' had sold fifty copies of the book, and there was a nice stack prominently displayed near the entrance. Certainly they were doing better than that place in Wisconsin.

When Tom got to the cheese and bagel quarters the red haired woman caught him.

"I'm interested in the writing process," she explained. She was good looking with a generous mouth and a hungry look. "How many drafts did you go through before the final camera ready copy?"

Tom waited until he had swallowed the bagel bit. His mouth was dry. Didn't they have any diet soda? "That's hard to say. We work on a computer network, and there are so many interim changes that it's hard to distinguish one draft from another. The process is too fluid."

"But you must print out hard copies sometimes. There must be quite a stack."

"Not really," Tom said. "The interim versions are on the computer, so there's no need to keep hard copies. When we got to the camera ready and proof stage I shredded the earlier hard copies. You can't imagine how small my work space is, no room for a pile of draft manuscripts."

"I would like to compare those drafts, as a study in composition theory," the red haired woman said.

"You must be a professor of English comp or creative writing. They're not available." She reminded Tom of one of his college English teachers, earnest and wrapped up in process more than content. "Would you like me to sign a copy of *Conspiracy!*?"

"I didn't bring my copy with me," she admitted. "I had it all ready before I left home and forgot."

"Too bad." Tom turned away only to bump into Trish, the tattooed lady.

"You still want to see my poems? I've got them at my place."

"No, really," Tom said. "It's been a long day and I have to be on the road again tomorrow."

"Where do you go next?"

"St. Cloud, then west. I'm working my way across the country for Nile Publishing Company."

"It sounds so exciting," she said. "I wish I had a life like that."

Tom shook his head. He was feeling like a book peddler. Instead of a bundle of copies on his shoulder he had his briefcase and a box in the trunk. Thank God he wasn't on foot. "One motel room begins to look like all the others. You wouldn't like it."

"And then all those people asking you dumb questions."

"They're not all dumb," Tom said in defense of his public. "Sometimes people ask things that make you wonder."

Like why this interest in his early drafts?

4. A Call to Jake Friedman

It was ten o'clock when Tom Godot got back to his room at the Minneapolis Marriot. Though the New York office was closed, he would work up his daily report to Nile Publishing and fax it to them. Their machine never slept. Jake Friedman did, but he was in Portland. It was only eight o'clock on the west coast.

Tom dialed the number and while it rang noticed the condition of his hotel room. The maid service at the Marriot in Minneapolis was better than Tom Godot expected. Someone who was being very tidy had hung up his shirt on a hanger and put the clothes he had strewn on the unused bed into a drawer. Even the papers he had left on the night stand had been neatly stacked. It was a wasted effort. He'd be repacking in the morning for the drive to St. Cloud.

For a change Jake Friedman and not his machine answered the phone. "Yes?"

"Hi. Tom Godot in Minneapolis. I just got back from a reading at the Mystery Lovers' book store."

"How'd it go?"

"The usual. Some guy videotaped my gig. Do we have a policy on that?"

Friedman laughed. "If you were a rock star or doing a one man stage show, taping would be forbidden, but nobody's going to pirate copies of your performance."

"I know that," Tom admitted. "It made me uncomfortable."

Jake Friedman spent too much time on the phones as it was, and the tone of his voice was flat. It was too late to be humoring authors, even if the author was Tom Godot. "Is that it?"

"No. I was curious. Which copy of the manuscript do you have at your office?"

"Jeeze. I don't remember. I have the copy you and Stevenson said was ready for submission. That's the one we used for the photocopies."

"Yes, but that was before Stevenson had second thoughts. We revised it before the final copy went to Nile. Then they said the manuscript was at least a hundred pages too long."

"So? Do you need it?"

"I don't, but a woman tonight showed a strange interest in early drafts."

"Why bother? The book is in print now. You're not Coleridge or Shakespeare. Conspiracy! ain't English literature. Nobody's going to want a blow by blow grad school analysis of the development of the characters and plot line. You're not getting delusions of grandeur, are you Tom?"

Tom appreciated the dig. "Not after doing a reading to an audience of one drunk in Wisconsin. Do me a favor. Check on which draft you have in your file."

Friedman sighed audibly over the phone, "These authors."

"Thanks, Mike. Is it raining in Portland?"

When they got to the weather report it was clear all substance of a conversation was over. "Do ducks swim?" Friedman asked, but didn't wait for an answer. He hung up.

Besides a stash of herbal tea bags and a copy of the book, Mike's commodious briefcase held his new laptop computer, his first purchase out of the advance on royalties. He plugged it in to keep the battery charged, then untangled the cord for the modem, found the phone jack in the wall behind the bed, plugged it in and got ready to prepare and fax his daily report to his editor, Mary McGann at Nile.

Mary McGann was insecure about her job. Nile had been bought up by a German communications conglomerate. She feared that the new German upper management would not treat women in publishing the way Nile had. She didn't trust the marketing people and was trying to micro manage the Conspiracy! account to at least stay abreast of the bean counters. Mid-fifties is a tough age to start looking for another job if the acquisition of Nile made her redundant. No wonder she kept a bottle of antacids in her commodious purse.

Tom had flown from his home in San Jose to New York and visited the Nile office in Manhattan for a power lunch with Mary McGann. Unlike the Californians he was used to, he saw at once that New Yorkers were a different breed. At MOM the engineers and tech writers seldom wore jackets or ties and blue jeans were accepted. McGann obviously spent a lot of money on clothes. Her coat could be worn like a cape and the cut of her business suit had flair. Tom realized it was a uniform. In Manhattan who you were was at least partly how you dressed.

Stevenson hadn't shown up for the lunch. Mary McGann considered it a command performance. She had her ways of getting even. Stevenson's no-show at lunch had been the reason why Tom's name was first on the title page. Though he didn't mind top billing, it made him cautious in his dealings with her. She expected performance and if she didn't get it, well...

Mary should be satisfied with his report of the St. Paul signing. Lotte Schmidt at the Mystery Lovers' book store had reordered the book and the radio broadcast at Minnesota Public Radio had provided more publicity, even though Inge Olsen hadn't been very friendly. Tom's report would be positive if not overwhelming.

Once the report was faxed Tom felt tired and empty. Maybe he should have taken Trish up on her offer to show her poems and maybe her tattoo. One night stands weren't his style, especially in the age of AIDS. He wasn't about to play Russian roulette with his dick. If he was going to shack up with anybody it would be with Sylvia Hansen. He imagined her small, tight, body, agile as a cat playing with a ball of string. But she was unapproachable, and besides, he was in Minneapolis and she was in California. Maybe later....

5. St. Cloud

Tom put breakfast on the bill, checked out of the Marriot and drove north to St. Cloud. Corn fields gave way to woods and lakes. Once you left the metropolitan Twin Cities, Minnesota was farm land, woods, and lakes with their accompanying bait shops promising huge muskies. By comparison to Minneapolis St. Cloud was a dreary place whose claims to fame seemed to be the penitentiary and a small college. Happily, he wasn't a tourist and it was only one night. The Super 8 in St. Cloud wasn't the Marriot, either. Nobody in this motel was going to hang up his shirts.

This time he was appearing at Barnes & Noble in a shopping mall at the edge of town. Mary McGann had set up the schedule for maximum exposure. Tom was supposed to sign books all afternoon, then do a reading in the evening.

According to his travel schedule the manager of the Barnes & Noble in St. Cloud was Kerstin Olofsdatter, a name he recognized as Icelandic. Unlike Tattooed Trish at the Mystery Lovers', he liked Kerstin at once. She had Nordic features, shoulder-length blonde hair, a high bosom, a direct look and a winning smile. If she made herself available, well....

Kerstin began with an apology, "I'm sorry to stick you at a card table all afternoon," and followed up with an invitation. "To make it up to you I'll buy dinner before the reading."

Better and better. Anticipation of dinner with Kerstin Olofsdatter kept him from being utterly bored as he sat at the table piled with copies of Conspiracy! while obese senior citizens and shoppers with baby strollers ignored him in search of bargains elsewhere. At twenty-five bucks a pop

28

Conspiracy! was out of their price range. He sold only five books.

One of the five buyers stood out from the rest. He was an intense man about fifty with short-cropped hair, a military cut, and a bright blue windbreaker worn over camouflage pants and combat boots. Clearly St. Cloud was not a center of high fashion. "I already read your book, Mr. Godot," the man said. "I'm buying this for a friend."

"Thank you," Tom said. "How would you like it inscribed?"

"For Rick. Things to come."

"Sounds ominous," Tom quipped and picked up his pen.

"Your book is the truth, Mr. Godot. There are plenty of people around here who consider it their bible."

Tom suppressed a shudder. "Sure you aren't confusing my book with the Turner Diaries?"

"I've read that," the man said. "Yours is better. You really know what you're talking about."

"My book is fiction, Mister, er..."

"But based on fact."

Tom hesitated. "The facts are my co-author's responsibility. My job is the fiction."

"Is Mr. Stevenson going to be at the reading tonight?"

"He's not able to travel," Tom said, reverting to his fictional persona for the man he'd never met.

"My name's Runner Preston," the man said. "I'll be at your reading tonight. Maybe we can talk after. Go out for a beer or something. My friends would like to meet you." Preston extracted a calling card from his wallet.

The card had the man's name in the center and across the top in block letters "The Freedom Constabulary" with a logo of crossed swords over a crucifix. The original phone number had been crossed out. There was no address.

Militia types gave Tom the creeps. He immediately searched for excuses for not joining this guy and his friends for a beer or anything else. A post-reading business conference with Kerstin Olofsdatter would probably suffice.

The dinner before the reading on her tab would give him an opportunity to reciprocate with a drink after. Then who knows? A bird in the hand....

6. Runner Preston

Since he told her Italian food was his favorite, Kerstin picked Romano's Restaurant near the shopping mall. Feeling his paunch Tom was dismayed at the size of his order of spaghetti and enormous meatballs. He'd pass on dessert. "Are there many Icelandic people in St. Cloud?"

"There are mostly Danes. St. Cloud University even has a branch in Denmark. Too bad you won't be in town long enough for me to show you around. There's more here than you think. You must get the impression that life on the road consists of hotel rooms and book stores."

"And fattening food," Tom added. He changed the subject. He showed her the visiting card Runner Preston had given him. "Ever hear of the Freedom Constabulary?"

Kerstin Olofsdatter wiped her mouth delicately with a napkin and studied the card. "It's not familiar. You should be warned that St. Cloud has more than its share of white racists and kooks. There was a branch of the Posse Comitatus here a few years back. Tax protesters. A few months ago we had a nasty case of vandalism. Someone painted swastikas on the local synagogue. You may have noticed there aren't many black faces in the mall."

"This guy Runner Preston wants me to meet some of his friends after the reading. If you'll accept my invitation to go out for a drink I'll be able to give him a good excuse."

Kerstin smiled. "You have an odd way of asking a girl for a date."

He hadn't had a date since he last saw Sylvia Hansen. Olofsdatter was also a blonde, but a different type. There was nothing vulnerable or fragile about Kerstin Olofsdatter. Comparing the two he identified one of Sylvia's qualities that he'd found elusive. Virginal. Sylvia had to be a virgin. That would explain her fear of intimacy. That wasn't the whole picture, but it had to be part of it. He wished he was with her so he could learn the rest.

He wasn't in California now and he was lonely. "You said yourself that my life is a sequence of motel rooms and bookstores. That's a pretty drab existence. A laptop isn't

31

much company even though I do have to use it for daily reports."

"That must be your security blanket," she said, not unkindly. "You never go anywhere without it."

"All my files for the trip are in it. Can't go lugging a pile of documents around. It's bad enough to carry a spare case of books in the trunk just in case a bookstore runs out."

Kerstin looked at her watch. "I'd better get back to the book store. If you're not going to finish that spaghetti, you can take back to the motel for breakfast."

"You've got to be kidding."

Barnes & Noble provided a big coffee pot and a plate of cookies.

Kerstin Olofsdatter was amused when Tom produced one of his tea bags and asked her to nuke a cup of water for him in the office microwave. While her clerk set things up Kerstin went over the Nile Publishing account and the sales of Conspiracy! "We get all our books through our own distributor," she explained. "Barnes & Noble is big enough to cut out the middle man."

"Yes, and even dictate prices to the publishers. My editor told me about the squeeze play the book store chains have put on."

"Does it affect your royalty?"

"I don't know. All the sales reports and payments stipulated in the contract go to Jake Friedman my agent. He takes his percentage off the top."

"Everyone takes care of their own. Now it's up to you to sell some books."

The chairs were set in a semi-circle around the Barnes & Noble lectern. It was such a small space that there was no need for a microphone. A few curious people gathered. As promised, there was Runner Preston in the second row. He had abandoned his camouflage pants and combat boots for a suit, but there was no mistaking that haircut and self-righteous look. He had two men with him. Both looked uncomfortable, like they might be embarrassed if someone knew they read books. Yet they were both holding copies of Conspiracy! Presumably they'd want them signed after the reading.

A woman in the back looked familiar. She resembled the red-haired woman who had asked all those questions in St. Paul, except this woman's hair was blonde and there was a lot of it. Could it be a wig? Or did the red haired lady have a sister in St. Cloud? Or was his imagination playing tricks? He had been on the road too long, Tom decided. The lonely life encouraged strange fantasies.

When Tom was introduced he opened with a joke about motel rooms and Gideon Bibles that wouldn't allow themselves to be in the same drawer as his book. Only one person laughed politely. St. Cloud was definitely not St. Paul. Were these what Garrison Keillor called the Norwegian bachelor farmers?

His book tour copy had bits of paper marking the various passages he might pick from, and tonight he chose one near the climax of the story when the hero was about to be confronted with the villain of the piece. Tom opened the book to it, looked up to get eye contact with the audience, then stopped.

There was a man at the back with a camcorder. Was it the same man who had been at the Mystery Lovers' in St. Paul? "Excuse me, but would you mind not taping this reading?" Tom asked. "If you're a reporter for a local station, you'll need permission of the store manager to record on the premises. Being on camera makes me nervous."

The man at the back shrugged in a pretense at apology. He took the camcorder away from his face, but held it steady against a book case. He might still be recording.

Who was he? Most of the audience wore casual clothing, except Runner Preston and his two uncomfortable companions in their ill-fitting suits. The man at the back had on a sport coat with a dress shirt, no tie.

There was no point in making an issue of it. Being hostile would only alienate the audience. He had already told one bad joke. Tom regained his composure and was soon back in his stride.

33

He felt he brought it off well, in spite of a bad beginning and the odd people in the audience. The questions were the usual ones, none this time about early drafts and what became of them. The woman with the big blonde hair asked a new one: "What's your next book, Mr. Godot? Is it a sequel? Another book about terrorists? Or are you working on something else?"

Tom relaxed, glad it was almost over. "Funny you should ask that. I'm tinkering with an idea about an author on a book tour and people who begin to follow him from place to place."

Someone laughed, thank you very much, but the man at the back with the camcorder was startled and turned away. Maybe it wasn't just Tom's imagination playing tricks.

The signing went well. Including the two friends of Preston, Tom sold eleven copies. Runner Preston was last in line.

"I'm sorry I can't accept your invitation, Mr. Preston," Tom said immediately. "I've got some business to do. My editor expects daily reports." He leaned forward in mock confidentiality. "If I don't make up something good she'll take away the company credit card." That was no joke.

Preston wasn't to be put off. "My organization is interested in a bulk order. If we buy several hundred copies of Conspiracy! can you give us a discount?"

"That's flattering, Mr. Preston. I refer you to Miss Olofsdatter the store manager. She might make you a deal. I'm just the co-author, not the publisher."

Preston wasn't satisfied, but he backed off.

Afraid Preston and his cronies might be hanging around the mall, Tom Godot prolonged his summary of the Nile account with Kerstin Olofsdatter. He let her do her job and he used the time before the store closed to prepare his daily report. Kerstin let him plug in his modem for the fax. He was now free for the rest of the evening and whatever it might bring.

Conspiracy

7. Wunderbar

Tom hung around while Miss Olofsdatter closed the book store and pulled down the steel grating that separated it from the rest of the mall. The place was deserted. The only other person in the emptiness was a maintenance man sweeping the floor. Dropping her keys into her handbag, Kerstin turned to Tom and smiled. "That's done. Now for that drink you promised."

"I don't know St. Cloud. What's a good place?"

"Tell you what. Leave your car here in the lot and I'll drive. We can talk in the car. I'll bring you back after."

"Why don't I just follow you?"

"Suit yourself."

She had driven him to dinner, so Tom knew where her car was parked. The vast lot was deserted except for a couple of cars and a big wheels pickup truck parked away from the lights. After some confusion he found his rental Neon, laid his ever-present briefcase on the front seat, and put the key in the ignition. Only after he'd buckled up, started the engine and turned on the headlights did he realize there was something under the windshield wiper. It looked like an advertising flyer, or so he thought. Irritated, Tom unbuckled, got out of the car, and lifted the wiper blade to remove it.

It wasn't a flyer. It was a note. "See you at the motel later," in pencil on a piece of paper torn from a small notebook. Who could that be? Not that Preston guy and his cronies, Tom hoped.

He looked around, but did not see anyone. Tom got back in the Neon and drove to where Kerstin was parked. She blinked her lights and he followed her into St. Cloud. There was little traffic at this hour, and it was not difficult for Tom to realize that while he was following Kerstin Olofsdatter, the big wheels pickup truck was following him.

The Wunderbar and Grill where Kerstin Olofsdatter pulled up was a supper place in mock Black Forest decor. Statues of German gnomes in lederhosen were chained to the entrance so pranksters couldn't carry them off. Inside, the ceiling was painted with quaint forest scenes. Tom half expected to see Snow White among the frolicking dwarves.

"This is the only place in St. Cloud with its own microbrewery," Kerstin explained when they had settled into a booth. "I thought you might enjoy the atmosphere. On the weekends the students from the college take it over but in the middle of the week it's pretty quiet."

The waitress wore an apron over a flouncy white skirt and a bonnet with built in blonde Brunhilda braids that didn't match her real hair. Tom ordered a round of the house brew.

"What do you make of this?" Tom asked, and showed Kerstin the note he found on the windshield.

"'See you at the motel after'? You have a secret admirer."

"I don't think so."

She gave him a direct look and quipped. "If you were planning to take me back to your motel room after drinks, I guess you'd have company." She made it sound more like a challenge than compliance.

"You're very direct," Tom said, feeling sheepish. He didn't feel comfortable with sex as a form of recreation. There had to be a relationship. What? Romance? Love? At the moment Sylvia Hansen was the only girl he felt drawn to.

"I haven't always lived in St. Cloud," Kerstin said.

"Hey, maybe in St. Cloud there's not much else to do but seduce visiting authors."

She laughed. "Visiting authors are rather thin on the ground here."

"I guess that makes me a rare commodity."

Kerstin looked past him. "You are in demand. We have company."

It was Runner Preston and his two buddies. Without being invited, Preston slid into the booth beside Tom Godot. One of the others pushed in beside Kerstin and the third man found a chair and pulled it up to the end of the table.

Tom nervously shifted his briefcase from the bench to the floor on the side away from Preston. "This is a private party," Tom protested.

"I didn't want you to leave town without having a chance for a talk," Preston said.

The waitress brought the two beers and Preston paid her, ordered three more. "Be my guest," he said with a chill smile that didn't reach his eyes. "I hope you'll forgive our intrusion, but we really want to talk to you about your book. We're genuine fans, Mr. Godot."

Tom gave Kerstin a furtive glance. "You're too kind."

"I've never been accused of kindness. The Freedom Constabulary is very concerned about what your book has to say."

"So am I, or I wouldn't have written it."

"We're also concerned that the plan you describe. It could be dangerous in the wrong hands."

Tom insisted, "You don't have anything to worry about."

Preston's face was close enough for Tom to smell the man's breath. "You're forgetting the Jews and the mud people."

"Mud people?"

"The blacks. This is a white Christian country, Mr. Godot. Don't you have pride in your race?"

"Not particularly."

Preston drew back. "You're not a Jew are you?"

"No." Since taking the job at MOM and moving to San Jose the only times he had been in a church were for a couple of office weddings. He simply wasn't religious, but he wasn't about to discus his personal thoughts of God with Preston. "I'm just a tech writer who got lucky." He hoped his luck wasn't running out.

"Your book has a powerful impact on people who are concerned for the future of this country," Preston said. "I'd like you to address one of our meetings. Not just one of those bookstore readings you do, but a serious lecture on state terror."

"My schedule is pretty tight."

"Where do you go next?"

Without thinking, Tom answered "B. Dalton's in Fargo," then regretted it immediately.

"We have people in Fargo," Preston said. "People who matter. It'll be worth your while to get in touch with them. They'll pay a nice honorarium, if money's your problem. I'll give you an address."

Tom protested, "No, really, I don't think there's time."

"Someone will contact you," Preston said.

"Sure, fine. Now would you mind excusing us? I'm busy trying to seduce this pretty lady here."

Runner Preston raised his hands in mock respect. "Sorry, Mr. Godot. I wouldn't want to put business before pleasure." He got up to leave.

"Before you go," Tom said, remembering. "You didn't put a note on my windshield, did you?"

For once Preston was confused. "Me? No."

The three men retreated to another part of the bar, but were still in sight. "I think we'd better leave," Tom said.

"Why? I don't think they'll bother us again. Enjoy your beer."

"I hope I didn't offend you with that bit about seduction. Preston looked like he wouldn't take a subtle hint."

She wasn't offended.

"Just where did you live besides St. Cloud?"

It was a safe direction for the rest of the evening. His report had already been faxed. After those dreary nights in hotels and motels, it was a treat to be sitting with a pretty girl over a beer. After half an hour Preston and his friends left, but Tom still couldn't relax. He remembered that back at the Super 8, someone else wanted to see him. Let them wait.

8. A Surprise visitor

Their cars were parked side by side in the Wunderbar lot. "Would you like me to guide you back to your motel?" Kerstin asked.

"That would be nice. I get lost driving around strange towns at night." Tom opened his car and put the briefcase on the seat.

She added, "I'm not coming in."

"If those creeps are hanging around you'd be safer if you didn't. Make sure nobody follows you home."

"I'll wait a half hour after you get in and call you. What's your room number?"

Tom had to get out his key to remember. "Eight."

He was glad Kerstin was thoughtful enough to lead him back to the Super 8. This time nobody followed him and he waved Kerstin Olofsdatter off before he pulled into the vacant space outside his room. It was too dark to see if someone was waiting in any of the parked cars. Tom put the key in the lock, looked over his shoulder, reached into the room to switch on the light and stepped inside.

His visitor was already there.

"What the hell is this?" Tom asked.

It was the woman with the big blonde hair, the one who had been at Barnes & Noble. "Don't get excited, Mr. Godot. Nobody's hired you a hooker to relieve the fatigue of your book tour." She opened her purse and flashed a leather folder with a picture ID "NSA National Security Agency."

"Let me see that," Tom insisted. "How do I know it's not just a driver's license?"

She held the ID in its folder close to his face but did not let go of it. The name under the picture was Mary Contrari.

"Contrari?" Tom asked. "Like in the nursery rhyme?"

"The bane of my existence."

She wasn't wearing a wedding band. Tom suggested, "Maybe you should marry someone named Smith."

"I haven't met a Smith I liked."

"What's NSA? Like the FBI or something?"

"NSA deals with communications. We're the code breakers. The FBI is the spy catchers. The agencies don't always talk to each other," she said.

Tom studied the picture on the identification card. "The lady in this isn't blonde. How do I know this is you?"

Agent Contrari took back her ID and pulled off the blonde wig.

"You're the red haired woman who was at the Mystery Lovers book store in St. Paul. I thought I recognized you."

The crows feet wrinkles around her eyes showed that she was a few years older than he was. The generous mouth he had noticed before was smiling now, but when she relaxed she did not have a happy face. She got right down to business. "You met some men from the Freedom Constabulary tonight."

"That wasn't my choice. I don't have anything to do with those creeps."

"Runner Preston's group is one of many. Some call themselves militia. In Fargo where you're going next they're the Sons of Liberty. Liberty and freedom are catch words they usually use in their titles, but the only liberty and freedom they're interested in is their own at the expense of everyone else."

"They sound like bait for the FBI, not the NSA. Aren't you treading on someone else's turf? What's the connection?"

She didn't explain. "I'd like you to humor them. Seem sympathetic."

"I have a very demanding schedule," Tom protested. "I'm just trying to sell books. Mary McGann at Nile publishing has me booked solid." He opened his briefcase and showed the appointment book. It was full. "Look. She even sends me maps so I can find the motels she's booked. She micro manages everything." He didn't need or want someone else standing over him.

"Those people are bound to buy a lot of your books, Mr. Godot. You can't let your fans down, can you? If the Sons of Liberty invite you to a meeting or a party, make time."

"What am I supposed to do? Give speeches for white power?"

"We're interested in names." Mary Contrari opened the flap of her purse and took out a white card. "If you get in trouble, here's my eight hundred number. Calls to it are forwarded to my cell phone. You can reach me anywhere."

"Wait a minute. What kind of trouble?"

"Some of those people are irrational and violent," Agent Contrari said.

"You mean like Runner Preston?"

"Don't be offended if you're being watched, Mr. Godot. Think of it as protection, not surveillance." The meeting was over. Agent Contrari picked up the blond wig and carefully put it back on, tucking away a few wisps of her own red hair. "I don't need to mention that you should keep our meeting confidential. You're bound by your security agreement."

"You know about that?" Tom remembered signing some papers when MOM became a government contractor. After that people came around to his neighbors asking questions about him. "That was for MOM." What else did she know about him? What magazines he subscribed to? What books he took out of the library? His medical records? What groceries he charged at Trader Joe's? His affinity for pasta and herbal teas? That he played tennis and sometimes got athlete's foot? Was anything private any more? No wonder people like Runner Preston were interested in revolution.

"Consider it extended. Goodnight, Mr. Godot. If you see me in Fargo, pretend we've never met."

Tom stopped her. "Wait a minute. That guy with the camcorder. Is he your partner?"

"Camcorder?"

"Someone made videos of my reading in St. Paul and in St. Cloud. Might have been the same guy. Is he with you?"

She was genuinely puzzled. "No."

"Maybe the Freedom Constabulary or the Sons of Freedom or whatever they call themselves are making a video without my consent. You sat near the front. Maybe you didn't see them."

"You may have some groupies, Mr. Godot."

"I thought that was just for rock stars."

"Maybe there's a new category. Goodnight." She slipped out into the night.

Tom double bolted the door and made sure the blind was shut. He sat down on the bed, his adrenaline rushing. First he had been bored and tired. Now he was keyed up. Groupies like hell. Preston had followed him. Contrari was following Preston. It was a game of tag and he was "it."

He remembered all those references to early drafts of his book. What time was it in Portland? Would Jake still be awake? Should he call? If NSA agent Contrari was watching him, she might have bugged the room. She'd had plenty of time to go through everything while he was nursing his beer at the Wunderbar. He had to be careful what he said from now on. He'd also better warn Stevenson that something fishy was going on.

The phone rang a long time before Jake Friedman answered with a "Yes?" that sounded more like "No, don't bother me."

"It's Tom Godot. I'm in St. Cloud, Minnesota. Did you find out which draft of the book is in your files?"

"What the hell is going on, Tom?"

Tom didn't want to say he was being stalked. That sounded too crazy. "I don't know. I think some crazy white racists are trying to recruit me."

Jake Friedman was worried. "I searched the files and even the slush pile. There's no sign of your original manuscript. The computer disks are missing, too. I don't know what happened to them."

"You think someone broke in?"

Jake hesitated. "I thought someone might have, but didn't notice anything missing then."

"Do you have a backup?"

Jake was plainly irritated. "Why do I need a backup disk for a book that's already published?"

Tom explained, "I thought maybe if I checked the early drafts I might find out what these people are after."

"Don't you have them?"

Tom shook his head. "Not on my laptop." Without thinking, he added, "All that's back in California," and caught himself before saying where.

He could almost hear Jake Friedman thinking. There was an audible sigh. "Might be a copy on my hard drive."

Tom suggested, "If there is, better download it to a disk and put it in a safety deposit box someplace. I'll see you when I get to the west coast."

"What's your next stop?"

It didn't matter if he mentioned it over the phone. Everyone else already seemed to know. "Fargo." Tom hung up.

He got out his laptop, unplugged the phone, and hooked up the modem. It was time he warned Harold Stevenson that something was going on. He powered up, dialed the network at MOM, entered his password, and prepared an e-mail message for Stevenson. "Harold: I'm being watched. Strange people are showing an unhealthy interest in the early drafts of our book. If you haven't deleted them, make sure they are secure. What can we do about security?-- Tom."

Should he warn Mary McGann? What kind of files did they keep at Nile Publishing? If he told her about the Freedom Constabulary she might put a spin on it for more book publicity, anything to sell a book, even if it meant news releases to the grocery tabloids. He didn't want to attract every white power survivalist screwball in the country to his readings. He wanted to make money on the book, but not pretend to be something that he personally abhorred.

Tom logged off, unplugged the modem and sat on the edge of the bed exhausted. When the phone rang he felt a surge of fear. "Hello?"

"It's Kerstin. I tried to get you before but your line was busy. Did your visitor show up?"

He remembered his security agreement. Tom hated to be evasive. He saw himself as an up front kind of a guy. "Yes, but it was nothing for you to worry about. Someone wanting to sell me something. I wasn't interested."

She wasn't convinced. "You're not a very good liar, Tom."

"Kerstin, I really appreciate the dinner and how you went out of your way to make my brief visit in St. Cloud a pleasant one."

"It's not every day I get to meet a celebrity."

"I'm not a celebrity. As for that kidding around about coming back to my place, I'm sorry. You're very nice, and in other circumstances we might have, but it wouldn't have worked out. I guess I have too much respect for women to take advantage of them."

"I might have taken advantage of you."

The suggestion gave him a twitch. When was the last time he had sex with anyone but himself? Too long. Tom changed the subject. "Listen, if you have any trouble with that guy Preston, let me know. You have my e-mail address. I usually check it every day."

"Preston wants to buy a lot of books," Kerstin said.

"Great. Give him a discount. But be careful. He gave me the creeps."

He hung up. That was that. An opportunity missed. Others might have acted differently, leapt at the chance to bed Kerstin Olofsdatter. Odd. He hadn't made any commitments to Sylvia Hansen, and here he was, being faithful to her. They weren't even lovers. Maybe he was just being stupid, clinging to a fantasy. He had felt comfortable as a quasi member of the Hansen extended family, but it ended when the memoir was done. He had no grounds for the relationship to be a lasting one.

Tomorrow he had more driving to do, but it wasn't a long haul-- about three hours drive northwest on the I-94. What was waiting for him in Fargo? Mary McGann had arranged a TV interview at the University of North Dakota and a signing at B. Dalton's. That was his official schedule. What about the Sons of Liberty?

9. Talk Radio

Tom got an early start, gassed up the Neon, got the grand slam breakfast at a Denny's, and headed northwest through a rural landscape heavy with dew. Near as he could tell, no one followed him, but with today's technology if Mary Contrari or her NSA partners had planted a transponder under the car they'd be able to track him by satellite. If Runner Preston's friends were keeping tabs on him, it was comforting to know that the NSA was in the wings, not that Mary Contrari gave him much confidence.

She made him feel like a goat staked out to catch a tiger, a decoy, live bait in someone's game. The trouble was bait is expendable. Bait usually gets eaten or mangled. Being bait wasn't part of his contract with Nile.

If Tom had not been so preoccupied he might have enjoyed the drive west from St. Cloud. It was a scenic route, but the early morning sunshine soon gave way to gloom. A dark front was coming from the west. As he got within range of Fargo-Moorhead, the radio in the Neon picked up a local station. Talk radio.

Tom seldom listened to talk radio, and now he got a full dose of conspiracy theories, off the wall rumors about the president, railing about taxes, and recollections of the Waco incident, now described as a massacre. If these were his own audience, no wonder the book was doing so well.

After the encounter with the Freedom Constabulary and Mary Contrari, he was almost willing to believe that drivel himself. It was a world away from the skyscrapers of Manhattan, Nile Publishing, and Mary McGann's Park Avenue wardrobe. The people calling in to the Fargo station might be from a different planet. He had started the book tour at the level of the New York Times and the Wall Street Journal. Now he was in the land of the Inquirer and the Sun grocery tabloids.

The Interstate skirted Moorhead and Fargo, so he decided to get off early and find a barber shop. He hoped the TV taping at the university would be more pleasant than the reception he got at Minnesota Public Radio in Minneapolis. People who came to bookstores expected an author to look a bit artsy. For television he would look presentable, no affectations like Kinky Friedman's cowboy hat.

While waiting for the barber he called the Days Inn motel where he had a reservation, just to make sure nothing had gone wrong. "This is Tom Godot with Nile Publishing. You have a reservation for me."

The voice at the other end of the line ruminated. "Yes we do, Mr. Godot. There's also a Federal Express package for you. Shall I keep it at the desk or have it put in your room?"

Did it make any difference? "At the desk. Does it say who it's from?"

"That part of the label's been damaged. I can't make it out."

"Thank you." Tom hung up.

While the barber snipped Tom worried about the parcel at Day's Inn. Maybe Mary McGann had some more appointments and readings for him, wanting to squeeze every book sale out of his travel expenses.

The walk from the guest parking lot on the university campus gave him a chance to size up the student population. They were different from what he saw in California when he visited Sylvia. In California half the students were oriental. The students in Fargo looked like farm kids. There wasn't a Hispanic or oriental face among them.

By the time Tom found the studio his arm was tired from lugging his briefcase but he didn't dare leave it in the trunk of the Neon. Today's event was a program "Talking about books" with a moderator and a panel which included a couple of academic writers from the university. Good Morning

America it wasn't. He wondered if anyone would be watching at all.

Tom took out his book tour copy of Conspiracy! and held it so whenever the camera was on him the book jacket would show.

The moderator was a flabby Midwesterner with a Finnish name, Pelanpaa, who wore a sports jacket over the light blue shirt favored by television people, but because the show used no long shots, below the waist Pelanpaa had on faded blue jeans. One of the professor panelists was a woman who had chosen a glittery, sequined blouse bound to drive the camera operator crazy. The other was an African-American with a black jacket and dark shirt and tie. Against the white background of the set, all viewers would see of his face would be his teeth. This was bound to be a disaster.

On signal Pelanpaa began with, "Today our guest is Tom Godot, co-author of the exploitative best seller, Conspiracy! and our panelists are Professors Janet Markhamn of the English department and Hugh Brown of political science and history."

The word "exploitative" was the indicator. If the woman at National Public Radio had given him a hard time, this couple looked like they were going to shred him. "Glad to be here in Fargo," Tom said, hoping he didn't look like a specimen bug wriggling on a pin. "This evening I'll be reading passages from Conspiracy! at the B. Dalton bookstore on 42nd Street here in Fargo. I'll be pleased to sign copies of my book at that time."

Professor Brown started off by asking, "Why did you write a blueprint for overthrowing the government?"

Tom countered with, "It's not a blueprint. This is a novel."

"But based on real conditions," Professor Markham interrupted.

"We always draw on real experience," Tom countered. "I work at a company that's connected with the communication satellite business." He tried not to look at the cameras to see which one had the red light on that said it was live. He wanted to lead the line of questions away from perceptions of his motivation. He had written the book because it was a challenge and an opportunity, not expecting it to sell, but these academic types wouldn't be interested in that level of the truth. "We all distort reality through the lenses of our own points of view. Look at how history distorts facts. If what you want is the truth, history is fiction, too. I'm sure you'll agree that Shakespeare's version of Richard the Third is no more accurate than a white man's history of slavery in America."

The tactic worked. Tom was able to pit the two professors against each other and sit quietly while they gnawed away and ignored him. When time was almost up and a frustrated Pelanpaa thanked the panelists, Tom held his copy of the book to the camera. "Remember: tonight at B. Dalton in Fargo."

Markham and Brown were still arguing as Tom put away his book, hefted his briefcase, thanked the exasperated Mr. Pelanpaa and escaped from the television studio. Time to find out what someone had sent him by Federal Express.

10. Pretty Good Privacy

Tom found the Day's Inn close to the shopping malls out near the I 29. B. Dalton's book store was close by. The proximity wasn't Mary McGann being efficient, he reasoned, but the natural placement of shopping and motels near a major highway. His briefcase felt like a heavy extension of his arm and he was glad to put it down on the receptionist's counter. "You have a reservation for Tom Godot," he said to the young clerk. The name tag said Lisa. She looked barely out of high school, not yet at ease in her Day's Inn jacket. "I'm told you have a parcel for me."

"Are you sure?"

"Yes. Federal express someone said."

Lisa looked under the counter. "I just came on duty. I'll ask."

Where was it? Conspiracy radio didn't help. With all the goings on the last few days his loneliness and exhaustion were turning to vulnerability that verged on paranoia. He realized that Mary McGann was smart in insisting on daily reports. They kept him in focus as he worked his way down the itinerary.

He had been living out of a suitcase for too long. His apartment in San Jose seemed so far away in both distance and time that when he did get back it might seem the home of a stranger.

"It's not here," Lisa said. "It must be in your room."

She showed him a map of the motel. "Your room is here." She returned the Nile corporate credit card with the reservation printout and handed him his key. "Continental breakfast is from six in the morning."

"Thanks, Lisa."

The parcel was on the bed. Apprehensive, Tom picked it up. The name on the return address was illegible, and the rest a post office box in Arlington, Virginia. It felt like a book. He tore open the wrapper.

It was a paper back manual with the title P.G.P. and a 3 1/2 inch computer disk in a blank protective mailer. A folded sheet of paper inside the cover had the explanation. It was a plain sheet of bond, no watermark, no letterhead. The message was flawlessly typed as if by an expert secretary who never made a mistake.

"Tom," the note began. "Got your e-mail message. You'd better use this Pretty Good Privacy encryption program for your e-mail to me and for your files. This is the freeware encryption program that is driving the FBI nuts because every militia, skinhead, racist, and criminal group can use it. The program is so powerful that it is virtually unbreakable.

"Basically, it works this way: you create a public encryption key which you send me by e-mail. Then I use your public key to encrypt my messages to you. Though anyone with your public key can encrypt messages, only you can decrypt the message made with your public key. Instead of a password you use a pass phrase, something you won't forget. Pass phrases are far more difficult to break.

"I'm also including on the enclosed disk a private key we can both use for our joint files at MOM. The pass phrase for those jointly edited files is 'The wages of sin is Death.' Note the capital letter on death and the period at the end. Memorize it and burn this note. Never write a pass phrase down anywhere.

"You can't send me a message encrypted with your public key, because I can't decode those. You encrypt your messages to me using my public key, which is on the enclosed disk along with the program. Install it right away, create your own public key, memorize your pass phrase, and send me an encrypted confirmation using my public key. That way I'll know you're not befuddled."

The note was signed simply "Stevenson."

It was the first time Tom Godot had seen Stevenson's signature. All their correspondence had been electronic. An actual signature was a step closer to seeing the man as a person, not just an unseen author on a computer network.

"That was fast," Tom said aloud. From Arlington, Virginia to Fargo, North Dakota in so few hours was a feat even for Federal Express. Stevenson must have paid a premium, or anticipated a need. But how did he know where Tom would be? So far as Tom knew, only Mary McGann at Nile Publishing knew the whole itinerary. Did everyone know his business, and how did they find out? "If I keep thinking like this," Tom said to himself, "I'll soon be calling Fargo conspiracy radio!"

Before doing his laundry in the motel's machine, Tom memorized the pass phrase and used the hotel ash tray as an incinerator. As he watched Stevenson's instructions blacken and turn into curls of ash he hoped he would remember "The wages of sin is Death."

While his laundry went through the cycles Tom studied the P.G.P. manual. If he hadn't spent several years as a technical writer familiar with manuals and programs he would have been intimidated. Fortunately, the author had used plain, direct language and had a sense of humor. Though the spy versus spy nature of encryption and secrecy could be befuddling, as Stevenson put it, it shouldn't be too difficult.

He might even have time to get started before checking in at the Fargo bookstore.

Following the instructions in the manual he installed the program and selected a pass phrase appropriate to the situation. "How does your garden grow?" As long as Mary Contrari was dogging his heels, he wouldn't have to write that one down.

The program at B. Dalton would have been routine, except that this time he expected to see a familiar face, Mary Contrari, with or without a wig. Would the mysterious man with the camcorder turn up again? And what about the Sons of Liberty or whatever they called themselves?

11. Fargo

Tom was glad he had packed a thin, nylon raincoat. He didn't have a hat and the cold rain soon penetrated to his scalp.

The bookstore in Fargo was similar to the one in St. Cloud, but the manager was no Kerstin Olofsdatter. He was a bored man about Tom's age with a name that could be on his tag in any combination, Nick Charles. Had his parents been mystery fans? No wonder he ended up in a bookstore himself. It was his karma.

"I see it's raining," Charles said, noting Tom's wet hair and dripping coat. "Stuck in the store from dawn to dark I sometimes wonder what the outside world is doing." His tendency to end a sentence on an up note made it sound like a question.

"You're right, Nick, or Charles. It is raining. Are we set for the reading?"

"I'm expecting a crowd. People saw you on television and there was mention on the radio of your appearance."

"If it's the station I heard coming in, they'll be asking about UFOs and who killed J.F.K." Tom's book had nothing to do with UFOs or who killed president Kennedy but to some people all conspiracies were equal.

Nick Charles wasn't worried. "If they buy books, what do I care?"

Tom went over the book orders, had a cup of herbal tea, and reviewed the passages of Conspiracy! to pick something appropriate.

A motley group gathered in the narrow aisles of the store half an hour before the reading. None of them wore camouflage pants and combat boots, but it was clear that they were not the usual crowd that hung around bookstores. They treated the books like foreign objects of some disdain, as if B. Dalton's sold forbidden sex toys or authors banned by the Church. Only the prominent display of Conspiracy! with Tom's publicity picture drew their interest.

While Nick Charles' made his introduction, Tom sized up the audience. He did not see Mary Contrari or anyone with a camcorder.

He decided a joke opening would be inappropriate for this bunch. Instead he chose to read the passage where the villain of the piece tries to justify his actions during the confrontation scene near the end of the book. "My plan," Tom read with a dramatic flourish, "will disrupt all government communications. The dependence on satellite communications for military navigation means that once the satellites are disabled, we can proceed with our coordinated overthrow of the Federal government." The passage continued in that vein. Harold Stevenson did have such a plan. Would it work in real life? Tom insisted the details be taken out early in the revision process. In the original the villain's harangue went on for fifty pages, like some of the diatribes in Ayn Rand's political novels. The audience Nile planned to reach didn't have the patience for such heavy prose. It had been Tom's job to make the writing more vivid, the characters more colorful, the action more gripping. The revision made for dramatic reading. Conspiracy! was a novel, not a turgid, repetitious, wacko unibomber manifesto. Conspiracy! was supposed to entertain.

It did. The audience was rapt. They actually applauded. If Conspiracy! had a cult following, he was an icon. The celebrity role made him uncomfortable. The question and answer follow-up began with someone in the back asking, "How can you express that point of view? Aren't you afraid of the government?"

"What I just read is a speech by one of the characters. That's his point of view, not mine." In fact, it was a passage Harold Stevenson had written and Tom integrated with the characters. Stevenson had provided the polemics, the technical details, and a rough plot outline. Tom had created the characters and their psychology. He also had to rewrite Stevenson's wooden passages. Tom didn't go into that aspect of their collaboration, deciding that was too much shop talk for an audience of readers, not writers. "What a character in a book says isn't necessarily what the author believes."

"But authors draw from their own experience," someone down in front piped up.

Tom recognized her. It was Professor Markham, the TV panelist of the sequined blouse. This time she wore a baggy sweat shirt with the emblem of the University of North Dakota. Had she come to take another pot shot at popular literature?

"Authors draw from the world around them," Tom said. "The world around us includes a lot of people like the characters in my book, people who are dissatisfied and angry with the government." He remembered Mary Contrari's request. "Is there anyone here from the Sons of Liberty?"

There were a few uneasy side glances and half a dozen hands came up. "How about the Freedom Constabulary?" Tom asked. No one. Maybe that was the Minnesota bunch. Moorhead might be on the other bank of the Red River, but this was North Dakota.

A man at the back held up his hand. He had narrow shoulders and looked like a preacher except instead of a dog collar he wore a string tie. "What views does your co-author, Harold Stevenson, have about the revolution?"

"You'd have to ask him yourself," Tom said. "Unfortunately he's not able to travel."

"He's smart," someone quipped. "Anybody who writes a book supporting a revolution better keep out of sight."

This was getting heavier than he expected. "I think Harold Stevenson's reasons for not doing public readings are more personal than political."

"Are you in favor of revolution?" someone asked from the back.

Tom hadn't seen who asked. It was a woman. Sure enough, she had come after all: Mary Contrari in her own red hair.

"I think revolution is a last resort. We're a long way from that in this country." With that he thanked the audience and invited them to bring their books to him for signing.

A line formed. Mary McGann would be pleased. The man with the string tie bought two copies. While Tom wrote his best wishes on the title page, the man said, "Revolution may be closer than you think. I'd like you to meet some of the Sons of Liberty."

This is what Runner Preston told him to expect. Agent Contrari told him to humor them. He complied. "That's possible."

"We're meeting tonight," the man said, taking up his two signed copies. "I'll wait for you when you're done here."

12. The Sons of Liberty

Tom Godot wrote down the sales figures Nick Charles gave him for Mary McGann's report and left the bookstore with the Sons of Liberty. The man with the string tie and narrow shoulders introduced himself as Pastor Carlson. He had hollow cheeks and a mouth that looked like it never smiled. With an audience like that Tom had been wise not to start his performance with a joke. No one would have laughed. "I'll follow you," Tom said as he unlocked the rental car and put his briefcase on the passenger seat.

He quickly realized that he was part of a convoy of cars, the other Sons of Liberty also following. He wondered if Mary Contrari's car was among them.

Fargo, like most American cities, is laid out on a grid and Tom tried to catch the street signs and numbers in the rainy dark so he could retrace his steps. The city map he had did not have much detail.

They were soon driving on a two lane road north of the city. The pastor's car pulled off into a lane and stopped in front of a white clapboard church. Did many such innocuous churches around the country also provide sanctuary to groups like the Sons of Liberty? Other cars drew up around his. Tired of lugging it everywhere, Tom locked his briefcase in the trunk and followed the men into the basement assembly hall.

It was a simple room with rows of tables that had no doubt served many post-funeral wakes. Several men and a couple of women were already seated. There were no cloths on the folding tables for this event. The hatch to the kitchen was open and a dozen or more pairs of salt and pepper shakers were lined up on the counter. An elderly woman was making coffee and Tom could see trays of cookies ready for later.

"Sit up here, Mr. Godot." Pastor Carlson motioned to a low platform with a speaker's table raised about a foot above the rest. "You're our guest of honor."

Tom didn't know why he had come. Curiosity. Mary Contrari's admonition to humor the natives. Boredom with having to go back to yet another sterile motel room. An urge to break away from the nightly routine of reports to Mary McGann. He could go out for a beer, but he hated drinking alone.

Two of the men put up a banner at the front of the room, "The Sons of Liberty," painted on white sheet material. Others, some reverently holding their freshly signed copies of Tom's book, settled on the folding wooden chairs. Satisfied that they were ready, Pastor Carlson called the meeting to order.

Though they themselves might be organized for revolution, the Sons of Liberty were not anarchists. They rigidly followed Robert's Rules of Order with motions to dispense with the reading of the minutes and to accept the tedious treasurer's report. By that time Tom was wishing he hadn't come, but then Pastor Carlson got up to speak.

"We are privileged today to have with us Tom Godot, author of the book Conspiracy! and authority on the revolutionary movements in the disunited states. He just did a reading at the bookstore in Fargo and agreed to come out with us. Perhaps he'll consent to say a few words later."

So, it was the Dis-united States, was it? Tom felt like an unwilling observer of a KKK meeting. The talk was all about the evils of big government, but it fell short of what Mary Contrari and the National Security Agency could legitimately call sedition.

When obliged to say a few words, Tom hushed the applause and began with his usual disclaimer. No, he was not a revolutionary or a terrorist. No, he was not trying to overthrow the government. He had written a book of fiction that had struck the nerves of many people. He was glad it was popular and maybe there'd be a movie. He didn't expect to get rich. The real inside information had come from his co-author, Harold Stevenson.

"What about the real conspiracy?" someone asked.

Tom would have said that it was all fiction, that there was no conspiracy, but he was no longer sure. Someone had taped his readings. NSA had sent at least one agent to follow him. Instead, he sighed and admitted, "You're right. I think there are hidden agendas, ulterior motives. I was listening to talk radio today, and there are obviously a lot of people who feed on this stuff."

An agitated man at the back stood up. "We've had it up to here with government interference." With that he launched into a string of hot button code words like NAFTA, exporting American jobs, illegal immigrants, religious rights, the superiority of the white race, the evil of homosexuals, corruption and immorality, that America was a Christian nation and the Jews should all go back to Israel where they came from. Jammed all together in one stream it sounded like what George Orwell in 1984 had called "duckspeak," to quack like a duck, mouthing catch phrases. It was amazing that anyone could spew out that much in one breath. Pastor Carlson might be the nominal leader of the Sons of Liberty, but the energies were elsewhere.

Someone else agreed, another shouted. The peaceful gathering was being transformed by frustration and anger. Tom could see how, if their numbers were great enough, these otherwise normal looking, peaceable North Dakotans could turn into a mob. If they turned on someone there was no telling how far they would go.

Tom wondered whether Mary Contrari had followed him to the church and slipped in to observe, but he did not see her. He was grateful for that. As raving and raging as these Sons of Liberty were, there was no telling what would happen if a federal agent turned up in their midst.

"I think I'd better be going," Tom whispered to Pastor Carlson. "I've got a long drive tomorrow and a sales report to write." He hoped he could find his way back to the motel in the rainy dark.

"You won't stay for the refreshments after?" Pastor Carlson asked. "My wife makes wonderful walnut brownies."

"Sounds terrific, but I'll pass."

Tom put on his raincoat and slipped out. It was still raining. He dodged the puddles in the gravel parking lot outside the church. Behind the car next to his someone was crouched with a flashlight. "Lose something?" Tom asked.

"Dropped my keys," was the mumbled reply, followed quickly by, "There they are." But the man didn't open his trunk or get in the car.

"You're missing all the action inside," Tom said. "It's getting pretty heavy in there." Tom got in the Neon and headed back to Fargo. Where was Mary Contrari, he wondered. Would she dog him all the way to Bismarck, his next stop? Or would the NSA switch agents now that he knew she was one? How much should he tell Harold Stevenson about this? Harold would want it encrypted. What was his pass phrase? "How does your garden grow?" The way this trip was going, it was full of poisonous plants.

13. San Jose

In San Jose at the apartment they shared Sylvia Hansen was embarrassed. She and her roommate Daphne had brought up the laundry from the machines in the basement and were putting their clothes away. Daphne stuffed hers in her bureau, but Sylvia was neat to a fault. Being neat gave Sylvia a feeling of control over her life.

Daphne watched Sylvia folding her underwear in neat stacks. "You are something else, gal. You are so up tight. Hey, what you got there?"

Before Sylvia could stop her Daphne reached into the drawer and took something out. "A vibrator! It's time you wrapped your legs around a real man, honey. That'll solve all your problems."

Sylvia retrieved the vibrator and hid it under the stack of underpants. "I believe in safe sex."

Daphne laughed and sat on the bed. "You mean self sex is safe sex? You on the pill?"

"What do I need that for? I don't have a boy friend."

"What about that guy you told me about, that Tom Godot? Ain't he your boy friend?"

"Yes, but..."

"What's he doing now?"

"He's on a book tour. I showed it to you, Conspiracy!"

"Why don't you get it on with him?"

Sylvia looked down at the floor. She didn't want to admit that she was a virgin. "It's not that simple." Daphne had lots of boys. Though they had separate bedrooms, the wall between them wasn't sound proof and Sylvia would lie awake listening to Daphne laughing and then moaning with pleasure. Sylvia would lie in her bed with a hand between her legs, a voyeur, pretending, wishing. It was awkward and embarrassing on those Sunday mornings when one or another male student would emerge from Daphne's room. With the memory of heard sexual gymnastics fresh in her mind, Sylvia had difficulty looking across the breakfast table at Daphne's latest conquest.

Daphne left the room, came back and dropped a fistful of condoms in Sylvia's lap. "Why don't you call this Tom Godot? Here. Like the Boy Scouts say, honey, be prepared. These come in all colors."

"Maybe you're right," Sylvia said. If she was going to "get it on" with someone, as Daphne put it, Tom Godot was a good prospect. He was gentle, compassionate, and understanding. Maybe with him she could get over her fear of intimacy.

14. Encryption

Tom Godot blundered while retracing his route back to Fargo, mistakenly got on the interstate, then had to double back. He would be glad to be back in San Jose where he knew his way around. He didn't get to the Day's Inn until almost ten o'clock. With the key poised at the lock to his room, he stopped to listen. As a matter of security he always left the television on so it sounded like someone was in the room. Would Mary Contrari be there this time?

He was relieved when she wasn't. He set the laptop on the round table, checked his notes, and prepared his daily report for Mary McGann. The book was selling briskly at the Fargo store.

After he faxed his report to Nile publishing, Tom dialed up the computer system at MOM in San Jose and logged on. There was e-mail from HLSteven@falcon.com, Stevenson. It was encrypted, a block of gibberish. "Well, we'll see how this works," Tom said to himself. He would have to save Stevenson's message, leave the e-mail program, decrypt the message, write and encrypt his own reply, then log on the e-mail again. This was going to be tedious.

Almost miraculously, the gibberish from Stevenson was replaced by plain text. "Got your message. You did good, Tom. How do you know the woman who called herself Mary Contrari really is with NSA? Could be a fake ID. Just in case, we'd better tighten our security. I'm attaching an encryption key we can both use for the files at MOM. The name of the key is Revolt.asc. You already know the pass phrase. Since you're on the road with your book tour, I'll take care of the encryption at MOM. When you've saved the Revolt.asc key to a separate file, use the destroy program to wipe your disk clean of this message. Do not record the pass phrase on your hard drive or anyplace else. That would be like leaving the house key under the door mat."

This is nuts, Tom thought. Stevenson is some kind of paranoid freak. But Tom knew that e-mail was not secure.

Poobah, the webmaster at MOM, could access anybody's files. Though Tom might delete old messages, there was no way for him to know if they were backed up someplace else for future reference. Maybe that was why Stevenson had waited until he could encrypt this message before he sent their joint key with its pass phrase.

Stevenson had signed his e-mail message with a little drawing made up of slashes and o's. Under it was a PS "Say hi to Sylvia."

So Stevenson knew who Sylvia was. He had to be a friend of Ivar Hansen's, someone who knew the family well. Curiouser and curiouser.

As if in confirmation to Stephenson's PS there was also e-mail from Sylvia Hansen at grad school. "Haven't heard from you in ages. How's the book tour going? Are those cute sales girls hitting on you? Where are you headed for next? Call me."

Tom logged off and dialed her number. After three rings her answering machine picked up. What time was it in California? Maybe she was out to dinner. "Hi. It's Tom. Got your e-mail. Tomorrow is Saturday and I'm signing in Bismarck, North Dakota. The tour started out boring, but now some weird stuff is going on. Stevenson is freaked out and makes me encrypt all his messages. I'll explain later. By the way, he told me to say hi. Do you know him?" End of message.

It was time for the eleven o'clock news. Tom studied the card on the television set listing the cable channels, couldn't figure out which was the local station, surfed until he found it. Channel Six late news.

They were into the weather report. An uncomfortable young woman who didn't know whether to read the TelePrompTer or her notes and wasn't sure how to point so her finger was at the right place on the map behind her reported that the rain would be ending and there would be strong west winds on Saturday.

Instead of sports the male announcer broke in with "Late breaking news. There's been an incident at the Church of the

Apostles in North Fargo. Police are at the scene as is Greg Thomas of Channel Six Action News. Greg, what's happening?"

The scene shifted to a three quarter shot of a young man standing in the rain in a yellow slicker. "The Fargo police are investigating an assault here after a meeting in the church. The police won't identify the person or give details on the injuries."

So much for small town reporting, Tom thought. Nobody knows anything but the TV crew are on the scene, wondering where to point their camera.

A yellow police line had been set up behind the TV reporter. In the background, lit by the dusk to dawn light, was a white building. Startled, Tom recognized the Church of the Apostles. "Looks like I left the Sons of Liberty just in time," Tom said aloud. "What next?"

Next was Bismarck and his Saturday appearance at what? He checked the elaborate itinerary Mary McGann had prepared. Cozy Corner book store, Roberta Whalen, manager. It was about two hundred miles to Bismarck, but he'd be bucking a head wind all the way. Tom didn't suspect he'd have to contend with a lot more than wind.

15. The road to Bismarck

The wind was as predicted on the late news in Fargo. The light weight Neon was buffeted and though the car handled well in normal conditions, in the gusty great plains the engine struggled. On one occasion when he reached the crest of a hill Tom Godot had a panicked moment when he thought it would be blown off the road. The two hundred miles should have been an easy drive on the I-94, but after a couple of hours Tom was stiff from the concentration it took to keep the car on the road. He was glad it wasn't winter.

He didn't notice the police car until it pulled alongside him with its flashing lights and the state trooper waved him off.

Tom pulled onto the shoulder, puzzled. He wasn't speeding. What could be wrong?

The police car stopped ahead of him and the trooper got out. He jammed his wide-brimmed hat tightly on his head and approached Tom's car warily with that measured step that comes from wearing too much hardware on your belt.

Tom rolled down the window.

The trooper was irritated and cautious. "Didn't you see my lights? I've been following you for two miles."

"Sorry. With this wind I was concentrating on keeping the car from blowing off the road. What's up, officer?"

"May I see your driver's license please?"

Tom got out his wallet and removed the license from its pocket.

"California. You're a long way from home, Mister Godot."

"Book tour," Tom explained. "I'm an author."

"May I see the registration for the vehicle?"

Tom opened the glove compartment where he kept the contract from Budget. "It's a rental. Must be in here someplace. Here you go. Is there some sort of problem?"

The trooper examined the Budget contract and returned it, but held onto Tom's driver's license. "Would you mind stepping out of the car, please?"

Tom unbuckled the seat belt and got out. The gusty wind shook the car. "What's this all about?"

"Place your hands on top of the car and spread your feet apart."

Tom couldn't believe he was being frisked for weapons. He hadn't been checked like this since there was a bomb scare on a flight to New York. Was this some kind of a shakedown?

"Would you mind opening the trunk?"

"Sure," Tom said. The latch could be released from the driver's seat. Tom dutifully opened the trunk.

"What's in the box?"

"Books. I told you I'm an author." It was the case of copies he carried in reserve if a bookstore ran out. With adequate notice Mary McGann could fill an order by UPS but she insisted that he carry some extras. There were sixty left. In Madison, Wisconsin the bookstore had needed ten.

The trooper picked up a copy and examined it. He read the title aloud as if he had uncovered damaging evidence. "Conspiracy!"

Tom wanted a close look at the man's uniform. The name tag pinned on the pocket said Peters. Peter, Peter pumpkin eater. He would remember that.

Trooper Peters gave him a suspicious stare. "Who's Harold Stevenson?"

"My co-author."

"Why isn't his picture here, too?"

Tom shrugged. "You'll have to ask him."

Trooper Peters forced a smile. It was not his accustomed expression. "Maybe I will. You have a briefcase on the front seat. Would you open it, please?"

"What's this all about?"

Peters asked questions. He didn't answer them. Tom didn't want his papers to blow away and started to open his briefcase on the seat, but the policeman looked like he thought Tom would pull out a gun. "Just put it on the hood of the car, Mr. Godot. Nice and easy."

"Careful," Tom said, stepping back. "Don't let anything blow away."

The policeman noted the laptop computer and made a cursory inspection. Tom felt violated. First frisked, the trunk opened, and now his itinerary and personal papers being checked.

Trooper Peters held up one of Tom's tea bags like he'd found a dead mouse and had it by the tail. It fluttered in the wind. He gave Tom a quizzical look.

"I don't drink coffee." Tom was clearly not one of the coffee and donut crowd.

Peters shook his head, an expression that might have been a comment on weirdo tea drinking Californians. He closed and latched Tom's briefcase and returned it. "Will you follow me, please?"

Tom was confused. He put the briefcase back in the Neon. "Have I done something? What is this? Can I have my driver's license back?"

"In Bismarck," Officer Peters said. "There's someone there who wants to ask you a few questions."

That was all the policeman would say. He steadied his hat against the wind as he returned to the patrol car.

Tom started the Neon and tried to keep up with the powerful patrol car. This wasn't a simple traffic stop, or he'd have been issued a citation. Tom was sure Peters had been waiting someplace along the highway and watching for the Neon. The search was to make sure that it was Tom Godot driving it. What did someone think he had done? What was this all about?

"A few questions"? He'd better call the Cozy Corner book store as soon as he got to Bismarck. If he missed the reading and signing Mary McGann would be pissed.

16. An interview

Officer Peters waited by the heavy, glass door to the Bismarck North Dakota state police post until Tom Godot went inside. Only then did he return Tom's driver's license.

"What's going on?" Tom asked, unable to hide his impatience.

A stocky man in a dark suit appeared from inside an office. He was about fifty years old and might have been anybody except for his demeanor that said he was at ease amidst law enforcement folks. The man had a Teddy Roosevelt style of brown mustache, but no Rough Rider hat. He had a file folder in his left hand. "Mr. Godot? Tom Godot?"

"Yes."

"We can talk in here." The man with the mustache led Tom down the hall into a small office. The mirror on the wall suggested it was one way glass and there was a tape recorder on the desk. "Have a seat. Cup of coffee? Coke?"

"I don't drink it," Tom said. "No caffeine."

Tea was not an option. "Suit yourself." The man laid the manila file folder on the table and opened it. He took out a faxed black and white photo which he handed across the desk to Tom. "Ever seen this person?"

It was a full faced head shot that might have been taken for police identification or for a driver's license. Since it was black and white, Tom couldn't tell the color of the hair. It was not a new picture, but Tom recognized the generous mouth. "Mary Contrari," Tom said and without thinking added, "How does your garden grow?"

"What's that?"

"Just a trick I use to remember names. When I met her I said something about the nursery rhyme."

"Just when did you meet her? Tell me about it."

Tom explained that he had first noticed her in St. Paul at his reading at the Mystery Lovers' book store, and that she had followed him to St. Cloud, Minnesota, but wore a blonde wig there. "She let herself into my motel room and showed me an ID that said she was with the NSA"

"NSA?" Surely the man knew what that was.

"The National Security Agency."

"Do you know who they are?"

Tom wasn't sure. "I think they snoop on authors who write provocative novels. Maybe she thinks I'm cute. You know how it is to be a famous author. Women keep throwing themselves at you."

The man with the mustache didn't catch the joke. If he did, he didn't think it was funny. "That's the last time you saw her?"

"I think she was in the crowd at the bookstore in Fargo. I'm on a book tour. As part of the contract with Nile publishing I had to agree to take part in the advertising campaign. My editor, Mary McGann, set up this itinerary. I'm supposed to read this afternoon here in Bismarck at the Cozy Corner book store."

"Did you speak to Mary Contrari in Fargo?"

"No. I didn't have the opportunity. Besides, she was working under cover and I was supposed to ignore her."

"Where did you go after the reading?"

"I was invited to a meeting of the Sons of Liberty."

"Was Mary Contrari at that meeting, too?"

Tom shook his head and stared at the picture. "Not that I know of. It was quite a crowd, mostly men. I didn't see her. Maybe she was wearing a false beard."

Tom's attempts at humor weren't any help. "What time did you leave the meeting?"

"About nine o'clock, maybe earlier. I left before it was over. Not my kind of place. Since I wrote my book some of the weirdest people think I'm their spokesperson."

"Since you published Conspiracy!" It was not a question.

"Right." It was time for Tom to take the initiative. "You didn't introduce yourself. What is this all about? Is Mary Contrari impersonating an NSA agent?"

The man with the mustache hesitated like he might be inventing a name for himself. Finally he decided. "I'm P. Henkel, the FBI agent assigned to Bismarck."

Henkel. No nursery rhyme to go with that.

"Apparently you're the last person known to have seen Mary Contrari before she was assaulted."

"Assaulted?"

"Some people think you might be the one who attacked her."

"That's ridiculous," Tom protested. "Where did this happen?"

"She was found in the parking lot of the Church of the Apostles."

"So that's what was on the late news last night," Tom mused. "It's a mystery to me. Is she all right? I mean, how badly was she hurt?"

"She's critical," P. Henkel said. "Do you think you could identify any of the people who were at the Church of the Apostles?"

"I can't remember their names. The man in charge was named Carlson, I think. A pastor. The Sons of Liberty are a pretty loony bunch. Very angry people."

"Angry enough to assault Mary Contrari?"

"I really don't know," Tom said.

"Can you think of anything else?"

Tom remembered the man with the flashlight. "There was a man in the parking lot. He said he was looking for his keys. Now that I think about it, maybe he was taking down the license numbers of all the cars parked there, or looking for a car to break into. Maybe it was one of your people. Mary Contrari said I might be under surveillance by the NSA"

"Why would they do that?"

"Beats me. I'm just selling books, nothing else." His mind was in overdrive now. Someone who had all the license numbers would know to watch out for a white rental Neon from Budget. Mary Contrari must already know what car he drove. She wouldn't have sent the police after him. It had to be someone else.

That ended the formal questioning. Agent Henkel retrieved the faxed photo and slipped it back into the folder. "What time is your reading at the... what was the name of the bookstore?"

"The Cozy Corner. Seven o'clock, I think. I'd have to look it up."

"Your book selling pretty well?"

Tom shrugged. "I haven't seen the current sales figures. Nile publishing is only obliged to furnish quarterly reports that my agent in Portland forwards to me. I may be the co-author, but I'm beginning to feel like a book peddler. Would you like to buy a copy? Twenty-five bucks. Free autograph."

"Sorry. I don't have much time to read in my job, other than reports."

Tom had a suggestion. "If you had the name of every nut case who bought Conspiracy! you'd probably have a roster of every would be revolutionary or terrorist in the country."

"Now there's an idea." P. Henkel stood up. "Where would we find your co-author, Mr. Stevenson I believe the name is."

"I don't know myself," Tom said. "I can give you his e-mail address. Maybe if you contact Mary McGann at Nile publishing. That address is inside the cover of the book. I have copies in the trunk of the car."

This time there was a smile under the mustache. "You really are a book peddler, Mr. Godot. I'll take that e-mail address and you're free to go."

Tom wrote it down on the back of his business card with the address of the MOM headquarters in San Jose. Handing the card to the agent, he said, "Mary Contrari told me to humor the Sons of Liberty. Does that mean anything to you?"

"Not to me, but it might to somebody."

"Is there a Sons of Liberty organization here in Bismarck?"

"They go by different names, Mr. Godot, but there are more of them around than you might think."

Tom stopped in the doorway of the office. "Someone was videotaping my readings in St. Paul and St. Cloud. Were those FBI?"

"Not to my knowledge." Now the agent had an idea. "Next time you do a signing, why not ask people to give you their names and addresses? Say it's for a fan club, a discount on multiple copies or something. The list might prove useful to us next time one of your followers gets assaulted." He gave Tom his card. The name of the organization didn't have to be in large print to have an impact. Federal Bureau of Investigation, with phone and fax numbers and an e-mail address that ended with .gov.

"Are you asking me to be an FBI informant?" Tom asked, putting the card in his wallet. He was getting quite a collection of business cards. P. Henkel was in with Runner Preston's Freedom Constabulary and Mary Contrari's with her 800 number. He should call and see how she was. Even if she was in the hospital she'd have voice mail.

"A fan mailing list might be helpful to Nile publishing." Tom wasn't eager to have something else to add to his daily reports. "I'll suggest that to my editor. She's always looking for a new sales gimmick."

The trooper who had brought Tom in was waiting in the outer office as Tom left the police post. The man had been polite and thorough. "Thanks, Officer Peters," Tom said. "See you around." He hoped not.

Tom settled behind the wheel of the Neon and tried to make sense of it all. First the NSA, now the North Dakota state police and the FBI. The Freedom Constabulary and then the Sons of Liberty. How badly was Mary Contrari hurt? The agent said "critical," but whatever he knew he didn't tell much.

It was time Tom talked with Harold Stevenson, actually talked. Not just encrypted e-mail. Stevenson knew more than he was telling. That stuff about encrypting all the files. There had to be a reason for that. And the original submission copy of the book manuscript missing from Jake Friedman's office. What was in that early version that someone wanted? How was he going to answer any of those questions from the wide open spaces of North Dakota?

Tom tried to get his bearings. Which way was it to downtown Bismarck from the state police post? He'd better call what was the name? He opened his briefcase and found it in the itinerary. Roberta Whalen. The Cozy Corner didn't sound like a hangout for Sons of Liberty types, but you never knew. That was the trouble. He never did seem to know anything.

17. Cozy Corner

Mary McGann had been thorough as usual. His reservation was all set at the Budget motel just off the I-94 on a windy hill south of Bismarck. He dropped his suitcase on the bed, consulted the itinerary in his briefcase, and phoned Roberta Whalen at the Cozy Corner bookstore.

She had a funny, breathy voice that Tom imagined might have been suitable for a 900 number phone sex connection. "I'm glad you called." She sounded relieved. "Did you have any trouble on the road?"

"Funny you should ask. I was stopped by the state police."

Roberta Whalen's sentences were oddly broken. "Were you speeding? Everyone speeds... on the I-94."

"A ticket would have been preferable. Someone thought I might be a suspect in an assault in Fargo last night."

"You sound like a... dangerous man, Mr. Godot. Are you sure you're just an author..., not some soldier of fortune?"

"Nothing quite so romantic or dramatic. Right now I'm a road weary book peddler who's ready for a shower. Need any more books? I have most of a case in the trunk."

"I might.... Your reputation has preceded you. I've been getting calls all... day about your reading, so many that I've arranged... for you to use the space next door here in the mini-mall. There's also a reporter wanting to interview you for the Bismarck Daily Gazette. Seems you're on the internet. Are you aware of that?"

Tom Godot kicked off his shoes and lay back on the queen size bed. "Nile publishing has web sites for all the books on their lists. I've seen it." It had his publicity shot, a copy of the cover of Conspiracy! and a sample chapter along with the usual ordering information. Mary McGann wasn't missing any bets.

"That's not... the site I mean," Roberta Whalen panted. Did she have emphysema, or was she jogging with a cell phone?

"I don't know about any other web sites," Tom said as he took off his shirt. His face felt greasy and grimy.

"Would you mind... if the reporter comes to your motel?

Tom stood up to drop his pants. "Not as long as I have time to get a shower. I'll see you at the store at six o'clock. Right?"

"Expect a crowd, Mr. Godot." She hung up.

Tom made it a long shower, changed from the jeans and sweat shirt he wore for driving to his best pair of slacks. A reporter would probably want to take his picture. He decided against the only tie he'd packed and put on a turtleneck sweater and the blazer he'd worn in St. Cloud for the taping of "Talking About Books."

He needed to talk to someone with a sympathetic ear. Jake Friedman in Portland hadn't appreciated the last call. Tom had the feeling that now that the book was published and the checks were coming in, Friedman's energies were elsewhere. The Nile offices in New York were closed on Saturday.

He tried Sylvia, but again she was out. This time he left the number of his Bismarck motel on her message machine.

There was a knock at the door, the reporter from the Bismarck Daily Gazette.

To Tom's surprise, she was a woman, Patty something-- he didn't catch her last name-- so young that she was either an apprentice out of high school or a new baked graduate from journalism school. She had short hair, wore no makeup, a butch look. Maybe nose rings and tattoos hadn't yet reached Bismarck, North Dakota. "Mind if I take notes while we talk, Mr. Godot?" She held up a steno pad.

"Go ahead. But no tape recordings," Tom said. "They make me nervous."

"That's just what I wanted to interview you about, Mr. Godot. Your recordings."

The motel room had only one chair and a little table by the window. Tom motioned for her to sit down. He pushed his suitcase to one side and sat on the bed. "What recordings? I was on National Public Radio in Minneapolis and on St. Cloud's TV."

"Whatever was put on the internet," Patty something explained.

"I haven't seen it."

"Maybe you should."

"That's easily done," Tom said. He took out his laptop, found the phone jack, plugged in the modem line and turned on the computer. "It'll just take a minute to log onto my server. It's a long distance call to San Jose." In a minute or two the familiar Netscape browser screen came up. "What's the web address?"

Patty something flipped pages on her steno pad and found it. It wasn't Nile Publishing. "Http:///www.whitepower/TomGodot.html." She spelled it out for him.

White Power? The page came up, first the text, then the pictures. The web site had a nasty logo, a swastika and the symbol Tom had just seen again on Runner Preston's Freedom Constabulary calling card, crossed swords and a crucifix. Odd that the atheist National Socialists would employ a Christian symbol, but since when did logic have anything to do with hate groups? There was a paragraph about him and a link to a film clip. Tom clicked on the link and waited. "This may take awhile," Tom explained. "It's over a megabyte. Lucky I've enough space on this hard drive."

While his laptop downloaded the film clip off the internet, Patty something continued her interview. Most of it was the usual questions. While she wrote, Tom got out his press kit and handed it to her. It had a nice photo of him, a dust jacket book cover, and the same list of questions he had offered to the woman in Minneapolis. "I don't understand how my reading at the Cozy Corner should generate so much excitement. In Oshkosh, Wisconsin I had an audience of one, a sleepy drunk. Now Roberta Whalen at the Cozy Corner says there's a big crowd coming. I'm not exactly Tom Clancy or General Powell."

"See the film clip," she said, and pointed to the laptop screen.

A chunk at a time the long file was relayed from the satellites and bounced to Tom's computer. Finally it was done. Tom clicked on the icon to play the video.

The voice on the film clip as heard through the tiny speaker in his laptop was hard to recognize, and the tiny window, only about two inches square, difficult to make out, but Tom recognized himself at a podium, reading from his book, and gesticulating. It was the first time he had seen a taping of himself doing his gig, and it looked awkward, the movements unnatural. It lasted less than a minute and was over.

"Did you make it out?" Patty something asked.

"No. It's me, all right, but I can't say where it was taped."

"Play it again," she suggested.

By the time Tom had watched the film clip three times he knew the passage. It was that bit he had read in Fargo only the day before, the villain's speech about revolution. Taken out of context and dropped into a white power web site it made him look like a Nazi.

"That is you, isn't it?" the reporter asked. Clearly she sensed a scoop.

Tom was angry. "It's me, but it's taken out of context. The passage is one of the characters' justification of his evil acts. Edited like this it makes me look like a..." For once he couldn't find a word.

"A white power revolutionary freak?" Patty something suggested.

"Hold it! Don't quote me as saying that," Tom cautioned. "When the lawyers at Nile see this clip they'll sue whoever put up this web site."

Patty was scribbling rapidly on her pad. "You're not the first public figure to be quoted out of context, Mr. Godot."

"I'm not a public figure," Tom protested. He had visions of movie stars pursued by paparazzi, journalists with long lenses hanging from trees outside hotel room windows.

"You are now," she said. "Are you saying you plan to sue whoever you claim misquoted you?"

"I don't know what I'll do." More than ever he was feeling trapped. "Maybe nobody will see the web site."

"Most people wouldn't find it by accident, but after the story is in the papers, you'll get lots of hits."

Hits, the term Mary McGann used for every time someone checked his web site on the internet. "Why don't you do me a favor, Patty? Whatever you write about my reading, leave out the white power web address."

"But that's the real story here, Mr. Godot, how you could give a speech in Fargo one day and by the next afternoon hundreds of people had seen it on the world wide web."

Tom groaned. He stared at the film clip's opening frame on the laptop screen. "Was there any mention of an assault in Fargo?"

She hadn't heard of it.

Tom shut the computer. His voice heavy with sarcasm, he told her, "Why don't you check the state police post here in Bismarck? Your local FBI agent grilled me about an incident last night in Fargo. Seems an NSA agent was assaulted at a meeting of the Sons of Liberty. That ought to get you on CNN, Patty. A story like this and you'll graduate to something more than the Bismarck Press Gazette. Now leave me alone while I call my lawyer." If he didn't control himself the next assault would be on a meddling reporter.

She was unfazed by his anger. "Thanks for the tip," Mr. Godot. "I'll see you at the Cozy Corner."

The door shut behind her and Tom stewed. He didn't have a lawyer. He didn't even have libel insurance. He was sinking deeper and deeper into a morass.

18. Sylvia

Tom still had a couple of hours to get a meal and consider what he might read at the Cozy Corner bookstore. Like the mother turtle who loses interest in her eggs once they have been laid, most authors lose interest in a book once it's printed. The joy is in the creation. He had enjoyed the intellectual exchange and occasional argument that went with collaboration with the invisible Harold Stevenson. That was over now and Tom was beginning to see Conspiracy! as a nagging, delinquent child. He wanted to be done with it.

At first the idea of a book tour had been exciting, a departure from life confined to a tech writer's cubicle at MOM. In California people called the Midwest "back east" the way immigrants to the United States had called their place of origin the old country. The Midwest was a vast open space one flew over on the way to New York. Now his view of the Midwest was redefined. San Francisco, like New York, was cosmopolitan and sophisticated, the proverbial melting pot of races and nationalities. By comparison the Midwest was white and bland.

It hadn't taken long for Tom Godot to tire of sterile motel rooms and restaurant food. He could predict what was on the menus. The standard fare was full of grease, sugar, and salt. The people asked dumb questions.

The weirdness, he realized now, had begun in Madison, Wisconsin and there was no telling where it would lead. He wouldn't mind calling it off right now, but the tour was part of the contract, and Mary McGann would hold him to it.

The phone rang. Tom picked up the receiver with apprehension. "Hello?"

"Tom?"

It was Sylvia. "What a relief to hear a friendly voice," Tom said. He tried to visualize her face, but his most vivid memory of Sylvia was not how she looked, but how she felt that evening when he had tried to kiss her and she reacted with uncontrollable trembling.

Her mental fragility was an odd contrast to her hands. Sylvia's knuckles sometimes bruised from a weekend of rock climbing. He was a head taller than she was. Even in heels she came up only to his chin with her hesitant smile and blonde hair. He regretted that he didn't carry a picture of her.

"How's the life of a famous author?"

"You mean infamous." He launched into a blow by blow description of his encounters with the Freedom Constabulary and the Sons of Liberty, climaxed-- so far-- by the white power web site. "Right now I'd rather be back in San Jose putting out the newsletter for the local chapter of the Society for Technical Communication." He was glad Ivar Hansen had given him a leave of absence for the book tour. When this was over he had a real job to go back to.

"The price of fame and glory," she teased. "Look at it this way: my uncle Ivar will be so impressed by your new marketing skills that he'll promote you at MOM."

"In the Horatio Alger books the hero makes good by rescuing the boss's daughter from a falling grand piano, marries her and becomes president of the bank."

"I'm not the daughter, just the niece. Do they count?"

"Who knows? If I get into any more trouble with those freaky revolutionary groups I'll lose my security clearance and be out on the street peddling remaindered books."

Now Sylvia was serious. "Do you think that could happen?"

"It might," Tom said. "People might make a connection between the plot Stevenson hatched for the book about disrupting world-wide communications and the computer chips MOM makes for communication satellites."

"Is that possible?" Sylvia asked.

"Possible? Anything's possible. What would I know? I'm not a programmer or an engineer, just a tech writer and editor. God, I wish this was over."

"What does Stevenson say about this?"

"He's gone spooky on me, wants everything encrypted. He says he's going to encrypt all our files at MOM. He even sent me a program and a manual for Pretty Good Privacy."

"He must have a reason," Sylvia suggested.

"Whatever it is, I'm getting stage fright about these readings."

"Where do you go next?"

"I was supposed to stop in Missoula, Montana but that's been canceled. I drop the rental car here in Bismarck and fly with United to Spokane and then drive to Coeur d'Alene in Idaho. Why don't you join me? I could use a little moral support."

There was a pause. Maybe Sylvia was thinking about it. "I've got to do a report for my industrial management seminar."

"Then join me in San Jose at the end of the tour. We can work on the Horatio Alger idea." He had an afterthought. "One more thing-- I don't have a picture of you. Why don't you scan one and post it to me by e-mail? Something to keep me company in these lonely motels."

"I thought famous authors were pursued by groupies," she quipped.

Tom thought about that would-be poet in St. Paul and Kerstin Olofsdatter in St. Cloud. He had had opportunities. "I'm saving myself for you," he said. "Besides, so far the only groupies I have are mean guys with swastika tattoos."

She laughed and rang off.

Tom couldn't laugh about mean guys with swastika tattoos. He decided for the Cozy Corner bookstore he wouldn't read at all, just field questions.

19. Live on Channel Five!

Roberta Whalen turned out to be as sultry as her breathy voice on the phone had suggested. The Cozy Corner book store was an artsy place that catered to Bismarck's natural foods, new age, gay-lesbian and otherwise fringe readers. The store had a special display section for each of those groups, besides the best sellers like his that probably paid the bills, even though Whalen's tastes were elsewhere. He saw no copies of the Turner Diaries or survivalist books.

Roberta Whalen decorated her honey-colored hair with interwoven strands of varicolored beads, wore slacks under a blouse that had been stylish once but now gave her a shopworn look. She lost no time in telling him that she had left her husband for a woman, but that didn't work out. Obviously she was still looking.

Tom was too worried about the impact of the white power web site on the local audience, the FBI man who had interviewed him at the state police post and whether the Freedom Constabulary and their network of contacts had called out the Bismarck survivalists. In the back of his mind he also wondered about Mary Contrari's condition. Had this been a rape, a robbery, or was it politically motivated? "I saw the web site," he explained. "I've been quoted out of context. This time I think I'll just answer questions. Is this a wine and cheese deal?" He had been spoiled by the Napa Valley California wines and dreaded the tanker truck red that was served at the Mystery Lovers' bookstore in St. Paul.

"How about herbal... tea and marijuana brownies?" she breathed.

Her panting was getting on his nerves. "Better keep it straight." Tom said. He'd already been interrogated and didn't want a repeat performance. "There may be police in the audience tonight."

If Roberta Whalen needed more books she could take the sixty copies still in the trunk of the Neon on consignment. Whatever didn't sell she could return.

She had borrowed a pickup truck load of folding chairs from a New Age church. Tom helped her set them up in the empty store next to Cozy Corner. While they were doing that Patty something from the Bismarck Daily Gazette showed up with her steno pad. Her butch appearance in the Cozy Corner setting suggested the connection. She was visibly disturbed when a crew from Channel Five TV showed up outside with their white truck, folding dish antenna, cables, and heavy cameras.

"There goes your CNN exclusive," Tom said.

The TV reporter was a hyperactive man in his forties. He was the only one wearing a jacket and acted like he was juiced on too much office caffeine. He treated his crew like slaves even though he called them "people" as in "Let's go, people" and barked clichés like "Get this show on the road."

There was only one camera which looked like it weighed as much as the perspiring cameraman who lugged it on his shoulder.

Roberta Whalen aimed him at Tom Godot and got Tom to move in front of the Cozy Corner store front for the subliminal advertising effect. Not to be outdone, Tom opened his briefcase and got out his copy of Conspiracy!

The TV crew acted like they were going on live. An assistant fussed with the earpiece the interviewer wore, checked her watch, then gave the signal to the man in the jacket.

"Tom Godot? Bert Jenkins, Channel 5."

Mary McGann would love this. Tom mumbled "gladdameetcha" and hoped his ears were on straight.

Bert Jenkins Channel Five wasted no time. No doubt he'd be edited down to no more than a one minute sound bite for the late evening news. "Tonight Bismarck`s Cozy Corner Bookstore hosted best selling author Tom Godot."

"Author of Conspiracy!" Tom added.

Jenkins wasn't interested in the book. "I hear you're the spokesman for the Aryan Nation which is headquartered here in Bismarck," Jenkins said.

Was that the outfit that ran the white power site on the WEB? "I never heard of them," Tom insisted. He was ready to form his own hate group, the I Hate Scoop-crazed

Journalists. "If you mean the people who put a film clip of me on the World Wide Web, the taping wasn't authorized. They took my statement out of context. I'm not in favor of revolution. I support motherhood, apple pie, freedom and the American Way of Life."

"Then you deny saying that America is ripe for revolution?"

"One of the characters in my book says that."

"A clever way to package your own views," Mr. Godot.

Were the people in North Dakota all nuts? In the movie Fargo they acted stupid, but weren't. In the case of Bert Jenkins, Tom didn't think it was an act. "The bible has Satan arguing with Christ," Tom said. "Does that make the authors of the bible Satanist?"

The question went right by Bert Jenkins of Channel Five. "You are alleged to have assaulted Mary Contrari in Fargo. Have you a comment on that?"

"Mary Contrari is an agent of the National Security Agency, a secret government agency that snoops on authors who give public readings," Tom announced. Her cover, if she had one, be damned. "I have no connection with the NSA, the FBI, or any other government agency."

"But you are an employee of MOM, a piece of what President Eisenhower called the military industrial complex."

"What's that got to do with it?" Tom asked.

"That's what we'd like to know, Mr. Godot. Is there a conspiracy within the government to overthrow itself?"

"Are you out of your cotton picking mind?" Tom asked.

Sarcasm hadn't worked. There had to be a way to stop this. He held his book up to his face so even with a close shot the cameraman couldn't avoid it. "Conspiracy! Twenty-five bucks at your favorite bookstore. Buy my book." With that he turned and walked away, knowing the last lines would be edited out.

20. Not such a Cozy Corner!

Roberta Whalen had found a big coffee urn and set up a table with a box of generic tea bags, a stack of insulated paper cups and a plate of cookies. No marijuana brownies this time. There was a lectern where he could keep his notes, but no microphone. Tom got the box of books out of the trunk and she set up a display.

While the crowd gathered Tom hid out in the Cozy Corner next door. It lived up to its name. Roberta Whalen had placed worn but comfortable chairs throughout her store to encourage customers to sit alone and read. It wasn't like Borders Books outlets where there was often a cafe where couples could hang out.

When Tom emerged, the space next door was full of people. The crowd was different from any Tom had encountered before. Whoever had put his film clip on the World Wide Web had made the reading an excuse for a demonstration. Besides earnest-looking men like the ones who had been at the Church of the Apostles in Fargo, Bismarck produced several skin heads in leather jackets, leather pants, and boots with spikes in the toes. Someone produced a placard with the words "White Power!"

If Roberta Whalen had wanted people to notice her bookstore, this particular crowd were more likely to burn books supporting the gay and lesbian and New Age lifestyles than to buy them. Maybe Whalen was naive, or maybe she, like the politician who says "I don't care what you say about me as long as you spell my name right" wanted publicity at whatever cost.

If she did, that would explain why there was a second contingent of people in the audience, the anti-hate group. If Tom had been posted as a proponent for white power, someone else was using his presence as an excuse to protest. Mixed in with the two factions were what looked like some of Roberta's regular gay and lesbian clientele. A couple of tough looking women were holding hands in the front row.

What was he supposed to do with this mix of audience? Any joke he might tell was bound to offend somebody. He was gun shy about being taped and quoted out of context, so he thanked people for coming and inviting him to Bismarck, then announced that he would dispense with a reading and take questions.

The first wasn't a question at all. "Mr. Godot, I want to thank you for expressing in your book the frustrations and anger so many people in this country feel about our government."

Was this a compliment? Tom protested, "I'm glad you liked Conspiracy! but that's not the purpose of the novel."

"What is the purpose?" someone shouted from the back.

Tom tried to locate the speaker. It was someone with a sign on a stick that said "People Power" which could mean anything.

Tom explained, "Besides being a work of fiction to entertain, Conspiracy! is a warning."

"And about time!" someone shouted.

"Yeh, right!" another yelled.

The shouting match didn't ring true. Was the audience rigged with agitators? Without a microphone, Tom couldn't make himself be heard. Someone was arguing loudly at the back of the room. Someone pushed. Tom saw a white power placard grabbed and torn up. In moments it turned into a free for all. If someone wanted a melee , they had one.

Tom decided that the best recourse was a retreat. He put his notes and copy of Conspiracy! in his briefcase and was closing the latches when he felt something hit him.

It was a glancing blow. Stunned, he turned to see where it had come from. One of the two women he had noticed had gotten to her feet. She was broad, wore a plaid shirt, had long black hair tied back. "Bastard!" she shouted and punched him hard in the face.

Someone grabbed him from behind. He was being kicked in the shins. He remembered someone saying, "Let's get him out of here," when he was struck in the face again and blacked out.

21. Taken for a ride

Tom came to in the back of a minivan. He was dazed, his mouth bruised. His head throbbed and his eye was swelling shut, so he could not see very well. He tried to get up. Someone said "Take it easy."

"What's this?" Tom tried to say through swollen lips.

The minivan smelled of spilled beer and dirty laundry. Occasionally the lights from an approaching car would briefly illuminate the faces of the men in the van, but the most he saw was a brief profile. Who were they?

"We got you away from those freaks," the man beside him said.

"Which freaks? I've been running into a lot of them lately."

"You're a funny guy, Mr. Godot."

"If you'll just take me back to my car..."

"You need medical attention," the man said. "We're taking you to a safe place."

They were somewhere in the open vastness of North Dakota. Tom felt the van slow down and turn onto gravel, then the rumble as it was driven over a cattle guard. For a few minutes they were on a rutted dirt road. They stopped. The door slid open and Tom was hustled and half carried by the elbows into a mobile home.

Which freaks? had been the right question. He had been too surprised to feel fear in the bookstore. Now he did, a queasiness in his stomach like the onset of diarrhea. He was apparently in the headquarters of a White Power organization. A Nazi flag hung over a fake fireplace. Empty beer cans stood here and there on the floor. A large, locked gun cabinet on one wall included a virtual arsenal. Though Tom Godot wouldn't know an M-16 from an AK 47 they looked like military assault rifles. As in most mobile homes the kitchen wasn't a separate room. What would normally be used as a breakfast bar was occupied by a computer with a large monitor.

Someone reached into Tom's hip pocket and took out his wallet. "Hey!" Tom protested.

Someone else had his briefcase and took out his laptop computer and opened it with the comment, "I hate these tiny keyboards." He was younger than the rest and didn't fit the mold. He wore a baseball cap backwards and, Tom noticed on closer examination, had a pierced eyebrow, the current sadomasochistic trend.

Tom saw that the young man with the pierced eyebrow had large hands with thick fingers. Tom's feeble protest, "Leave that alone," was ignored.

They sat him down none too gently in the middle of a threadbare couch. "What are you guys doing?" Tom asked, his mouth sore. "Rescuing me or kidnapping me?"

"That depends on you, Mr. Godot."

"Right now it feels like a kidnapping," Tom said, gently feeling his left cheek.

"Let's just call this a private interview," the captor who appeared to be the leader said. He was a bald man of medium height with a narrow chest. Though the others wore short blue jean jackets reminiscent of World War II, the leader wore a hunting jacket in khaki with lots of pockets.

Tom asked him, "Got any ice?"

"Sure. Rick, see if we've got any ice."

The young man who was fiddling with Tom's laptop got off his stool and went to the fridge, broke out some ice cubes which he wrapped in a dirty dish towel and handed to Tom. "Here."

"Thanks, Rick," Tom said. Now what were the names of the others? He pressed the towel to his swollen cheek. "What sort of interview?"

One of the men, a skinny fellow with cowboy boots, jeans, and a big belt buckle had Tom's wallet. "I'm curious about the cards you got here in your wallet. People reveal so much of themselves by what they carry around. The Nile Publishing Company corporate Visa card tells me someone trusts you with a lot of money, Mr. Godot. But no picture of a girl friend? And these business cards... Runner Spencer of the Freedom Constabulary, P. Hinkel of the Bismarck FBI office, some bookstore cards and... Now here's an interesting one. Mary Contrari, National Security Agency, with an 800 number. This is heavy stuff, Godot."

Rick had returned to the counter, but turned to say, "Contrari. I heard that name. Something in the Fargo news."

Someone laughed. It was the fourth man. At first he had been sitting at Tom's left, but he had gone to the fridge for a beer. "She got beat up. Snooping around the Sons of Liberty in Fargo."

Tom shifted the towel to his swollen lip. The ice felt cool and soothing. "Hinkel, the FBI guy, thinks I did it."

The man popped the beer can. "And of course you didn't."

"I don't go around beating up women. Or anybody else," Tom said.

"You obviously don't have much experience in barroom brawls." The man in the cowboy boots looked at Tom. "Who the hell are you, Godot?

"I'm just an author on a book tour."

"Bullshit," the man beside Tom on the couch said.

Tom tried to get up, but was restrained.

Cowboy boots leaned down into Tom's face, holding up the fanned business cards. "You're like flypaper. Wherever you go, things stick to you.

"I'm just a popular guy."

"Who set up this so-called tour?"

"Mary McGann, my editor at Nile publishing."

"Do editors normally set up book tours?

"I don't know," Tom said truthfully. "This is my first trade book. Before it I did a private family memoir and a few short stories, stuff like that."

The one called Rick was fiddled with Tom's laptop.

"Hey," Tom protested. "That's none of your business. You might erase something important."

Rick was clearly the computer jock of the group. "Don't worry. I'm not going to delete anything. I see Nile here."

"That's correspondence with the company about the book contract. What are you looking for?"

Rick didn't answer. "What about your book? Is it in here?"

"Of course not," Tom answered. "The book's published."

"I mean, you didn't delete the text?"

Tom shook his head. "It was never on this computer. I bought this with the advance from the publisher. I worked on the book in San Jose." He didn't tell his "hosts" that he had a computer in his apartment and he and Stevenson worked through MOM's computers, just as he had with the Hansen memoir.

Bald Man had taken the business cards from Cowboy Boots and studied them. "What about Harold Stevenson?"

"My co-author."

"Yes, the man with no face on the book jacket."

"What about him?"

"Tell us about him."

"Nothing to tell," Tom said. "I never met him. I don't even know his phone number."

Rick turned from the counter. "E-mail? You communicate by e-mail?"

"Yes."

"What's Stevenson's e-mail address?"

"I don't remember. It's in the e-mail list of addresses."

Rick grunted and fussed with the laptop, cursing the tiny keys. "Got it! HLStevens@Falcon.com. Where's Falcon?"

"Falcon?"

"Falcon is the server ID"

"No idea."

Rick shook his head. "I'll find it." He powered up the big computer on the counter. "I can find anything."

"Are you the one who put that film clip of me on the World Wide Web?" Tom asked.

Rick turned and gave Tom an evil smile. "Yeh, that was me. Pretty slick, eh?"

"Where'd you get it?"

The bald man intervened. "That's our business. Tell us about Stevenson."

"I honestly don't know."

Tom saw from the big monitor display that the man's computer was running Windows 95. Rick said, "Now that we have his e-mail address we'll find him."

"If you do, you're a better man than I am," Tom said and meant it. Stevenson's identity was something he wanted to know himself.

22. E-mail to Stevenson

"The place to start is the major domo of the server," Rick explained. Using his computer he sent a query asking for Stevenson's name and address. "You could have tried this yourself."

"I didn't know you could do that," Tom admitted. He turned to the bald man. "Can I have my wallet back now?"

The man pondered, then reluctantly handed it over. Tom checked the business cards. They were intact. So was his credit card. As soon as he was free of these men he was going to call Contrari's voice mail and the FBI man in Bismarck. "How about your own business card for my collection?" Tom asked the bald man.

"You don't need the Aryan Nation alongside the NSA"

"Suit yourself." So these guys were the Aryan Nation. How many such organizations were there? Were they all separate, or was there a national movement? "I wouldn't mind a beer."

"Help yourself."

Tom got up, still nursing his swollen eye with the ice pack, and went to the refrigerator. Obviously these men didn't do much cooking. There was a supply of sandwich meats, half a loaf of white bread, bacon and eggs, and several brands of beer. Remembering his paunch, Tom chose a can of Coors lite, popped the tab, and stood behind the computer jock to eavesdrop.

The response to Rick's request was almost immediate. HLStevens was not known at Falcon.com. "How is that possible?" Tom asked.

"It's a fake. The messages are relayed from somewhere. I'll try Finger."

The Finger directory could locate millions of e-mail addresses. This search came up with a dozen Harold Stevensons. Which one was it? Or was Harold Stevenson none of the above? It would take time to check out each one.

"Maybe you should send each of the dozen Harold Stevensons a message," Tom suggested. "'Are you Harold Stevenson the author?'"

Rick turned to Tom Godot. "I'll do that. In the meantime maybe you should ask him yourself. Here." He pushed the keyboard to the side and motioned to Tom to take a seat on the stool beside him. "Ask Stevenson for his phone number and snail mail address."

Rick was using a different program than Tom was used to, but it was as the computer jocks at the MOM plant said, "intuitive." Tom entered the address. For the subject line he put in one word: "urgent." Then he typed, "Harold. The Aryan Nation in Bismarck, North Dakota want to know your phone number and mailing address. They've put a film clip of my reading on the World Wide Web. Now they're insisting that I cooperate with them. I need to talk to you." He ended with his name and before Rick could stop him clicked the mouse on "send." Now from phone line to satellite his message in plain language was out in cyberspace where hackers or other snoops could read it. Tom hoped so, for if Hinkel or Contrari's people were watching, they'd know who he was with and they could trace the e-mail message he had just sent to its origins. But what if Rick, like Stevenson, had somehow relayed all his messages through a third party to protect his anonymity? It was like the old Mad magazine comic, Spy versus Spy, for every action a counter action.

Tom looked at his watch. It was a freebie he'd gotten from the credit card company for paying his bills on time. Nothing fancy, but it worked.

What time zone was Stevenson in? In New York it was past ten o'clock on a Saturday night. If Stevenson worked out of an office, he might not get the message until Monday. "We may have a long wait," Tom said. "I've got to be in Coeur d'Alene, Idaho, on Monday."

"You may have to cancel," the bald man said.

"Look," Tom pleaded. "So far you've been reasonably cordial hosts, gave me an ice pack for my eye, offered me a drink. But if you keep me against my will, it's kidnapping. That's hard time."

The bald man laughed at him. "If you witness against us, you might make that stick, Mr. Godot, but what if they never find your body? What about that?"

Tom tried to steady his hand and sip his Coors. "They may not find me, but they'll find you. Nile publishing will sue you for loss of my services. Stevenson will send the cavalry." Tom tried to imitate the trumpet call they always played in those old western movies when the cavalry arrived in the nick of time. His lip was too sore to make it sound anything but feeble.

"E-mail coming in!" Rick announced triumphantly.

Tom was astonished. Did Stevenson sit at his machine twenty-four hours a day? Who was on watch at Falcon.com, or wherever the messages really originated?

Rick the computer jock clicked on the message, subject line "Tom Godot, Eyes Only." Harold Stevenson's reply flashed on the screen.

"What's this?" Rick's voice had a tone of mixed incredulity, anger, and satisfied surprise. "It's encrypted."

"I thought he'd do that," Tom said, pleased with himself.

"So decrypt it," the bald man said, and put a hand on the back of Tom's neck.

"Can't," Tom said. "It's not on my machine. It was sent to your computer, and while we fool around Stevenson will be tracing it to us right here."

Now the bald man had both hands on Tom's throat. "You are a smart ass, aren't you?"

"I'm just suggesting that for your own protection you take me back to Bismarck now. You haven't done anything criminal. Like you said, people stick to me like flypaper. Everybody's watching me, the NSA, the FBI, the Freedom Constabulary, Sons of Liberty, and now the Aryan Nation." Like that reporter Patty something had said, he was a public figure. It might mean he'd lost his privacy, but there were certain advantages to having a high profile: everyone was watching. He remembered Mary Contrari said he could view surveillance as a kind of protection. He hoped her people were good at it.

The man in the cowboy boots agreed, "He's right. Take him back. We've got Stevenson's e-mail address. Given time, Rick will trace it."

Tom put his can of beer down on the counter. "May I have my laptop and briefcase back, please?"

Rick looked at the bald man and got the nod to return the laptop.

The bald man wasn't finished. "Make no mistake, Mr. Godot. We'll get what we want one way or another."

Only when they were in the minivan on the road back to Bismarck did Tom remember that the e-mail message had been sent to Harold Stevenson from Rick's computer and the answer sent as a reply to that same server. He had no idea what the address was or what the encrypted message said. There was no way he could get it.

23. The Budget motel

The man with the cowboy boots drove Tom Godot back to Bismarck. Still holding the ice pack to his left eye, Tom tried to get a look at the odometer to gauge the distance from town. He doubted if he could find his way back to the Aryan Nation's trailer if the FBI man asked him to. He was glad enough to be away from those men and considered himself lucky to escape with a black eye and a swollen lip. They hadn't beaten him up or robbed him of his money or corporate credit card and had returned his laptop and briefcase. So far as he knew, nothing was missing. He didn't dare check until he was free of them.

They rode in silence back to the city. The driver was not the talkative type, and Tom didn't want to press his luck by asking questions. He was grateful for the ride. They could as easily have dumped him at the side of a deserted highway and left him to find his own way back in the dark.

The Neon was parked where he left it near the Cozy Corner bookstore. Bits of glass littered the sidewalk. A new sheet of plywood had been fastened over a broken window at the store front next door where the reading had turned into fist fights. The Cozy Corner itself was dark except for a single light at the back showing the cash register with the drawer open, Roberta Whalen's way of telling would be burglars there was no money inside.

The window display had a stack of his books and his picture with a sign, "Meet the author." Some meeting! He would try to call Roberta Whalen at her home about the books on consignment. If she hadn't sold them he might have to pick them up before his trip to Idaho.

The ice pack had helped and he could see to drive, but he was going to have a nasty black eye. His lip was sore. Ah, the perils of an author on tour, he thought. Getting punched out and kidnapped were not in the contract with Nile. What next?

He remembered vaguely that his next stop, Coeur d'Alene, Idaho was a center for racist activity in the Northwest. If Bismarck was any indicator, this was one event he would prefer to cancel. Playing the successful author over wine and cheese in Madison, Wisconsin with the literateurs was one thing. Getting beaten up was another. Maybe his next project should be a cookbook.

With his luck, even a cook book could precipitate violence. He imagined being pelted with turnips by vegetarians protesting meat dishes. Only his sense of humor kept him from packing it in.

Back at the Budget motel, Tom got a bucket of ice from the machine for another ice pack, double locked his door, drew the blinds, and made several phone calls.

He left a voice mail message for Mary McGann at Nile, but got no answer at the Bismarck FBI office.

Mary Contrari's 800 number at NSA was answered by a real person. "Hello?"

"I'm trying to reach Mary Contrari."

"Who's calling, please?"

"Tom Godot. I heard she got hurt. I just wanted to see how she'd doing."

"I'm sorry, Mr. Godot, but I can't give you any information about that. Can you leave a number where she can reach you?"

"No. I'm at a motel. I won't be here very long." Tom was certain that NSA would have caller ID. He suspected that the person he talked to knew nothing, probably didn't even know who Mary Contrari was or that she was in a hospital in Fargo. People stuck at a switch board for the night shift couldn't be expected to know much.

He couldn't do the sales report for the fiasco at Cozy Corner. Mary McGann would have to wait. But he had to reach Harold Stevenson.

Stevenson had been right in his concern about security. Rick the Aryan Nation computer jock had not been able to access Tom's old e-mail messages. They weren't on the laptop, but in his electronic mail box back in San Jose at MOM's server. If he got grabbed again, he didn't want anyone to be able to read any of his stuff on the laptop hard drive.

Until he got used to the program, encrypting was tedious and clumsy, but it had to be done. Tom wrote an urgent message for Stevenson. "I got kidnapped by four men of the Aryan Nation. They wanted to contact you. Wasn't able to get your message because it was encrypted and on their computer. You should be able to trace them through the headers on the mail I sent you. I can't."

Tom paused. As co-author Harold Stevenson was not much of a partner. Stevenson hid while Tom literally took it on the chin. Did Stevenson know, was he in any way aware of the trouble Tom was getting? Why was Stevenson hiding? Why didn't he just come out in the open? Who the hell was he?

At the beginning the project had been an intellectually rewarding challenge. He hadn't thought about the money. The book's acceptance meant more hard work with the revisions. When he got the check for his share of the advance the rarefied experience of those early morning hours at work alone in his apartment were transformed to a new reality. Then came the author's copies with his picture on the covers of all those books, and displays in bookstores across the country. He was a celebrity. What a kick! Now he felt like a chump who had been tricked, a pawn in some larger game. Why him?

He tried to backtrack. Stevenson had gotten to him because of the Hansen family memoir. Besides the family members, Ivar Hansen had given copies to all his business associates, which included government contractors and satellite manufacturers. Could Stevenson be among them?

Or was Stevenson a friend of a friend of Ivar Hansen? In a world where everyone is only six degrees of separation from every other human being, we are all connected. With today's communication, maybe there were only three degrees of separation. A friend of a friend of a friend of Ivar Hansen could be anybody.

The reality made Tom Godot angry. He wrote, "Where the hell are you, Stevenson? People keep asking me about the early drafts of the book. You say you've encrypted everything in the file at MOM's. What's in there that somebody wants? And what will they do with it if they get it? We've got to talk. I need your phone number."

The plot of Conspiracy! was a scheme to blackmail the world with a threat to disrupt all communications. It was, to Tom's mind, plausible science fiction, the kind of thing someone would make a James Bond movie of if Jake Friedman could sell the rights. It was a good page turner, a fast read, a hit at the beach. Trouble was, people couldn't tell the difference between fiction and fact.

Maybe someone out there believed it was possible. What would they be willing to do to get the real information? Burglary? Kidnapping? Murder? Jake Friedman had said the presentation copy before the Nile revisions was missing from the office. If Jake hadn't simply misfiled it in the slush pile, there might have been burglary. The Aryan Nation had kidnapped him. Would someone murder for information they thought he and Stevenson had shared early on?

At first he thought the idea stupid, silly, but remembered how Stevenson reacted: encryption.

The package with the P.G.P. encryption manual and disk had been sent from Arlington, Virginia. The obvious next step was the information operator. There was no listed number for a Harold Stevenson. Listed or unlisted, there was no certainty Stevenson was in Arlington. Someone else could send the parcel for him. Stevenson himself could be anywhere. If the Falcon e-mail server's major domo denied having a Harold Stevenson, maybe it was a pseudonym, or the major domo had special instructions to deny. Why should Tom have to be the public figure, getting punched out and kidnapped, while Harold Stevenson remained safe and anonymous?

Tom encrypted the message for Stevenson, called up the MOM server, moved the cursor to the "send message" button and clicked on it.

Before logging off he checked his incoming mail. Sylvia Hansen had scanned a picture of herself by her Uncle Ivar's swimming pool and sent it as an attachment, "with love, Sylvia." Too bad he didn't have a portable printer. He would save this on his hard drive for later.

She looked so sweet in the picture. He wanted to put his arms around her, hug her, get lost in her embrace, sweep her up in his arms and carry over the threshold. How he longed for a warm caress. The trouble with our culture, he reasoned, is that nobody touches anybody, except maybe a handshake, or, he thought ruefully, a punch in the eye.

San Jose might be only a few hours away by plane, but it felt like a million miles. How long had it been since he slept in his own bed? He admitted that after all these nights in strange towns and sterile motels he missed the mess in his apartment and morning jogs. Even being back in his office cubicle at MOM would be a relief.

After he unplugged the laptop modem line and replaced the phone cord he realized the red light on the phone set was blinking. He had a message at the desk.

The night clerk took a long time to answer. A bored, male voice said, "Yes, Mr. Godot, you have a couple of messages. Some reporter from the Bismarck Daily Gazette wants you to call and there was a message from a Sylvia Hansen."

"I'll come down and get it," Tom said. He had no desire to talk to Patty something from the Gazette. He'd be glad to put Bismarck, North Dakota behind him.

The written message for him from Sylvia was cryptic. "Be ready for a big surprise in Coeur d'Alene."

This book tour had been full of surprises, most of them unpleasant. It was too late to call her now. She should be in on Sunday morning.

His head buzzed with mundane details. He had to reach Roberta Whalen, get the sales figures, do Mary McGann's report, pick up books, pack, drop the car at the airport. The United flight left at 2:20 with a change in Denver. He wouldn't get to Spokane until almost seven in the evening after an airline snack of what? Peanuts and pop? It was a roundabout way to get to Idaho, but would save him two days of driving. As long as Mary McGann didn't cut off the credit line on the Nile corporate card, he didn't care. Mary McGann didn't have a black eye and a sore lip.

After the melee in North Dakota, Tom wondered what surprise awaited him in Idaho.

24. Welcome to Spokane

The United connecting flight out of Denver was fully booked and the departure delayed. Air travel was getting worse and worse, the seats smaller and smaller, the leg room suitable for midgets. Tom had a window seat, his precious briefcase wedged under the seat in front of him. To avoid people staring at his black eye he wore his dark driving glasses.

The man in the seat beside him weighed at least three hundred pounds. Tom was grateful to be protected by the armrest between them or he would have been crushed by the overflow of flesh.

The plane bounced heavily as it hit the runway in Spokane. Tom waited until most of the passengers had cleared the aisle before he attempted to extricate his feet where they were jammed by his briefcase. He wriggled out from under the overhead bin and moved stiffly toward the exit.

The flight attendant's smile had been fixed so long it looked pasted on. "Thank you for flying United," she said.

"Great peanuts," Tom said. "All two of them."

The surprise was waiting for him at the gate.

"Welcome to Spokane." She was wearing purple Lycra pants and an electric blue Gore-Tex jacket with a hood. She probably wore it for climbing, along with the Sorrel ankle-high boots she favored. The color of her jacket set off her blond hair and deep tan. An overnight bag was on the carpet beside her.

"Sylvia!"

She looked tentative, nervous. He put down the briefcase and threw his arms around her with a sense of relief that surprised himself. She relaxed in his embrace. Her first kiss was cool but then she melted into his arms. The next kiss was passionate and promised more, later. "I thought you had a report to write."

"I do, but I can work on it in Coeur d'Alene. I brought my notes."

"How did you know my flight number?"

She gave him one of those looks she reserved for people who should know better. "You sent me a copy of your itinerary. How did it go at the Cozy Corner?"

His answer was to take off the sun glasses. "Some of the audience wasn't happy. I got punched out by a dyke. I think the whole thing was staged to get me out of the place. I'll tell you about it while I get my baggage and pick up the rental car."

While he waited by the baggage carousel for his suitcase and the remainder of the carton of books, he explained what had happened, about the Sons of Liberty and the Aryan Nation, about the fight. He found himself out of breath. There was so much to tell.

At first he had envisioned the book tour as an escape from his cubicle at MOM, a great opportunity to see the country. Now travel had become a test of endurance. He was glad his suitcase had wheels and a handle so he could balance the carton of books for the walk to the Budget car rental desk. There was a line.

"So the Cozy Corner wasn't as cozy as the name suggested," Sylvia said.

"It was Cozy enough. The crowd I attracted wasn't in tune with the place."

"What about the bookstore in Coeur d'Alene? What cute name does it have?"

Tom shook his head. "Book World. I've no idea if it's a new wave, gay and lesbian, mystery lover's, general interest, or what. I just know that Mary McGann picked it out of her list. It's her call."

"And you have nothing to say about it?"

"What do I know about Coeur d'Alene? Never been there."

The car rental agent was practiced and efficient. The name tag said "Arthur." There was no quibble about the corporate discount. Tom signed for the car, went over the contract, took the keys and the paperwork, said "Thanks, Arthur," and they searched the lot for the car, a red Toyota Tercel.

Tom loaded the box of books and his suitcase in the trunk, then took Sylvia's overnight bag. "How well do you know your Uncle Ivar?"

"Depends," Sylvia told him across the roof of the Toyota. "Are we back in interview mode? I thought the memoir was done."

"There's something your Uncle Ivar knows about Conspiracy! that he hasn't told me. I'm sure of it. Harold Stevenson's being cagey. I'm looking for the connection. Any ideas?"

"I'll think about it," Sylvia said. She buckled her seat belt. "Have you got a reservation in Coeur d'Alene?"

"Comfort Inn," Tom said. "They advertise free breakfast."

"Can you have a guest in the room?"

That was a surprise. She was more free-wheeling than he thought, or she had made up her mind about something. Maybe she just wanted to keep her expenses down. A grad student's budget didn't include money for plane tickets. Tom looked across at her with a smile. "Nile publishing and I will be pleased." For a change, things were looking better.

25. Comfort Inn

If Tom hadn't guaranteed the room, their late arrival at Comfort Inn might have lost the reservation. The room was more upscale than the Super 8 and some of the other franchise motels where Tom had stayed. This one had two queen size beds. Sylvia took the one near the window. He hoped her choice was a formality. He was keyed up, tired, and hungry. A pizza delivered to the room would not do. Among the information cards on the night stand by the phone there was a restaurant list. Great. Coeur d'Alene had an Olive Garden, his favorite Italian chain.

Tom didn't unwind from the stress of the last few days until he and Sylvia finished the second carafe of wine. Sylvia insisted on driving back to the motel.

She hadn't been able to tell him anything about Harold Stevenson. She didn't see her uncle Ivar often. The last time had been at a clan gathering to celebrate her uncle's fiftieth birthday. She had remarked about how many eligible silicon valley millionaires were among her uncle's friends and associates. "He told me to take my pick," she said. "I'm not into that kind of shopping just yet. Most of those are nerdy guys who get up in the middle of the night to check their e-mail."

"How do you know that?" Tom asked.

"Just guessing," she said, playfully. She had taken off the blue jacket. Under it she had on a tank top. Her braless breasts were small and perky, in proportion to her stature.

"You shouldn't have reminded me," Tom said apologetically. "I've got to see if Stevenson sent his address and phone number."

"You think you'll get it?"

"Good question. The Aryan Nation computer jock said the address was a fake, that Falcon.com had no record of a Stevenson. It's getting ridiculous." Using the motel phone line Tom rang up MOM's server, entered his password, and called for the e-mail. "There's nothing from Stevenson," he said, disappointed, "but there's something from the system manager. What the hell?"

It was a message from Poobah. Tom had once visited the office where the system manager hung out. He was a Gilbert & Sullivan fan, with pictures on the wall from the Mikado. That explained his choice of pseudonym: Poobah. That Ivar Hansen didn't mind a little levity at the office, even encouraged it, made life in the warren of cubicles more tolerable.

The subject line of Poobah's message was WARNING in all caps. Occasionally he'd send notices of system shutdowns for maintenance or changes in the service, or reminders to change passwords, but this one was different. "There are daily attempts by hackers around the world probing our system. So far we have been successful in blocking them with our fire walls. MOM's secret files are secure, but your own personal project has been penetrated. I don't know whether anything has been copied. Your files are write and delete protected, but someone has been snooping. When did you encrypt your files?"

"It sounds like the Aryan Nation's hacker is busy," Tom said. "Of course, it could be anybody. The world is full of teenagers with nothing better to do than try to break into computer systems, snoop around, and sometimes do damage."

"What are they after?" Sylvia asked. She had taken off her Sorrels and was lying on her bed with her feet straight up. The tight Lycra pants revealed the lines of the scanty briefs she wore under them. It was distracting.

"From the kinds of questions I've been asked, I'd say it was the first draft Stevenson sent me when we started the collaboration. It was technical and clumsy stuff, a long way from fiction, certainly no novel."

She put her legs down and turned toward him. "So Stevenson's no writer."

Tom thought back to those early days of the collaboration. "He's a writer of some kind. I think he writes reports and is likely to put in wry comments someone else has to edit out. I'd say he has a rebellious nature. He's also didactic and kind of boring. All his sentences are about the same length."

"Who would write like that?"

Tom sighed. "Maybe a computer programmer. Some of those guys are weird. They spend all their time writing code, all those computer languages. Can you imagine? Thousands of lines that look like scrambled alphabet soup?"

"It's not alphabet soup to them," Sylvia said. "Maybe that's why he's comfortable with encrypting files and you're not."

"Maybe I should retrieve that first draft. It was pretty wooden. What I find strange is that your Uncle Ivar encouraged the project. Stevenson has to be someone he knows, some friend of his."

"Ask Uncle Ivar," Sylvia said. "Go to the source. He was eager to have you write his family memoir, about his parents and all that, so why not tell you about his friends?"

Tom hesitated. "When you write a book like I did for your uncle you are bound to find out things you can't publish, stuff about mistresses, infidelities, nasty divorces, and failures. Take your uncle Erik Streicher, for instance."

"Don't," Sylvia said, growing cold. "Not Uncle Erik."

"Why? What's with this Erik Streicher?"

Sylvia drew herself together and took a deep breath. "Erik Streicher is persona non grata."

"If you don't want to talk about it, you don't have to. A family memoir isn't supposed to be an expose. That's why I'm hesitant about asking your Uncle Ivar too many probing questions. Remember, Sylvia, your uncle Ivar is my boss. If he gets mad at you you're still his favorite niece. He can fire me."

"Then don't ask him."

Tom took her hand and remembered the surprise he felt when this petite blond who weighed not much over a hundred pounds could have the callused knuckles of a rock climber. The book tour had made him vulnerable and alone in strange towns among people he did not know. "I'm glad you came, Sylvia. I feel so out on a limb, no one to talk to. Stevenson's a non sequitur. You don't get any sympathy out of a laptop computer."

Sylvia looked at her watch and took a deep breath. "I think it's time for some of that sympathy."

She picked up her overnight bag and went into the bathroom. Tom didn't know what to expect. They had never been intimate. He was so close to the Hansen clan that seducing Sylvia was like a breach of trust. If she was seducing him, did that make any difference? He had wanted to see her, but she had invited herself to his motel room.

He didn't even pack pajamas, but slept in his jockey shorts. Self-conscious, he hung his shirt and slacks over the chair. He was distracted by all the events of the last few days. He sat, worried and tense on the edge of the bed.

Sylvia hesitated in the doorway as if mustering her courage, then came out of the bathroom wearing just the pair of briefs the Lycra pants had promised. The tan lines showed they were even smaller than her bathing suit. She modestly covered her breasts with her arms and went to the light switch by the door. "God, your eye looks awful," she said.

"Does it?"

She sat on the bed and put an arm around him. "Let's kiss it and make it well."

Tom let himself melt into her embrace. Book World, Harold Stevenson, the hackers and the creeps could wait until tomorrow. He reached over to turn off the bedside lamp and noticed the Comfort Inn clock. He had forgotten the time zone change now that he was in Idaho. Tomorrow was already today.

He slid his hand down her naked back until he reached her tiny briefs and started to slip them off.

Sylvia froze. "Don't do that. I take off my own panties."

26. Flashback

The moment Tom had touched her in the small of her back and slipped his hand down onto her bottom the nightmare came back. She was five. Uncle Erik had been playing with her on the living room carpet. Then his mood changed, and he put his hand down her panties.

She pulled Tom's hand away and held it. "I'm sorry. It's a bad memory. When I was a little girl. Five years old, I think. Uncle Erik was, well, too affectionate. Nowadays the polite way to describe it was that he fondled me. He... he took off my pants. He showed me his penis. I had never seen a man's penis before, sticking out like that." She shuddered at the recollection. "I was terrified. My mother caught him and there was a row. I think that's behind the divorce and his leaving the company. I got a lecture about what was proper and improper touching. But that episode with Uncle Erik really messed me up."

"You never mentioned this before."

"Molesting children isn't appropriate information for Uncle Ivar's family memoir," Sylvia said.

"You're not a child any more."

"No." She looked at him, sitting there in his shorts, saw that he was ready. She was, too. She stood up and crossed the motel room to her overnight bag. "Got a condom?"

Tom licked his lips. He was obviously embarrassed. "No. It's not part of my book tour equipment."

"I thought you were a Boy Scout," she said, and pressed a packet into his hand. "Be prepared."

27. Parade!

If this is Monday, I must be in Coeur d'Alene, Tom thought. He put his feet on the floor, saw his jockey shorts lying there, and realized that he was naked. Then he remembered. Sylvia!

In packing for the book tour he did not plan for any sexual adventures. She had surprised him. She hadn't taken that flight from California to Spokane just to say hello. He understood her motives better now.

Their first attempt at sex had been a failure. She was frightened and he had been too excited. He guessed that the medical term for it was premature ejaculation. "Fiasco" was how he felt. He had joked that it was like it was his first time. She admitted that for her it was but that it was long overdue. They tried again, with less urgency. They had all night, didn't they? Once they knew each other better, once they got over the tenseness and felt comfortable with each other it would be different.

It was. By the third time he was no longer premature and could stay with her, helping her along as she was aroused. When she climaxed she nearly fainted with joy and pleasure.

He heard the shower running, went to the wash basin where he had put his shaving kit, threw cold water on his face and tried to get in focus. His lip was OK, but the black eye looked like some a ghastly birth defect. Maybe Sylvia had some makeup that would cover it.

The shower door opened and she came out, rubbing her hair with a bath towel. "I see you're awake."

Tom turned to her, uncertain and shy. "Morning." He was not used to seeing nude women in his motel room.

"Such a hunk," Sylvia said, and stroked his back. Whatever inhibitions she had had the night before had been swept away by their intimacy. "You are up," she observed. "Let's have some more of that."

It was amazing that she could be transformed in one night from someone so frightened to a woman of, how could he put it? experience. Her long pent up inhibitions were blown away. She guided him willingly back to the bed. They romped and cuddled another hour and might have started on another round when the phone rang.

Tom was spent. He groaned, "Who could that be?"

"Who knows you're here?"

"Too many people. Mary McGann..." He picked up the phone. "Hello?"

"Tom Godot?"

111

"Yes."

"Ted Brewer here. I was wondering if you'd ride in the parade today."

"Ted Brewer?" Who was that?

"Ted Brewer, Book World. You're reading this afternoon. Have I got the right Tom Godot, author of Conspiracy!?"

"Yes. I'm that Tom Godot. Sorry. You caught me at an awkward moment. What's this about a parade?"

"There's a parade today here in Coeur d'Alene. I thought you might ride with me. Book World has a float. I've got a big sign on it to publicize your talk. It would be great if you'd be part of it. Might sell more books."

"I'm all for selling books, but I'm not prepared to sit on any float with a grin pasted on my face. I'll leave that stuff to the politicians and beauty queens."

"You're too modest, Mr. Godot."

He didn't feel modest, sitting naked in the bed with Sylvia Hansen nibbling at the hair on his chest. "I guess I can ride in the car with you. Can I bring a friend?"

Brewer was agreeable. "Sure. Bring him along."

"Her."

"All the better."

"Where and when does all this happen?"

"One o'clock. I'll pick you up at Comfort Inn. That's where the letter from your publisher said you'd be staying."

"Mary McGann doesn't miss a bet," Tom said. "See you at one." Tom hung up and turned to Sylvia. "We're going to be in a parade."

"What kind of parade?"

"Damn if I know. Maybe it's the Girl Scouts jamboree. Ted Brewer of Book World has a float for it and wants to ballyhoo my book. Can't turn the guy down. It might be fun. We don't have to ride in the float, just in the car. There'll probably be a high school band or something. American Legion color guard. Fire trucks. Small town stuff. Maybe Brewer will have us throw candy to the kids. Let's get some breakfast before the Comfort Inn buffet closes."

They dressed and went in search of the breakfast buffet. As they passed the registration desk Tom noticed the rack displaying tourist information and offering the local newspaper. The Coeur d'Alene News Chronicle had a prominent headline. "Oh, shit," Tom said loudly enough to catch the attention of the desk clerk.

"What is it?" Sylvia asked.

Tom took a copy of the paper. He handed a dollar across to the desk clerk and showed the headline to Sylvia. "It's not the Girl Scouts jamboree," he said. "Look at this. 'Aryan Nation on the March.' It's a goddam white power demonstration."

Sylvia didn't respond at once. She studied Tom's troubled expression and searched for an appropriate comment. "I didn't even bring my Nazi armband."

"That's not funny, Sylvia. These people are nuts."

"Then it's a good thing you told Mr. Brewer we'd ride inside the car and not on the float. There's bound to be hecklers throwing fruit."

Tom threw up his hands. "Spare me. One black eye is already too many. Let's have breakfast and see what this rag has to say about the Aryan Nation."

28. Mary McGann

According to the story in the News Chronicle the parade would go down East Sherman Avenue and end at Blackwell City park for the rally. The parade was co-sponsored by the Aryan Nation and the local KKK. There had been a protest about a parade permit, but the mayor was sympathetic to the marchers. The irony was that the ACLU was prepared to take the case to court on behalf of the Aryan Nation to defend their rights of free speech and freedom of assembly.

"You're worried about this," Sylvia commented as she refilled her coffee cup.

Tom had stuck to his herbal tea. "For good reason. My gig in Bismarck turned into a fist fight with me as the prize. No telling what will happen at a white racist parade."

"Why are they so interested in you?"

"It's because of the book. It was Stevenson's idea to make it a conspiracy of white racists to coerce the government into expelling all blacks and Jews. You know the old line, send the blacks back to Africa and the Jews to Israel. I tried to soften that, and the editor, Mary McGann, agreed. Didn't want to make it a niche publication sold only to racists. It had to appeal to a more general audience. I wanted to phone Mary McGann from Bismarck, but the office was closed." Tom looked at his freebie watch. "She should be there now if she hasn't taken off early for one of her power lunches. I've got to call her. You can wait here and finish your coffee, if you like."

"I'll take it with me."

Sylvia carefully balanced her cup and they went back to the room.

Tom was reminded of their night of love when he saw the unmade bed. The disarray of sheets and pillows looked like the scene of battle. The other bed was untouched. In the light of day it was obvious to anyone who looked what had transpired. The maids at the hotel must be adept at reading the stains on sheets and feigning ignorance when they passed the tenants in the hallways.

Tom made a perfunctory attempt at tidying the bed spread, looked up Mary McGann's direct number in his address book and dialed.

Mary McGann's answer was tentative. "Hello?"

"Mary McGann? Tom Godot in Coeur d'Alene."

Now her voice brightened. "Tom! I expected to see a report about the Bismarck reading. How'd it go?"

"It got complicated. Turned into a fist fight, with me as the punching bag. Then I got snatched by some guys from the North Dakota branch of the Aryan Nation who claimed to be rescuing me. What they really wanted was information."

"Really."

"You're not surprised. You should be surprised."

Mary McGann's voice had a hard edge. "I'm from Manhattan. Nothing surprises me."

"I'll get the sales report for Bismarck to you today. I didn't do a signing. The figures are disappointing."

"But the publicity must have been good. If the incident made the newspapers, people will flock to the bookstore." Mary McGann hesitated while she looked something up. "That was the Cozy Corner, wasn't it?"

Tom felt bitter and put upon, a pawn in Nile's campaign to build profits. Mary McGann had gotten very pushy about sales after Nile was taken over by that German company. "Sometimes I think you'd be happy if people really did start a war against blacks and Jews if it sold books."

"I wouldn't go that far," she said. "Some of my best friends are Jews, and we have several African Americans working here at Nile."

Where, he wondered, in the mailroom? That wasn't what Tom wanted to talk about. "Today I'm going to be in the Aryan Nation and KKK parade, no less. This isn't my style, Mary." He didn't usually call her by her first name. She was too commanding a figure for him to be comfortable on a first name basis. "I'm not going to put on a white KKK robe just to sell books. Looking at the travel costs, I can't see how this book tour is going to make expenses. Nile must have deep pockets."

"One of those pockets is yours, Tom. It's in the contract. Read the fine print."

Tom could imagine her in that office with a window looking out at Manhattan's skyscrapers. What could she know in New York of what went on in Idaho and North Dakota? What did she think the Comfort Inn cost? Ten bucks a night? He had a sinking feeling in his bank balance. Using the Nile corporate card he'd forgotten his responsibility for a portion of the book tour expense.

Tom made a quick calculation. The book sold for twenty-five bucks a copy. Royalty was $2.50, of which twenty-five cents went to Jake Friedman the agent. The remaining $2.25 was split between him and Harold Stevenson. Tom's share was a dollar and twelve cents a book. For this he got a black eye and who knows what next. If he signed ten copies that didn't even pay for his dinner at the Olive Garden. "It's not cost effective. I think we should cut out the travel unless it's for appearance on a talk show like Good Morning America. I don't want to spend my royalties on the expenses of riding in a racists' parade."

"It's not as bad as you think," Mary McGann said. "Harold Stevenson is matching anything you have to pay out of pocket. Since he can't do the tour with you, it's the decent thing to pay his share of the publicity expense."

"It's still not enough."

Mary McGann hesitated and her voice lowered. "Nile is keen on your book's being a success. It's attracted some high level attention. There's additional financial support. I can't say from whom, but where travel money's concerned, you shouldn't worry."

"What do you mean, 'high level attention'?" Tom glanced at Sylvia and passed on a quizzical look.

"Someone's sweetened the money pot," Mary McGann said.

"You don't know who." It was a realization, not a question.

Now what? It was coming back to Harold Stevenson again. So he was paying his share of the book tour expense. What else was he paying? "This isn't a subsidy publication, is it? Some corporate manipulation of the media?"

It was impossible to track these things. With the communications corporations controlling television, magazines, book publishing, and the movies, a story on ABC television news about a film might be a scam to sell movie tickets. How could you tell what was news and what was manipulation?

Mary McGann was offended. "It's not a subsidy publication. Nile is not a vanity press."

"But someone's interested in our book being a bigger seller than it frankly deserves to be," Tom said. "Conspiracy! is not that great a book."

"You're being modest, Tom."

Clearly she knew more than she was telling. Her job security at Nile put book sales above everything else.

He realized that a book didn't have to be good to sell. It had to be hyped enough to get attention. That explained why there was so much trash on the market. "One more thing, before I ring off," Tom said. "I need to talk to Harold Setevenson. I left his number back at the office in San Jose. Can you give it to me?"

"I have a number. I don't know if he's there, but you can leave a message." She gave it to him.

At last, Tom said under his breath and wrote the number down inside the back cover of his address book. He said goodbye and hung up the phone. He turned to Sylvia, still sipping her Comfort Inn coffee. "Curioser and curioser, like Alice said down the rabbit hole. Someone's bankrolling my book and I don't know who."

Sylvia cocked an eyebrow over her coffee cup. "Sounds like Conspiracy! is a conspiracy."

29. MacArthur Foundation

Tom dialed the number Mary McGann had given him. It was picked up immediately. "MacArthur Foundation, Alice speaking, may I help you?" It was an African-American, southern accented voice.

So that was it. MacArthur Foundation. "The same MacArthur Foundation that gives out the genius awards?"

"No," she said. "Ours is spelled differently."

Was the misleading name a mistake or deliberate? "Can you connect me with Harold Stevenson, please?"

"Who?"

"Harold Stevenson. This is his co-author, Tom Godot."

"I don't think we have anyone here by that name."

"This was the number I was given by our editor at Nile publishing. Maybe he's out to lunch. Are you in New York?"

"Arlington, Virginia."

So it was Arlington, where the package with the P.G.P. encryption program came from. He was getting closer to the truth.

"Just a minute," Alice of Arlington said, and put him on hold. Now he had to listen to elevator music while she found Harold Stevenson.

After a long wait a hesitant male voice came on the line. "Who's calling, please?" The accent was hard for Tom to place. East coast, white, educated.

"Tom Godot. Is this Harold? Harold Stevenson?"

"How did you get this number?"

"I got it from Mary McGann."

"Who's Mary McGann?"

Just when he thought he was getting through. Nuts! "You're not Harold Stevenson."

"No. I'm one of his, er, associates."

"Is he there?"

"I can take a message for you. What's the problem?"

Tom sighed in frustration. "It's too complicated for a simple message, but you can say someone's hacked into my file-- correction, our file-- at MOM. I have to talk to him."

"What's your number? Perhaps Mr., er, Stevenson can call you."

Tom thumped the night stand in frustration. "I'm at the Comfort Inn in Coeur d'Alene, Idaho." He read the number off the phone. "I can't just sit around the motel waiting for him to call back. When is he in so I can reach him?"

The man's voice was tentative. "That's, er, a bit problematic. Mr. Stevenson is... out of the office."

"Does he have a beeper number?" So many people had beepers nowadays, and cell phones.

"I couldn't say."

Couldn't, wouldn't, or can't? "Who am I talking to?" Tom asked.

"Why don't you call back later, say four o'clock?"

When had Tom run into such a blank wall? The only real information he'd gotten was Alice from Arlington, and he was willing to bet she wasn't supposed to say. "I may be in a parade at four o'clock Eastern time," Tom said. He had an afterthought, a long shot. "Is MacArthur Foundation associated with NSA?"

"MacArthur Foundation is what some people call a think tank. Why don't you call again later, Mr. Godot? Perhaps Mr., er, Stevenson will be in then." He hung up.

Tom looked at Sylvia in bewilderment. "A think tank, he said. Every time I asked him something he gave me an evasive answer."

"At least you got the number where Harold Stevenson is supposed to be," Sylvia said. "That's something."

"Yes, and I found out the name of the city and MacArthur Foundation."

"See? You did good, Tom."

"Maybe. But the way the guy talked it makes me wonder if there is a Harold Stevenson. Maybe Conspiracy! is a book written by a committee like Naked Came the Stranger."

30. CMOS

Tom looked at his freebie watch. "We have a couple of hours before Mr. Brewer picks us up for the parade. Let's take a walk around Coeur d'Alene. Get the lay of the land."

"You going to take your security blanket with you?" she asked, pointing at his briefcase.

"It's too heavy to carry, and I don't want to leave it in the trunk of the Toyota." He remembered the hackers and what was his name? Rick, the computer jock in Bismarck. "The computer's insured, but I'll make it a little more difficult in case someone gets hold of this." He pulled the heavy briefcase onto the little table and got out his laptop. When he turned it on the computer went through its self test and setup routine. Before it could complete it, Tom hit the delete key.

"What are you doing?" Sylvia asked.

"Fixing the CMOS. I'm adding a password so nobody can access anything on this without it."

"What if you forget the password?"

"Then the computer won't run at all. I'll be shit out of luck," Tom said. "The password's got to be something I won't forget." There were so many passwords to remember, one he used to get to MOM, another for his own files, the pass phrase he needed to encrypt e-mail to Harold Stevenson and yet another to get to his own Conspiracy! files.

"How about 'Sylvia'?"

"I won't forget that," Tom said. He reset the CMOS and closed the laptop, put it back into the briefcase. The briefcase had combination locks he never used. The trouble with all these security measures was they hindered your own easy access. "Let's check the parade route. I want to see what we might expect."

"And buy some candy to throw to the kiddies?" Sylvia asked, remembering.

Tom shook his head. "Don't I wish. I'm afraid there won't be many kiddies at this parade."

31. Book World

The main street of Coeur d'Alene looked like any other small American town. One might have expected an alpine theme in a city whose environs were so similar to Switzerland. It had been dusk when Tom's flight from Denver arrived, and he had not seen the place in full daylight, the wooded mountains, the brilliant blue lake. Coeur d'Alene was a jewel.

Unfortunately, the jewel had been discovered. Besides the headline about the parade, the News Chronicle tackled the pollution of the mountain lakes by silver mine tailings. The native Americans wanted to repossess the land and reclaim the lakes. Other letters to the editor decried over-development. The same story was repeated all over the country. As soon as someone discovered an ideal location, it was ruined by people flocking to it like flies on a fresh carcass. First the trappers, then the miners, and now the yuppies had come.

Tom and Sylvia parked the red Tercel at Blackwell City Park and watched as workmen set up a platform for the rally. A man in khakis and an over-the-shoulder belt reminiscent of the old German brown shirts was doing a sound check of the PA system. A couple of workmen were setting up folding chairs. Tom and Sylvia stood under a tree and observed as a large Nazi flag was stretched between two posts.

A few curious onlookers watched from a distance. It was easy to spot the alert bodyguards, men with looks to match their hard bodies. They were the enforcers who would not hesitate to pound anyone who protested their constitutional right to speak against the rights of blacks and Jews.

A couple of police cars were parked not far away, a low key but visible presence. The decals on the doors read "Coeur d'Alene police, to Serve and Protect." The uniformed drivers stayed in their vehicles. Tom wondered how sympathetic the Coeur d'Alene police were to the Aryan Nation.

Tom's home state of California had first been populated by indigenous people, was invaded by the Spanish, became a Spanish province, then was invaded again by whites seeking their fortunes. The new tide of Mexicans seeking survival had made California's majority brown. Idaho was white. So far he had not seen a black face.

"This could get nasty," Tom said. "I'm glad I'm not on the podium for this one. I was uncomfortable enough in St. Cloud. The punch-up in Bismarck would be nothing compared to what may happen here." He pointed to two of the bodyguards. The men had hunched shoulders and thick necks, like they'd been working out with steroids. "Look at those guys. They're aching for a fight."

They drove around the city, found the book store. Ted Brewer wasn't in, just a male clerk who wore a Book World tee shirt and looked like a high school dropout with skin ravaged by acne. Tom was pleased to see his book prominently displayed in the window. Ted Brewer had plenty of copies, stacks of Conspiracy! inside as well. He was dismayed to also find The Turner Diaries, still in print, and copies of the Protocols of Zion and books that denied the Holocaust.

"You're not in very good company," Sylvia commented. "Has it been this way all along?"

"I can't figure it out," Tom said. "Conspiracy! is just a run of the mill thriller. If it sold ten thousand copies in hard back I'd have been satisfied. It would be on the store shelves a couple of months and disappear. But there's been heavy advertising, radio commercials, reviews by critics I wouldn't have expected to have any interest at all. Honestly, Conspiracy! has no business being on the best seller list. It just goes to show what can be done when a communications conglomerate manipulates the media."

"Who owns Nile?"

"Some German conglomerate," Tom said.

"You think it's political?" Sylvia winked at him. "Some neo-nazi plot?" She was teasing him.

Tom wouldn't tumble. "You think I'm paranoid? Full of my own conspiracy theories? Nile's list is huge. They bring out a book a day, cook books, sports, mysteries, even a textbook division. Conspiracy! is no more than a footnote, filling space near the bottom. My book isn't political or racist at all. It's just the usual formula stuff, villain versus hero and a bang-up confrontation scene at the end. Light reading, not what I'd expect the Aryan Nation to latch onto."

"There's got to be an explanation," Sylvia said. "You haven't looked deeply enough."

"I've been too busy peddling books. Let's go back to the motel. How about lunch before the parade? Brewer's picking us up at one o'clock."

"I wonder what he looks like."

"If he has a little black mustache, black hair down on his forehead, and a swastika arm band I'll skip the parade."

32. The Parade

The man who called from the desk of the Comfort Inn to pick them up did not have a mustache or an arm band nor was he a thick-necked bruiser or a brown-shirted thug, but a mild man with a receding hair line, an unhealthy paunch that obliged him to wear suspenders to keep up his Dockers, tan, buckskin shoes and a ready smile. His button-down shirt collar was cinched with a bolo tie, the slide a polished lump of silver. "Tom Godot? I'm Ted Brewer, Book World." He looked at Sylvia. She still wore her electric blue Lycra pants and Gore-Tex jacket. "And this must be your fiancée, right?"

"No," Tom said, feeling sheepish. Did the morning sex show on their faces? "This is Sylvia Hansen, Ivar Hansen's niece."

"Ivar Hansen?"

"My boss at MOM. When I'm not writing books I work in San Jose as a tech writer for Machino Office Machines, what we call Big Momma."

"That's very interesting." Brewer turned to Sylvia. "You're perfect for the parade, Miss Hansen-- a classic Aryan type."

"Swedish and Norwegian." Sylvia got right to the point. "What's your part in the parade, Mr. Brewer? Are you the organizer or something?"

"Or something," Brewer said with a conspiratorial grin.

Tom protested. "Sylvia and I were down at the park. We saw the thugs that call themselves the Aryan Nation. If you don't mind, we'll skip your parade."

"Mr. Godot, be reassured. It's not my parade. I'm just tagging along. We have quite a clientele at Book World, lots of special orders. If you look at our float you'll see it isn't about the KKK or Aryan Nation at all. It's about freedom to read without censorship or some government agency snooping into your book purchases. We're very jealous of our freedom here in Idaho. Surely you can't be against that."

Head games, Tom thought. He's trying to justify himself. Brewer isn't a Nazi himself, just a collaborator. Instead of being hostile to Ted Brewer he would be merely cautious and suspicious. "Let's see that float."

They followed Brewer to the parking lot. For once Tom felt safe leaving his briefcase locked in the room.

Tom always felt a person's choice of a dog or a car was an extension of his personality. He was surprised that the mild-looking middle-aged Ted Brewer was driving a red classic four door Cadillac convertible with white leather upholstery. He had expected a man with Brewer's appearance would drive something more sedate and subdued. "There it is," Brewer said.

The book store float, a flat platform, was hitched to the rear bumper. A large mock up of an open book stood six feet high with "Freedom to Read" in block letters. American flags on poles were stuck on each corner of the float and signs along the sides said BOOK WORLD. "Nothing wrong with that, is there?"

Tom reluctantly agreed.

Taped to the doors of the red Cadillac convertible were posters advertising Tom Godot, author of Conspiracy! complete with his picture. There was no mistaking who would be in the back seat. He had hoped to ride in a closed car with the windows up. If he sat there he would have to smile and wave at the crowd after all.

"Where's your adventurous spirit, Tom?" Sylvia asked.

Ted Brewer was earnest and pleading. "Don't let me down, Mr. Godot."

Once you put on a clown suit, you must act like a clown. Tom's unaccustomed role as a celebrity had momentum that pushed him against his better judgment. He got in the back seat of Brewer's convertible.

The parade assembled a mile from the city park. "We're near the end," Brewer explained. "A footnote, you might say." He turned in the front seat to face his passengers. "Once you think about it you'll realize that Book World's float is a subtle dig at the Aryan Nation. They think I'm in favor of their freedom to read, but I'm opposed to their brand of censorship."

"You think people will figure that out?" Sylvia asked.

"I'm flying American flags, not burning them."

"A real patriot," Tom said and hoped his sarcasm wasn't too obvious.

Up ahead a high school band had begun to play, the snare drums leading, followed by brasses that missed the drum major's cue. "They're moving out," Brewer said and started the engine.

The trouble with being in a parade is that you cannot see it yourself. Behind the Book World float was a contractor driving a huge truck bearing a newly washed Caterpillar bulldozer and behind that the first of several local fire engines. Being near the end, Tom and Sylvia had no idea what the marchers at the front were like. If the decorations they had seen at the park were any clue, it was an ugly display of arrogance and hatred, militia types in their "cammies" and survivalists. What came next? Book World with Tom Godot, author, with a wave and a smile. Guilt by association.

There were few spectators at the start of the parade, but as they made their slow progress down E. Sherman avenue more and more people stood at the curb, senior citizens in folding lawn chairs, silent spectators, a few people with cameras and camcorders. Tom wondered who was taking all those pictures and if they went into an FBI file with the caption, "Tom Godot riding in a white racist parade." He supposed Mary Contrari, whatever her NSA motives, would be pleased that he was humoring Ted Brewer as he had accommodated the Sons of Liberty. Peters the FBI man would not be pleased. The contradiction between NSA and FBI gnawed at him. Did they talk to one another? Someone had asked, "Which side are you on?" It was like the false dilemma, "Are you with us or against us?" He wasn't "with" anyone. By their definition that made him an enemy.

The jeering started when they got to Fourth Street. Idaho was not populated solely by white racists. It had its moderates and liberals. By Second Street he saw placards opposing racism. Coeur d'Alene wasn't all lunatic fringe.

As they neared the park the crowd on both sides of the street pressed in from the curb. Someone called "Hi, Mr. Godot!" but he could not see who it was. Another said, "Loved your book."

"Thanks!"

The parade ended at the park. "Let's get out here," Tom suggested. To Mr. Brewer, "You don't need us any longer, do you?"

They got out of the convertible and were immediately caught up in the crush of spectators. "I hope this doesn't get ugly," Tom said, gripping Sylvia's hand. "If we get separated, let's meet by the police cars parked over there."

The high school band had assembled to one side and struck up The Stars and Stripes Forever. People pushed from behind to get a closer look at the men on the platform.

Four men appeared to be speakers. Three were wearing khakis with swastika arm bands and Sam Brown belts. A bodyguard was stationed at each end of the podium. The fourth speaker was in a double breasted business suit, an old fashioned cut.

The energies of crowds feed on themselves until they reach a critical mass. A sprinkle of applause was followed by catcalls and jeering. Sylvia was so short that her view was blocked. "Can you see anything?" Tom asked.

"No."

"Let's work our way over to the side. Excuse me, can we get through? Excuse me. Coming through...." Pulling Sylvia behind him, he tried to thread his way through the crush.

Someone was pushing and someone else pushed back. The speaker tried to be heard above the noise. Whoever was running the PA system tried to turn up the sound, but got a squeal of feedback instead. More shouting. Looking toward the platform Tom saw a folding chair being thrown and the bodyguards rushing in. He didn't want to get caught in another riot. He let go of Sylvia's hand, told her "Stick with me," and bulled a path away from the center of the action.

When he got to the edge of the crush of spectators the crowd had become a mob. Where was Sylvia? Somewhere in their midst.

33. Brewer's Caddy

Sylvia felt someone take her hand in a firm grip and heard them say, "Back to the car." It was Ted Brewer. "You won't get through that way."

He wouldn't let go of her hand and pushed his way back to the parked red Cadillac. "We'll meet Tom at the bookstore," Brewer said.

"Everything OK, Ted?"

It was a large man whose belly threatened to push his pants down off his hips. He was not all fat. The beefy shoulders were broad and his arms thicker than Sylvia's thighs. He had a pudgy face and heavy eye brows that met in the middle of his forehead. He got into the back seat of the car, sitting behind Sylvia.

She heard an electric motor running and realized that Brewer was raising the top of the convertible. "In case someone throws rotten fruit," Brewer explained with a false smile. "Don't want to ruin this white upholstery."

"But Tom's meeting me at the other side of the park," Sylvia protested.

The engine was running and the Cadillac, the Book World float in tow, was in motion. Sylvia sensed something was wrong. She reached for the door handle but a strong arm held her from behind.

"Don't get out, Miss Hansen. We'll just make a detour to the motel. Mr. Godot expects us to pick up his briefcase and his computer and meet him at the bookstore. Nothing wrong with that, is there?"

It might be believable if the man behind her weren't gripping her shoulder so tightly. She tried to shake him off. "Let me go!"

"It's all right, Kilgore," Ted Brewer said. "Miss Hansen is very cooperative. She won't give us any trouble."

34. Missing

The Coeur d'Alene police held back until the scuffles threatened to turn into a general riot. From a safe distance behind one of the patrol cars Tom tried to spot Sylvia's blue jacket, but she was so short there was no sign of her.

The police sirens whooped and squealed like jackals surrounding a kill. A uniformed policeman with a bull horn ordered the crowd to disperse. At the podium the microphone stand had been knocked over. The three men in khaki and swastika armbands had melted into the crowd or escaped.

"Go home!" the voice on the police bullhorn demanded. "The party's over. Anyone who remains will be arrested!"

The crowd dispersed, leaving a confusion of folding chairs which had been set up so carefully before the parade. Pamphlets, circulars and trampled placards littered the grass. A man with blood running down his face was being taken away by two policemen.

The business end of a policeman's baton poked Tom in the shoulder. "The order is to leave the park, Mister."

"I'm looking for my girl."

"Your daughter? You didn't bring a kid to this."

"No, my girl friend, Sylvia. She was right behind me. She's wearing a blue jacket and blue slacks. Blonde, about so tall." He pointed to his collar bone.

"She's probably gone home."

"I told her to meet me here if we got separated."

"The order is to leave the park. Now."

Sylvia had been swept away by a tide of angry people, sucked under in swirls of hostility and anger. Where was she now?

Tom made his way as slowly as he dared across the park to Mullan road on the north side. The high school band had been gathered up by their leader like a flock of multi-colored chickens and were boarding their bus. Tom glimpsed Ted Brewer's red Cadillac with the Book World float in tow as it pulled away. Brewer had put up the convertible top, probably for protection. Tom couldn't see who was in the car.

If Sylvia missed him she would go to the Comfort Inn, he supposed. He had to walk several blocks before he found a pay phone to call a cab.

At the Comfort Inn desk there were no phone messages. Troubled, Tom walked the deserted hallway to his room. He had left the TV on as was his practice, but he did not hear it as he put the key in the lock.

The maid had turned off the TV and done the room. The bed he and Sylvia had left in disarray was made. Fresh towels and soap in the bathroom. His suitcase on the low bureau where he had left it. Sylvia's overnight bag beside it. What was missing? The bottom fell out of his stomach: the briefcase.

"Shit!" Tom exclaimed. It was not in the closet or under the bed. All his notes, his itinerary, and Mary McGann's maps and instructions were in it, his dog-earned and boookmarked copy of Conspiracy! and of course the laptop.

Tom called the front desk. "My briefcase is missing."

The clerk was indifferent. "The hotel is not responsible for valuables left in the room, Mr. Godot. We do have a hotel safe."

"Someone's been in here and taken it."

"Are you sure you left it in your room?"

"Of course I'm sure."

"Perhaps your companion has it."

"Sylvia?" Why would she do that?

In a moment of paranoia Tom allowed himself to suspect her, but dismissed the thought. Maybe Sylvia had gotten back to the room first, decided that, considering the riot at the park, it would be safer not to leave the briefcase in the room and taken it with her. But where would she go?

He rejected the idea as absurd. If Sylvia had come back, which he doubted, she would not want to lug ten pounds of briefcase.

Maybe she'd taken the car. Tom rushed from the room to the parking lot and searched for the red Toyota Tercel. It was in the lot where he had parked it. He opened the trunk. The box Beth Whalen had packed with the unsold copies of his book was in it, but no briefcase.

Tom looked up the number in the yellow pages and called Book World. Ted Brewer was not in. The assistant had not seen anyone that fit the description of Sylvia.

It was too early to file a missing person's report with the police. In any case they'd insist he wait at least twenty-four hours. Her plane reservation to return to California was for tomorrow. He had seen the ticket.

Tom got in the car and drove back to Blackwell City park. The crowd was gone, the platform being taken down, the folding chairs loaded in a truck. One police car remained, just in case. There was no sign of Sylvia Hansen.

What next? With the briefcase gone, all Tom had was his address book and the cards in his wallet. Who could he turn to? For now all he could do was go back to the motel and wait. If she didn't return to Comfort Inn she would turn up at Book World for his reading.

35. Book World

Tom parked the red Tercel behind the bookstore. Without the briefcase and all his records, without the modem connection to his e-mail he felt cut off and naked. Brewer was not in the store. Tom fidgeted, aimlessly browsed the book display, made sure there was a good stack of Conspiracy! on hand for the signing.

His annotated copy with all the slips of paper marking the passages he selected was in the missing briefcase. He would have to borrow a fresh copy from stock and leaf through it. It was hard to concentrate. In the scruffy employees' bathroom mirror he saw that his black eye was at its peak. He would have to read in dark glasses again.

Ted Brewer came in, apologized for the mix-up at the park, was surprised that Sylvia had disappeared. "Maybe she's gone shopping," he suggested. "Women do."

"Sylvia's compulsive," Tom admitted. She did join him in Spokane on an impulse, hadn't she? "I don't think she'd leave the park to shop when a riot is breaking out."

Brewer had nothing to add. "Did you get supper? You have some time before the reading. There's a burger joint around the corner."

Tom had seen the Burger King. He wasn't hungry, but it would give him something to take his mind off his anxiety. He left the store. Was someone watching? A van like the one he'd been taken in in Bismarck was parked across the street, the tinted windows hiding anyone who might be inside. A woman who might have been Mary Contrari, except it couldn't be her, was window shopping outside a boutique a few doors down. He was suspicious of everyone.

Tom started to order hot tea at the Burger King, then remembered his herbal tea bags were in the missing briefcase. He felt miserable and sick to his stomach. He couldn't finish his Whopper and fries and left the remains on the table.

Ted Brewer had a surprise for him when he got back to the bookstore. "Someone brought this in," Brewer said, holding it up. "Said it was yours, that you had misplaced it."

It was his traveling copy of Conspiracy! "Who brought this?" he demanded. Tom studied Brewer's expression. Was the man lying?

Brewer's shrug was unconvincing. "I don't know. They gave it to my assistant. He's gone on break."

Tom opened the book expecting a message written inside the cover. None. He was beginning to doubt himself. Maybe he hadn't had the book in the briefcase after all, but left it somewhere, like in the Comfort Inn breakfast buffet. Had he done that? He was in such disarray over Sylvia's disappearance and the apparent theft of the briefcase that he couldn't be sure of anything.

The usual crowd gathered, if there was such a thing as usual. Pretending to sip his glass of water, he studied the spectators. He half expected a bunch of thugs in Aryan Nation uniforms or hecklers. To his surprise, nobody fit that description. He hoped Sylvia would turn up. She didn't. After Brewer's introduction Tom found the bookmark near the middle of the book, the passage he usually read.

He stopped cold. Something was written on the slip of paper. He turned it and stopped breathing. "If you want to see your friend Sylvia again, you'd better cooperate."

Tom made a startled sound that drew curious looks from the people in the audience. "Excuse me," he stammered. "Conspiracy! is so thrilling sometimes I get carried away myself."

To his relief, someone chuckled, but though he was sure afterwards that he continued with the reading and signing, he couldn't remember any of it. He read the passage like an automaton. No hand gestures or body English this time. He could only think "They've got Sylvia. What do they expect me to do?"

Before his closing remarks and invitation to have their copies signed, Tom asked, "Is there someone here with a message for me?" He searched the faces in the crowd. None.

He tried to collar Brewer's assistant to get a description of whoever had brought in the book, but Brewer put him off.

36. Calls for help

Tom Godot sold twenty-one copies of Conspiracy!, a record, then went behind the checkout counter to show Ted Brewer the slip of paper with the note.

Mr. Brewer's bland face darkened. "What are you going to do? Call the police or wait for another contact? This isn't a ransom note."

What am I going to do? Tom thought. The bastard's denying that he had anything to do with it. Getting us in the parade put Sylvia in front of that crowd. I should never have agreed to it. "Ransom or not, this a kidnapping," Tom said. "Can I use your phone?"

"Sure."

Tom closed Brewer's office door so he could not be overheard. Through the window in the door he could see across the store to the checkout counter. Brewer was busy with a customer, not listening in on an extension phone.

A man's personal space reveals a lot about him. Ted Brewer's office at the back of Book World was surprisingly tidy. It was done in dark paneling. Two hunting trophy heads were displayed on the wall, an antelope and a big horn sheep. Tom wondered whether Brewer had shot them himself or found them at a garage sale. He also appeared to collect old silver mine stock certificates. Several were framed on the wall, ten shares from the Lucky Lady mine, a hundred from the El Dorado, five hundred shares in Bonanza. Funny what people named their mines-- Lucky Lady, El Dorado, Bonanza, as if a name would make the dream come true. All looked antique and were elaborately engraved so whoever bought them got the feeling there was value in those sheets of paper. Now they were mementos of high hopes and disappointments.

The telephone book was under a chunk of ore mounted on a piece of varnished mahogany. Who should he call first? The police? That would have been his first choice, but he didn't want to go into long explanations. He needed to talk to someone who already knew what was going on. What about Mary Contrari? She hadn't responded to his last message. He'd try again, the 800 number.

This time the switchboard person had been alerted. "Mr. Godot... yes. I've been told to put you through. That may take a minute."

He was put on hold. What was happening? Was Contrari in the hospital, on a beeper? Was she being paged?

"Mr. Godot."

"Is this Mary Contrari? I heard you were injured."

"A concussion," she admitted, her voice labored. "Sorry if I sound dopey. I'll be taking lots of pain killers for a few days. Fortunately I haven't needed an operation. Where are you calling from?"

"Coeur d'Alene, Idaho. Sylvia Hansen, Ivar Hansen's niece, joined me here and she's been kidnapped. I got a message warning me to cooperate."

"Then cooperate."

"What is this? Cooperate about what? Whose side are you on?"

"It's rather complicated, Mr. Godot. You have to be patient and cautious."

"I'm cautious enough, but I'm not patient. They've got Sylvia. What am I supposed to do?"

"Give them anything they want."

"You mean like ransom money" That was ridiculous. Tom lived from pay check to pay check.

"They won't be after money, not from you, Mr. Godot."

"But I don't have anything. What do they want?" Tom imagined Contrari in a hospital bed, her red hair wrapped in bandages. Maybe part of her skull had to be shaved if she'd been hit on the head. Sometimes doctors had to remove part of the skull to relieve the swelling caused by a concussion or the brain could be crushed. Wherever Contrari was, she was safe. Sylvia wasn't.

Contrari's answer was not helpful. "Since you don't have anything, you have nothing to lose. You can't tell whoever has Sylvia Hansen things you don't know."

"You're talking in circles," Tom said. Looking up at Brewer's stuffed animal heads, he felt like he was locked in someone's telescopic sights. "Kidnapping is a federal crime. I'm calling the FBI." He hung up before she could comment.

At least he still had the calling card for the guy in Bismarck. P. Henkel.

This time there was an answer. "Federal Bureau of Investigation."

Tom assumed they had caller ID and could see he was calling from Book World. "This is Tom Godot. Is this Agent Henkel?"

"Yes."

Tom remembered the stocky agent with the Teddy Roosevelt mustache. "You remember Mary Contrari, the NSA agent who was assaulted? The one you asked me about?"

"What about it?"

"I just talked to her. She's recovering. But she's not being very helpful."

"Calm down, Mr. Godot. Of course I remember our conversation about Contrari. Why are you calling me from... er, Coeur d'Alene, Idaho?"

They did have caller ID. "Because that's where I happen to be at the moment. Excuse me if I'm not making any sense. My girl friend's been kidnapped."

"There's nothing I can do for you from here, Mr. Godot. There's an FBI agent assigned to Spokane. I can give you the number."

"I'm sure this has to do with the Aryan Nation. There was a sort of riot at the parade today in Coeur d'Alene and Sylvia Hansen disappeared. Now someone is holding her."

"Are they asking for ransom?"

"No. They're asking for my cooperation."

Henkel shifted into another operational mode. He didn't risk that Tom would hang up and not call another office. Instead he asked Tom where he could be reached in Coeur d'Alene, the details of Sylvia's disappearance, her description, and ended with "Is there anything else you think I should know?"

"I'd like to know something," Tom said. "I'd like to know if the FBI is investigating the Aryan Nation here in Idaho."

"I'm not privy to that information," Henkel said, "and if I was I couldn't tell you."

"Should I call the local police?"

To Tom's surprise, Henkel said no. "Go back to your hotel, Mr. Godot, and sit tight. Someone will contact you."

Tom hung up, confused. He sat back in Ted Brewer's ample swivel chair and stared at the trophies on the wall. Contrari said cooperate. The FBI said don't call the local cops. The NSA weren't talking to the FBI and the FBI didn't want him to talk to the local police. If the FBI were investigating the Aryan Nation, maybe the local cops were part of it.

It was too soon to call Ivar Hansen or Sylvia's parents. It would only cause the Hansen family a lot of worry, and it might be for nothing. There was nothing they could do from California.

Tom returned to the Book World checkout counter and waited while Ted Brewer served a customer. "Did you call the police?"

"No," Tom said. Besides being uncomfortable because Brewer had talked him and Sylvia into riding in the parade, Tom was suspicious. He studied Brewer to see how he would react. "I called the FBI."

Brewer flinched. "Really?"

"Not very helpful," Tom said, testing Brewer. "They get lots of crank calls."

"Especially around here," Brewer said, "considering our clientele. Too many people crying wolf. Soon no report has credibility."

"Sure. That must be it."

There was only one other person he needed to consult: Harold Stevenson. Maybe Stevenson would call back at the Comfort Inn.

37.

Tom returned to the Comfort Inn. The young man whose face bore the ravaged scars of adolescent acne was working the desk. No messages. No packages. Tom half expected another mystery parcel, this time with proof of kidnapping, like Sylvia's blue jacket or maybe a lock of her hair. With the Getty kidnapping they had sent the victim's ear.

The room was as he had left it before the reading. It was like so many of the motel rooms where he had stayed on the book tour-- impersonal. If it weren't for Sylvia's overnight bag next to his she might never have been there.

Tom was a bundle of emotions, frustration, anger, worry, uncertainty, fear for Sylvia's safety, resentment and helplessness. He unzipped her overnight bag. Her return ticket was there, notes for a report and a textbook, Management Ethics. That sounded to Tom like an oxymoron. She had a change of clothes, a short dress that could be packed without ironing, underwear, and a pair of light weight lace-up shoes with stiff rubber soles. He was embarrassed, invading her privacy and going through her things, but he hoped for some clue to what he might do.

He could not just sit around waiting for Stevenson to call. E-mail was out. At least he now had Stevenson's number in Arlington.

The office of the MacArthur Foundation think tank would be closed at this hour, but someone, probably an answering service, took his call. This time when he identified himself and asked for Stevenson he was put through.

Again the hesitant, cultivated, Ivy League voice. "Mr. Godot. We were about to call you."

We? Who's we? Tom thought. "Sylvia Hansen's been kidnapped."

"Sylvia Hansen?"

"Ivar Hansen's niece. I got a note telling me to cooperate, whatever that means."

"That's serious. We didn't expect this."

Again the "we." "I've got to talk to Harold Stevenson."

"Just be patient, Mr. Godot. Who else knows about this?"

"The manager of Book World. He handed over the copy of my book with the kidnapper's note. I talked to Mary Contrari, the NSA agent, and to a guy with the FBI, but I was told not to notify the local police."

"That's unfortunate. You should have called us first."

"Us?" Who was us? "You've made it damned difficult. I couldn't send you e-mail, either. They've got my briefcase, my laptop, everything."

"But not this number," the voice said.

"No. Since you say it was unfortunate that I notified the NSA and the FBI, what do you suggest I do?"

"Stall them until we get things together. Is your system secure?"

"Do you mean my computer files? I put a password on the CMOS," Even as he said that, Tom realized that a good password was not a name or a common word, or even any word in the dictionary. A hacker could use a spelling checker dictionary to try every word in the book until he broke in. A good password was a unique combination of random numbers and upper and lower case letters. He had chosen "Sylvia." That was dumb. He admitted, "It's not a very good one."

"It will delay them."

"Not for long," Tom said. "Sylvia Hansen knows what it is. She might tell them, whoever they are."

"They can't get the information they're after," voice said.

"What the hell information is that?"

"You don't know?"

This was infuriating. He hadn't a clue. What should he do now? Bluff? Pretend he did know? Or forgot? "Which information? Refresh my memory."

There was a sigh and a hesitation. "It's too bad you called the FBI. It makes things complicated for us. If you are contacted by the kidnappers, stall them. It will give us time to get things in order."

"What things?"

Again he didn't get a straight answer. The receiver at the other end was muffled. Finally the voice came back on. "Coeur d'Alene has a municipal airport near the firing range. Be there at midnight. We'll have someone pick you up."

With his picture on the dust jacket of his book, anyone could know him. "How will I know who ever shows up is for real? Will they hold up a sign or something?"

"Someone carrying a bible will engage you in casual conversation and give you Harold Stevenson's pass phrase. I won't mention it over the phone."

He remembered the P.G.P. pass phrase for his public key. It was "How does your garden grow?" Stevenson's was more sinister, "The wages of sin is Death." Capital D. "OK."

"Don't check out of the Comfort Inn," the voice said. "Miss Hansen's kidnappers need a place to contact you."

"What if I'm not here?"

"Then they'll have to wait."

Wait. But what would they do to Sylvia in the meantime?

38. Coeur d'Alene airport

Tom hadn't realized Coeur d'Alene even had an airport. His United airlines flight had been to Spokane, the nearest commercial connection. He got a local map at the motel desk, hoping to find the place without having to ask someone. He didn't want to leave a trail. The rack of local tourist information was there as he remembered it from the morning. A few copies of the News Chronicle were still unsold, the headline the one he had seen at breakfast, "Aryan Nation on the March." Now the story had a new context.

Back in the room he sat at the little table and examined the note that had been slipped into his copy of Conspiracy! "If you want to see your friend Sylvia again, you'd better cooperate." But how?

His other slips of paper marking favorite passages were still intact. There were no other notes. He felt helpless, frustrated.

He did not want to call Ivar Hansen or Sylvia's family, not yet. Ivar Hansen was dynamic, aggressive, flamboyant, and conspiratorial, but he could also be a loose cannon, hard to predict. Under the wrong circumstances he could leap to a bad decision. If Ivar Hansen's ego was bruised Tom didn't want to be in the neighborhood of the man's wrath. He could be vindictive and unforgiving. That was a side of him the staff at MOM seldom saw, but Tom had witnessed during his interviews for the Hansen memoir. Best if he could solve this without causing them anxiety.

He studied the map of the town and the news story for names he might want to remember later. No one phoned, not anyone from the FBI, no kidnappers. Waiting for a telephone to ring was worse than waiting for a kettle to boil.

Tom tried to kill time by watching CNN. The Israelis had sent up an experimental satellite on a French rocket. The Serbs were still battering their Moslem neighbors. A flood ravaged Pennsylvania. He realized they could replay the same news year after year and no one would notice the repetition. The same stuff was always reported. If it bleeds it leads. Would Sylvia be the next bleeding headline?

At 11:30 Tom got up to leave for his meeting at the airport. What had the man at the MacArthur Foundation meant when he said someone would pick him up? What kind of organization was it? Did they have people everywhere? Or did they have someone on his tail, like Mary Contrari for the NSA? It made him feel like that old nursery story where the first person to grab the goose gets stuck, the next one sticks to him, until there is a whole string of people tagging along.

If he was to be picked up, where was he going? Some safehouse? Besides the copy of Conspiracy! with the kidnappers' note, Tom decided to take the copy of the newspaper for any clues it might contain. He slipped out the side door of the Comfort Inn. The security door's latch snapped behind him.

The airport was not difficult to find, a small air strip with a few private planes parked near the hangar. It had to be one of those airports created by a World War II veteran with dreams of cross country air connections. Now the clientele must be the rich who bought expensive lakeside property.

There were no other cars in the parking lot. Tom walked around the deserted terminal building. No one. The runway lights were dark. The only outdoor illumination was two dusk to dawn security lights, one at each side of the terminal. Tom returned to the parking lot, expecting someone to drive up.

"Mr. Godot?"

The voice startled him. A tall man stepped out of a doorway. He wore a leather bomber jacket that made him look like the ghost of the flier Tom supposed created the airport. He was carrying a book.

Feeling foolish, like a character in a parody of a spy movie, Tom asked, "Is that a bible? I heard there's a prayer meeting near here, but I got lost."

"You wouldn't want to do that. Like they say, 'The wages of sin is death.'"

"Since I'm not a sinner, am I exempt?" Tom asked.

"Nobody's exempt," the man in the leather jacket said. "This way."

Tom followed the man to the tarmac where the private planes were lined up, some with their wings tied down against a possible wind storm. At the end of the line of small planes a white corporate Lear jet was parked. The door was open.

Tom hesitated. "What's this?"

The man held out his hand. "Give me your car keys. I'll drive it back to your hotel. I'll leave the keys for you on top of the left rear tire."

So that's how they do it, Tom thought, and complied.

Tom handed the man the car keys and got into the plane. The door shut and sealed behind him. There was no turning back.

He had never ridden in a private jet before. His flight on United had been a torture, that narrow seat with no leg room and the fat man spilling over the arm rest at him. This was deluxe first class, the seats leather, everything done up in pearl gray. There was a bar and a low coffee table.

There were no other passengers. The door to the cockpit was open. He glimpsed the lit instrument panel in the darkness. A voice told him to fasten his seat belt.

"Where are we going?" Tom asked. He couldn't tell if there was a copilot or not.

"Get some sleep," the anonymous pilot said. "We'll probably refuel in Desmoines. If you want, there's coffee in the thermos."

"I don't drink coffee," Tom said. "When will we get to wherever it is we're going?"

"Depends on the jet stream. Should be at National by nine o'clock."

"But I have to be here in Coeur d'Alene. I can't just leave now."

Tom could not see the pilot's face or guess his age. "With any luck you'll be back in twelve hours. Nobody will know you've been gone." End of conversation.

With that the cabin lights were shut off, leaving some blue, courtesy lamps. Tom buckled up and looked out the small window. Apparently the runway lights could be switched on by radio control from the plane, for they were suddenly on. The jet engines kicked in, revved up to a whine, and the plane eased forward onto the runway.

Tom had heard about the Lear jet. They were so powerful and the planes so lightly built for fuel economy and speed that a careless pilot could literally fly their wings off. The takeoff convinced him. One moment they were at the end of the runway revving up the engines against the pull of the brakes. The next moment the acceleration pressed him back into the soft upholstery of the seat. They were in the air, climbing nearly vertically.

The lights of Coeur d'Alene dropped away and were as abruptly blotted out by clouds. For a long moment he could see nothing. Then the mist disappeared. Below him Tom could see a moonlit cloudscape spread like tarnished silver and broken by the tops of mountains. The jet turned east and accelerated, trembling with the power of the engines like a frightened bird.

39. A meeting in Virginia

Tom woke up as they landed to refuel, but he didn't get out of the plane. The copilot, hunched over in the low cabin, passed him, commenting, "You don't drink coffee. Tea?" What was the accent? German? Danish?

Tom stretched and yawned. "Please."

The copilot left the plane and returned with a tepid cup of water, a Lipton tea bag, and a sack with two Danish. "They're yesterday's. We're too early for the morning delivery."

Tom grunted, watched the tea bag sink, grimaced at the taste, and set it aside. Before he could try the stale pastry they were taking off again.

He wondered where Sylvia was, and if her captors were feeding her. The men who grabbed him in Bismarck had been barely civil, threatening but not violent. He had been able to talk his way out of that. He had no confidence now.

He read and reread the note, "If you want to see your friend Sylvia again, you'd better cooperate" as if by rereading he might find something else in it.

Reviewing the Coeur d'Alene News Chronicle he concluded that the mayor was sympathetic to the Aryan Nation. The name of the parade organizer was mentioned, Otto Royer and the ACLU lawyer who had defended the right of the Aryan Nation to march, Isadore Plotnik. What kind of a Jew defended the rights of American Nazis? Had Royer been one of the men on the podium in the park? The one with the suit, or one of those in uniform?

The sun was high when the jet landed at National airport in Washington, DC. It did not pull up to the terminal, but taxied to a hangar where a black Lincoln Town Car was waiting.

In the open door to the plane Tom turned to the copilot. "Will you be flying me back?"

"I fly wherever they tell me to."

"Then maybe I'll see you later."

The non-committal expression on the copilot's face said he didn't care one way or another. Tom Godot was just another item to be ticked off on a report. Perhaps they didn't even mention his name, but listed him on the flight plan as A. Passenger.

The uniformed, black chauffeur leaned against on the hood with a piece of paper in his hand. Tom realized it was his picture.

"Mr. Godot?"

Tom nodded and got in the back.

He had hoped there would be someone inside he could talk to, but there was no one.

After they left the airport the driver said, "There's an electric razor in there and some little towels if you'd like to freshen up."

Sure enough, a little battery operated electric razor. Tom gratefully shaved while he looked out the window and tried to figure out where they were going. He had not been in Washington, DC before. The little packages with moist wipes were a nice touch. Lear jet, chauffeured car. Whoever the people at MacArthur were, they had class and paid attention to details. They also didn't tell more than absolutely necessary.

"All this needs is a shower," Tom joked, but the driver couldn't be persuaded to talk.

Tom recognized the Pentagon as the car drove south. Most of Washington's morning traffic was headed in the other direction, toward the District.

"Are we going to the MacArthur Foundation?" Tom asked.

"No, sir."

That was it. No explanation, no conversation.

The driver made a call on a cell phone and when the Town Car pulled into the underground parking garage of a large apartment complex there were two men waiting.

They were both in their thirties. One had remarkable blue eyes like Dan Quayle, except this man showed a keen intelligence. He wore a dark suit and a red, silk tie. He was deeply tanned, like someone who spent a lot of time on the beach or, more likely, on a boat. His handshake was firm but not crushing.

The man with the blue eyes did not introduce his companion, who hung back, watchful. He reminded Tom of those men who always stayed close the president, but kept their eyes on the crowd. This one had an athletic build and walked on the balls of his feet like a boxer, ready to move quickly. He was not someone you'd turn your back on.

The blue-eyed man did not introduce himself. "Good morning, er, Tom." He said it as if Tom Godot were a made up name. "I hope I can call you Tom. Did you, er, have a comfortable flight?"

Tom couldn't distinguish Eastern accents but the speech pattern was familiar, those, er, pauses. Was the blue-eyed man the one he talked with on the phone? Tom stretched. "Sure beats United."

"We'll talk inside."

He followed the two men to the elevator. He did not see what floor button was pushed.

It was an ordinary upscale apartment building like many built to house the army of office workers who kept the wheels of government turning. The door opened into a comfortable furnished living room that had no personal touches, no family pictures, no souvenirs from Key West Florida, no tennis trophies, no books. It reminded Tom of a motel room. Obviously nobody actually lived there.

"Ah, Mr. Godot!" a voice called from the galley.

Tom glimpsed an arm in a red sleeve, a tray with four cups, a tea pot and a plate of cookies. She entered the room, an elegant woman in her fifties. It was not a cocktail dress, but would do well enough in case one had to go from the office directly to a stand up party.

What Tom liked immediately were her friendly eyes. This was no hard bitten Mary McGann, but a woman secure and confident, someone not about to be displaced. "So glad you were willing to come."

"I wasn't offered a choice," Tom said.

She put the tray down on the coffee table. "You drink herbal tea," she said. "I think you'll like this. And there's some Scottish shortbread direct from Princess Street in Edinburgh."

"Thanks." What else did they know about him?

They sat around the coffee table. Tom couldn't wait for them to get to his problem. "This is the note I found in my copy of the book when I did the reading at Book World in Coeur d'Alene." He passed it around. After everyone had seen it the second man took a plastic bag from a briefcase and put the note inside.

"That was your only contact?" the blue-eyed man asked.

"That's it. I should be back in Idaho waiting for instructions. I don't understand why you brought me here." Tom sipped his tea and waited. Finally, impatient, he asked. "How are we going to get Sylvia Hansen released?"

"It's time you were briefed on this," the blue eyed man said. "If we're to get what we want out of this we'll need to know a bit more. Who else did you contact? Did you call the police?"

"I'd been approached by someone called Mary Contrari who claimed she was an NSA agent. She's in the hospital, I think, back in North Dakota."

These people must be great poker players, Tom thought. The mention of Mary Contrari and the NSA didn't register. "I also called the FBI in Bismarck."

"Why Bismarck?"

"I was questioned in Bismarck about the assault on Contrari."

"Who did you talk to?"

Tom extracted the FBI agent's business card from his wallet. "Here's his name and phone number."

This time the information made a difference. The blue-eyed man was troubled. "The FBI complicates things."

The woman sat down on the couch across from Tom. He noticed that she had skinny legs and narrow feet in flat shoes. "Yes. We don't want people tripping over each other on this. Does anyone else know about this kidnapping?"

"Ted Brewer at Book World. I showed him the note when I found it. He knew I was looking for Sylvia."

There was a long silence. Finally the woman asked, "Where would you start in your search, Mr. Godot? Obviously you can't just wait passively in a motel room?"

Tom still had his copy of the Coeur d'Alene newspaper. "Otto Royer organized the Aryan Nation march and the ACLU lawyer, Isadore Plotnik. That's all I can think of. Even if Royer isn't personally involved, if this is an Aryan Nation job, he should know someone in on it."

His two hosts agreed. The third man didn't take part in the conversation. Tom had the uneasy feeling that the third man was there to make sure he cooperated. Why wouldn't he?

They could not have brought him all the way to Washington, DC just for this, Tom thought. Harold Stevenson could have conferred this much by phone. "Why didn't Harold Stevenson just call me? Could have saved a lot of time." Was this man Harold Stevenson?

Tom caught the blue-eyed man's glance. Tom had been making up excuses for Stevenson's absence from book readings for so long that he was beginning to believe his own stories, that Stevenson was shy, had a stammer, or was crippled and couldn't appear. At first Tom thought Stevenson was a computer programmer, a nerdy guy in cut-off blue jeans and a shirt with a pocket protector for his colored pens. The blue-eyed man was definitely not in that category.

The blue-eyed man did not look like a computer programmer. All the programmers Tom had met at MOM hated jackets and ties, were more likely to bicycle or roller blade to work than to ride in Lincoln Town Cars. The big guys with stock options drove BMWs. He couldn't imagine the blue-eyed man playing Myst or Duke Nukem on his coffee break. "That's not you, is it?"

The woman in the red dress gave Tom an apologetic smile. "I'm Agnes. Peter here calls me Lady A. As for Harold Stevenson, that's a bit awkward, Mr. Godot." She glanced at the others before proceeding. They were noncommittal but compliant. "I'm afraid that Harold Stevenson is dead."

40. Judas Goat

"Dead? I just got e-mail from him. What happened?"

Agnes, a.k.a. Lady A, poured herself a cup of tea. She studied Tom's face while she decided what to tell him. "Harold Stevenson was killed in prison five years ago. He was a computer hacker who broke into an international bank's computer system and helped himself to ten million dollars."

Peter, the blue-eyed man, added, "Trouble was, Stevenson didn't know how to spend the money once he got it into an account he'd created in Switzerland. He tried to buy diamonds from the Russians, who alerted INTERPOL. Diamonds weren't his game. You never play someone else's game. What's your game, Mr. Godot?"

"Tennis, now and then. I was on the company soft ball team for a while, but I'm not very good. I got tired of being put out in left field, and they got tired of me striking out. How did Stevenson die?"

"A prison fight. He wanted to teach the prisoners how to break into computer systems. He wouldn't join the prison skin heads and he obviously wasn't a black Muslim. It's not safe to be a loner in prison."

"But if he died five years ago, that's before my collaboration with him on the book. So who have I been working with; who pretended to be Harold Stevenson?"

Peter glanced at the woman. "Harold Stevenson is a pseudonym. Lady A has assisted from time to time when your real co-author has been ill. It's a complicated story we'd rather not burden you with. Just go on as you did before."

"Then the real Stevenson had nothing to do with the book at all?"

Agnes, the lady in red, interrupted. "Not exactly."

Thinking out loud, Tom said, "Well that explains why he's not on the dust jacket or on the book tour. Can't very well do that if you're dead. You can't write books, either, or send encrypted e-mail messages."

None of his hosts said anything.

"I don't understand why you've flown me here. I work with Mary McGann at Nile Publishing, not the MacArthur Foundation, and considering the expense and nastiness I've encountered, I'm ready to forget the book tour, write it off as an unpleasant experience."

Agnes agreed. "You could do that, Mr. Godot, but the stakes have been raised."

"What stakes? Is this some kind of a game?"

"You might never have known about us if it weren't for Sylvia Hansen. She wasn't part of the plan, so now we have damage control. You're the one who can get her released. But we also want to turn her kidnapping to our advantage. Be patient and bear with me. It's all right for you to know that Harold Stevenson is dead, even to know that all this time you've been teamed up with someone else. If you pursue this Mr. Royer or whatever his name is, he or the kidnappers will be determined to find Harold Stevenson. We've already seen that in Bismarck."

"Then you saw my message to Stevenson about what happened there." What was this plan she alluded to? What did it have to do with selling books? It didn't make sense. Were they in cahoots with Mary Contrari and the NSA?

Tom was about to ask, but she interrupted him. "The less you know the safer you will be. I am concerned for your safety as well as Miss Hansen's."

"Then I'm not to meet the person who's claimed to be Harold Stevenson?"

Peter shifted uncomfortably on the couch. "The person you know as Harold Stevenson has been, er, difficult. When his intentions were discovered we had to intervene. He resisted. We had to be persuasive. So for the time being at least, until this is over, you can't meet Harold Stevenson."

Agnes tried to divert him. "You should be satisfied. The book's making money, isn't it? You're not just a tech writer working out of a cubicle any more. You might even write another book."

Tom quipped, "I thought of writing a book about an author on a book tour who finds himself entangled in some national intrigue."

Peter's blue eyes could be chilling. They were now. "I wouldn't advise that, Mr. Godot. Maybe you should be content to be a one book author." He glanced at the other man.

Lady A cut him off. "Let's not alienate Tom. His girl friend has been kidnapped. Her life may be in danger. He doesn't even know what the kidnappers want from him." She turned to Tom. "Do you know what a Judas goat is?"

"I think so."

"That's you. But we're not going to feed you or Sylvia Hansen to those wolves if we can prevent it. Here's what we want you to do...."

41.

He was back on the plane, heading west. The team from MacArthur Foundation had given him only first names, Peter and Agnes, a.k.a. Lady A, which might not be real. He had seen no one else or left the safehouse until time to go down in the elevator to the parking garage and return to Washington National airport.

They had not even risked going out to lunch, but sent the other man out as go-fer to fetch something to eat. There was no food in the apartment. Tom would have preferred a vegetarian pizza and soda, but the man came back with a sack of tuna sandwiches.

He also brought an L.L. Bean canvas shoulder bag with Tom's survival kit. It was not what he might have expected.

They gave him a watch.

The watch was heavier than the freebie Tom had gotten from Visa for paying his bills on time. It did not look like something a mugger would want to steal. It looked no different than the ten dollar, made in China sports watches you could buy in K-Mart, complete with calendar, timer, light and plastic band. The difference was this watch had a built in EPIRB emergency locator, a miniature of what was carried on all airplanes. Any passing aircraft would pick up the signal. Wherever he was, in an emergency, someone would find him. Whether they would find him in time or alive was another matter.

Besides the EPIRB watch, the L.L. Bean shoulder bag contained a dozen souvenir flashlights. The miniature flashlights looked like stock promotional gadgets with split rings so they could be used to carry keys.

Tom put one of them on his own key ring. His keys no longer looked familiar. He identified the key to his apartment in San Jose, the security front door, mail box, storage locker and his car keys. Those keys reminded him of how far away from home he was and how long it had been, not just in time, but in accumulated experience. He was a different person than the Tom Godot who had left so excitedly at the start of the book tour.

The souvenir flashlights were a cunning device. In the little plastic sleeves an advertiser could slip in a label with the company logo and phone number. In this case, someone had prepared labels: "Conspiracy! A best selling book by Tom Godot." The flashlights looked like something Mary McGann would dream up, though she would make sure that Nile Publishing would be included in the fine print.

What wasn't obvious was that each flashlight included a transponder. The blue-eyed man had explained, "To activate the transponder you twist the cap. See? That breaks the seal and makes the connection. It can't be turned off. The transponder sends out a pulse signal. You may have heard of them. They're used on the radio collars of trapped wildlife. Some day we'll have these, er, on our kids so they can be found if they wander off or, in the case of your friend Sylvia Hansen, if they're, er, kidnapped. See if you can get one of these to her."

Blue-eyed Peter had explained that the transponder wasn't as elaborate as radio collars that sent out pulse rate and temperature or, if the animal did not move within twelve hours, a signal indicating that it was dead.

With those in his bag, Tom Godot felt like James Bond, except he carried no explosives, no underwater breathing apparatus, no pocket size parachute, or any of the stuff of heroic fiction.

If they had given him a gun, he wouldn't have known how to use it. Tom Godot had never fired a real firearm. As a kid growing up in Oakland he had played with a neighbor, Toby, who had a BB gun and they had shot at tin cans and paper targets. Once they had gone into the hills and hunted harmless California lizards, pretending they were miniature dinosaurs. They had killed three before Tom had felt remorse for murdering the poor things and quit. Killing gave him no pleasure.

He wasn't into fighting, either, and avoided school bullies. Once, when confronted, he had diverted the bigger boy with a question about homework and offered to help with the teacher's tough assignment. There were ways to deal with people like that and avoid violence.

In Bismarck his willingness to cooperate had helped him out of a bad situation. He hoped his non-combative, joking nature would be an adequate alternative when dealing with Sylvia's kidnappers.

They might at least have given him mace or pepper spray, the sort of thing women carried to defend themselves against rapists. Maybe he could buy pepper spray when he got back to Coeur d'Alene.

Tom helped himself to soda from the fridge of the Lear jet. Where would they refuel this time? he wondered. He also wondered where Sylvia Hansen was, who was holding her, and exactly what they expected from him.

He knew now that there was a shadowy war going on between two invisible antagonists. Just as the AIDS virus lurked for years in its victim's body before breaking out, this disease was growing in the country. Agnes, the woman in red, had mentioned a plan, but what was its purpose? Obviously his book had something to do with it, something the MacArthur people knew and others were trying to find out.

42. Pepper spray

Tom dozed on the flight back to Idaho. He hadn't been to bed for more than thirty hours and felt like the blood had drained out of him. By the time the day was out he would have traveled across the United States and back again. His legs ached. He just wanted to lie down flat and sleep.

This time they had enough fuel to make the flight non stop. It was late Sunday afternoon when the Lear jet landed at Coeur d'Alene. They taxied up to the little terminal building but the engines were never shut down. Tom thanked the pilots, took his new L.L. Bean bag with his copy of Conspiracy! and the promotional flashlights, and stepped down onto the tarmac. He had hardly entered the terminal when he heard the engines rev up and turned to see the plane taxi down the runway.

He found a pay phone and called a cab from the terminal. By the time he got to the Comfort Inn his body told him only one thing: sleep. His mind told him otherwise: find Sylvia. At the desk he asked the same acne-scarred clerk he had talked to before if there were any messages.

The desk clerk's scarred face went through several pained expressions. He wasn't accustomed to lying. "Some guy came by looking for you."

"Did he leave a name or number?"

"No." Again the guarded expression. "Said he'd check back later."

"If he shows up again, tell him I've gone to get something to eat."

The red Tercel was parked at the end of the Comfort Inn lot. Just as the man in the bomber jacket had promised, the key was hidden on top of the left rear tire. He drove to Pizza Hut, ordered spaghetti and meatballs, and asked about a gun store.

There was one. He was relieved to find it open on Sunday. The store front he was directed to was a fortress with heavily barred windows, a steel front door and a simple sign: Guns & Ammo. It was not the kind of place Tom was comfortable in. Tom knew nothing about guns.

When he entered he found a strange world, racks and racks of locked long guns, shotguns, assault rifles, and glass display cases with hand guns, laser sights, and other things he could not identify.

"How do I go about buying a hand gun?"

The gun shop owner wore a plaid shirt and a conspicuous holster. Obviously some of the people who came into his place needed to be intimidated by heavy hardware. "You from Idaho?"

"California," Tom said.

"I'll need your driver's license. You'll have to fill out a form. There's a five day waiting period. The Brady law."

He had forgotten about that. If he filled out the form, the records would be searched to see if he had been convicted of a felony. The FBI would know. Who else would?

Tom not only didn't know how to use a firearm, but he couldn't get one without the waiting period-- not legally. "I forgot about that. What have you got for self defense?"

"How about a shotgun? If you're worried about home invasion, there's nothing like a 410. It won't blow big holes in the walls, but it will stop an intruder." The man talked like blasting away at burglars was a sport and anyone who broke into your space should be gunned down like a rabbit.

"Too big," Tom said. He couldn't imagine shooting anyone.

He was shown a display of wicked looking assault knives, punch knives you could carry in a little pouch on your belt, hunting knives and commando daggers with finger grips. They made him queasy. "You got anything else?"

"Mace. Pepper spray."

Tom settled for a little punch knife in a leather holder that was easy to conceal inside his belt and a pocket canister of pepper spray. The gun store manager explained how to use it, that the spray could shoot up to twenty feet. He was cautioned that it was illegal to take pepper spray or mace on a commercial airline.

Remembering how everyone seemed to know everything about him, what he did, where he went, and what he bought, Tom didn't want to put the transaction on his Visa card, but he didn't have enough cash for both purchases. He paid cash for the pepper spray, charged the knife and returned to the motel. There was a cash machine in the lobby. He wondered who had come looking for him and why the kid at the desk had been so cautious with his answers.

If he didn't get contacted by the kidnappers he'd pursue those leads from the newspaper story. The longer Sylvia was held, the greater the risk. At least he was better prepared than he had been in Bismarck.

43

He looked around the lobby of the Comfort Inn and the now deserted breakfast room where he and Sylvia had enjoyed the buffet. He wondered if someone was waiting for him. It was a normal, quiet Sunday afternoon, a serene contrast to the turmoil, anxiety, and fatigue that wracked his mind and body.

He remembered the newspaper. The fat Sunday edition of the News Chronicle with all its advertising inserts had a front page story about the Aryan Nation KKK parade and the riot. The sidebar told another story: about the funds raised by a tolerance group. They had turned the hate march into a fund raiser. The farther the Aryans marched and the more marchers they brought out, the greater the sum that was collected to oppose them.

Otto Royer, the leader of the Aryan Nation, was incensed by the tactic and quoted as saying the mongrelizers of the white race wanted freedom of speech only for themselves, but would deny it to others. His Jewish ACLU lawyer could not be reached.

Normally the incident, though sinister, would be remote to anything in Tom's personal life. Now he was in the middle of it like a sparrow mistaken for the birdie in a vicious badminton match. He felt whacked. This time he could expect worse than a black eye.

When he reached the top of the stairs he saw a man waiting by the window at the end of the hallway. He wore a business suit, had neatly trimmed hair, and a look of impatience. Tom kept an eye on him as he put his room key in the lock. Ever since that surprise by Mary Contrari in St. Cloud he was nervous when he opened his motel room door.

The room seemed empty. When he turned to close the door, it bumped into the shoulder of the man in the business suit.

"Tom Godot?"

"Do you have a message for me?" Tom asked. "Is this about Sylvia?"

The man flashed an ID. "FBI."

Tom held out his hand. "You mind if I have a closer look? I heard you can buy those by mail order."

The man was not amused. "This one's authentic, I assure you."

Tom read the name. "Philip Gaiser, Special Agent." He needed a way to remember that name. Gaiser, like Old Faithful. "You the guy from Spokane?"

"Yes. You called one of our agents in Bismarck."

"Come in." Tom shut the door. "Have a seat."

They sat down on opposite sides of the little table. "My girl friend Sylvia's been kidnapped, probably by someone from the Aryan Nation."

"How do you know she's been kidnapped?"

"I got a note. It was slipped to me at the bookstore when I did my reading last night." God, it was only last night, wasn't it?

"May I see this note?"

Tom made an open handed gesture. "I haven't got it."

"Where is it?"

"The people from the MacArthur Foundation took it."

"Who are they?"

Tom felt foolish. "I don't even know. They flew me to Washington in their Lear jet last night and brought me back this afternoon. I showed the note to them and they kept it."

Philip Gaiser's stony face was unsympathetic. "You say you were flown to Washington and back in a Lear jet? From where? Coeur d'Alene?"

Tom sighed. "I suppose they must have filed a flight plan at the air strip. You could check that. Then maybe they didn't. They're awfully secretive. Wouldn't even tell me their last names."

"Then you have no note, no proof of your friend's disappearance or of your alleged flit across the country?"

The choice of words wasn't a mistake. The L.L. Bean canvas bag was on the bed. Tom opened it and took out one of the little flashlights. "They gave me a dozen of these. See? There's a transponder inside. Once you twist the cap it sends out a locator signal. I'm supposed to give these to the kidnappers so they can be tracked."

Agent Gaiser took the flashlight and held it up by its split ring like it was a dead bug. "You say this is a transponder? Looks like a flashlight to me."

"That's what they told me."

"Mind if I keep this?"

"No. But don't twist the cap if you don't want to be tracked. Once it's on, it can't be shut off."

Agent Gaiser put the flashlight in his pocket. He leaned forward and put his face close to Tom's. "I think you're making this up. That's your book on the bed? Conspiracy!?"

"Yes. I'm on a book tour. Readings, interviews, TV appearances. Everything's gone crazy. It started in St. Paul, I think. I was videotaped and a film clip put on the internet by the Aryan Nation. I got punched out in Bismarck. My eye is still black."

"I noticed." At least Gaiser did believe the black eye was real. "I think you've got conspiracies on the brain, Mr. Godot. I don't appreciate being called out on a Sunday wild goose chase. Do you know the penalty for filing a false police report?"

"I haven't filed any false reports." Tom held up his wrist. "Look. In Washington they gave me a special watch with a EPIRB built into it."

Gaiser gave it no more than a glance. "Looks like a cheap watch to me." He took out the promotional flashlight and read the label. "'Conspiracy! A best selling book by Tom Godot.' You people will do anything to sell a book."

"Check the transponder yourself," Tom said. He had hoped that the agent in Bismarck would follow through, but this was hopeless. "You must have a lab for those things."

He could not be sure himself. Maybe Peter the blue-eyed man was faking. Maybe the flashlights were nothing more than cheap publicity gadgets. Maybe the watch didn't work as an EPIRB. Maybe the whole thing was a big practical joke. This was maddening. He felt like a fool.

"I'll send it to headquarters," Gaiser said.

"But what about Sylvia Hansen? Aren't you going to investigate that?"

Agent Gaiser got up. "Before I investigate this alleged kidnapping I'm going to investigate you, Mr. Godot. I don't recommend your playing games with the FBI. We have serious work to do, serial killers, terrorists, the real thing, not some fiction cooked up by authors trying to make some money."

"Where do I reach you?" Tom asked. Not that it would do any good.

There was no business card this time to join the others in his wallet. "We're in the blue pages in the Spokane phone directory," Agent Gaiser said, and paused in the doorway. "You just stay out of trouble."

Tom locked the door behind him. "Oh, shit," he said aloud. He finally got the attention of an agency that should help him and instead he might be investigated himself. In the meantime, Sylvia was God knows where. He would have to solve this one himself. He wasn't a detective. He didn't have any resources. He couldn't even reach MOM by e-mail. He didn't want to worry Sylvia's family. What he had to do was find out what the kidnappers wanted, give it to them, get Sylvia back safely and be done with it.

He looked up Otto Royer in the motel phone book and dialed. The phone rang five times, six, ten. Royer wasn't answering his phone. Maybe he had gotten too many heckling calls.

Without his briefcase and laptop computer, with no e-mail and no access to his files at MOM he felt naked.

The phone rang. Tom snatched it up, knocking the cradle off the bureau. "Yes?"

"Tom Godot?" It was a voice he did not recognize.

"Yes. Who's calling?"

"That doesn't matter. There's someone here who wants to talk to you."

The phone was muffled, then she was on. "Tom?"

"Sylvia. Where are you?"

"I don't know. They want your password."

"Tell them I'll give it to them in person if they let you go. Are you OK? You're not hurt or anything?"

"I'm all right." She didn't sound convincing. "For the time being." The phone was taken from her.

The man's voice came on again. "Right, Mr. Godot. The password."

"Not until I see her safe."

"Be at the park where the rally was held in an hour."

"See you there," Tom said. "Let me talk to Sylvia again."

No such luck. The phone was dead.

44.

The setting sun was swallowed in a blue haze over the mountains as Tom got ready for his meeting with the kidnappers. He slid his belt through the holster for the little punch knife so it was on the inside against his waistband. If he was frisked it was small enough to be missed.

In case they wouldn't let Sylvia go, he twisted the cap on one of the transponders and slipped it into her overnight bag with her toiletries. If the kidnappers wouldn't release her he could use the excuse that she'd need fresh clothes.

He put the pepper spray in his pocket. He had drawn a hundred dollars from the cash machine and had change for a telephone. He looked around the room. Was there anything else? He couldn't think of anything, so went back downstairs, found the car, and drove to the park.

The clean up crew had done a good job. A family that had a picnic on the grass was packing up. Their children were tossing a Frisbee. A jogger in a Lycra running outfit startled him. For a moment he hoped, he wished, it was Sylvia, but of course it wasn't. Tom made three circuits of the park before someone came up to him.

He was a big, rough-looking man with a paunch. His baggy trousers were at a funny angle, pushed down in front by his belly and hiked up in back to cover his butt, a good candidate for suspenders and a heart attack. He looked to be in his fifties, with heavy eye brows that met in the middle of his forehead. "Mr. Godot?"

Tom nodded. "Everyone seems to recognize me. Where's Sylvia?"

"Over there in the truck. What's in the bag?"

"Her stuff. Toothbrush, underwear. Her plane ticket. She's got to fly back to California."

The man scratched his chin. "She ain't goin' no place until we get what we want. I'll take the bag."

Tom was relieved to hand it over. If the little flashlight down in the bottom among Sylvia's toiletries really was a transponder, the signal was going out. To whom he had no idea. Maybe nobody. Maybe the FBI guy... what was his name? Philip Gaiser, as in Old Faithful, was right and the transponder story a fake.

They walked to where a dusty, black pickup truck with a camper box on the back was parked. There were two men, one in the truck, the other standing behind it as a lookout.

"Just what the heck is it that you want?" Tom asked. "I don't understand any of this."

"You can play dumb all you like." The man stopped behind the pickup and took hold of the latch that opened the camper box on the back. He opened it far enough to toss Sylvia's bag inside. "So what's the password?"

"The password that gets you into the computer?"

"Right."

"It won't do you any good," Tom said. "Where's Sylvia?"

"The password," the man insisted.

Tom hoped he was right. The CMOS password would get them to his computer files, but without the password to get into MOM's system, they still had nothing. And if they did get into MOM's system Harold Stevenson or whoever he was, had encrypted the files. They were secure. "The CMOS password is Sylvia," Tom said. "I'm surprised you haven't figured that out yourselves. Now where is she?"

"Right here." The man lifted the hatch to the camper box.

Inside in the shadows Tom could see a hog tied figure. She had duct tape over her mouth and a desperate look in her eyes.

"Sylvia!" Tom called to her.

Before he could say anything else someone hit him in his other eye and he went down. Before he could get up, the pickup door slammed and it drove away. His eye smarting from the blow, Tom wasn't even able to glimpse the license plate.

45. Nice Doggie!

Tom ran to where the Tercel was parked, did a U-turn out of the space and drove in the direction the pickup had taken. It was nowhere in sight. He beat on the steering wheel in frustration, "Damn!" then returned to the motel. He went to his room, got a bucket of ice from the machine in the hallway, made an ice pack for his face and tried to focus on the numbers in his address book.

What was the number of the alleged Harold Stevenson? This time he got a recording. The office would be open on Monday at 9:00 AM.

Otto Royer of the Aryan Nation had not answered his phone, but his address was in the book. The Jewish ACLU lawyer, the other name mentioned in the newspaper story, wasn't listed. Probably didn't live in Coeur d'Alene.

Tom bought a map of the city at the motel desk and looked for Otto Royer's street. It was in a working class neighborhood, single family houses crowded together on forty foot lots. Some of the houses had been identical when built, but as time passed some acquired different siding, altered front entrances, new roofs. The better ones squeezed a narrow driveway at the side leading to a garage in the back.

Otto Royer's house had a six foot chain link fence and a prominent sign, "Beware of the Dog." There was no sign of any pickup truck, but an old Buick was parked in the driveway. Royer had used the rear bumper to advertise his views: "They can take my gun when they pry my cold dead finger off the rigger" and "I heart my pit bull."

Tom took out the pepper spray and had his hand on the button when he cautiously opened the gate to the chain link fence. Tom had seen film clips of pit bulls that wouldn't let go of a stick even if they were lifted off the ground by their jaws. Once they got a grip with those teeth they didn't let go until they were dead. Would pepper spray make any difference to a pit bull?

The moment Tom came up the front steps he heard a growl and bark and an evil-looking dog's face appeared at the living room window.

The front door opened about three inches and the dog's muzzle appeared in it, the jaws dripping with saliva.

"Quiet Suzy!" a man's voice commanded from inside the house. "Shut up." Then to Tom, "Whaddaya want? You a reporter? I already talked to the reporters, the TV and the radio, too."

"I'm Tom Godot. The author of Conspiracy! Could I talk to you? Without the dog?" Suzy? What a name for a pit bull.

"Tom Godot? Yeh, I was at your reading last night. You even signed a copy for me. Got it right here."

Tom could not see the man's face, just his eyes, wary behind the chain that kept intruders out and the dog in. "I'm sorry. I don't remember. There were so many people, and I was distracted. My girl friend's been kidnapped. There was a note. I thought you might be able to give me some advice."

"What would I know about it?"

Suzy lunged at the crack in the door and was yanked back. There was a yelp, cursing, and the sound of a door slamming somewhere inside the house. The front door shut, the chain rattled and the door opened. "Come in."

Tom wouldn't enter the house until he saw that Suzy wasn't in sight.

"It's OK. She's in the kitchen. Suzy's really a sweet tempered softy once she gets to know you." The man's smile showed yellow teeth. The canines were unusually long. Maybe it was true that people looked like their dogs.

Aside from his ugly teeth, Otto Royer seemed pleasant enough, sixtyish with gray hair and a high widow's peak. He wore a soiled striped shirt and a vest. Tom couldn't tell whether he was one of the men who had been on the podium at the Aryan Nation rally or not. They had been too far away for a good look.

Royer sat down in a threadbare recliner opposite his TV and motioned Tom to a battered couch cluttered with doggy toys and shed dog hair. Tom shifted the gnawed toys with visions of his own legs similarly chewed.

He explained that Sylvia had been kidnapped, there had been a note in his book at the bookstore reading, and he had seen Sylvia tied up in the back of a pickup truck. Did Mr. Royer know anyone who drove a truck like that? Any members of the Aryan Nation that might resort to kidnapping?

Otto Royer gave him a thin smile of insincerity. "Now really, Mr. Godot, much as I admire your work, do you think I'd admit to being a kidnapper? You know yourself that the government is out to get all of us. It's in your book. How do I know you're not working for the FBI?"

"Look, Mr. Royer. I'm just trying to get my girl back safely. Sylvia and I are engaged to be married." It wasn't true, but it might persuade the man. Just saying that they were engaged brought back memories of their lovemaking. Marriage hadn't been mentioned. Suddenly it felt like a certainty.

"It's love is it?" Royer looked like he might have a soft spot for love. He loved his dog, didn't he? Teeth and claw?

"Mr. Godot, I want you to understand that my role as leader of the Coeur d'Alene Aryan Nation is strictly political. I have a right to my views of niggers and commie kikes. I even have a Jew lawyer who defends those rights in court. I'm not interested in kidnapping anybody, just in protecting my rights as a white, Christian citizen in a Christian nation. Understand?"

"I understand." Tom had heard this line before, not that he believed it or had any sympathy for the man's intolerance. He would use a Jewish lawyer to attain his goals, then deport the man to Israel or, for all Tom knew, to the gas chambers, all in the name of racial purity. "But I know not everyone is as reasonable as you are, Mr. Royer. If you have any suggestions for me at all about finding my fiancée, I'd appreciate it. Anyone I could call?"

"What did you say the pickup looked like?"

"Black, with a camper box on the back. The man I talked to had a belly that looked like it was pushing his pants down off his hips. He has funny eyebrows that meet in the middle."

In the kitchen Suzy barked again and scratched furiously at the door. She clearly wanted to take a chunk out of Tom's leg or his throat.

"Shut up, sweetie," Royer shouted, then turned in the recliner. "I think I know someone that fits your description. Drives a truck, too, though I don't know if has a camper box in the bed." Royer got up and went to his phone, took an address book from under it, turned pages, found what he wanted, and copied a name onto a slip of paper. "Try this. You can say I gave it to you."

Tom took the paper. There was a name and address and a phone number, Kilgore Smith, Lay-Z-Boy Ranch. "Thanks. Any idea where this ranch could be?"

"Somewhere in Silver Valley near Smelterville."

Silver Valley. Maybe that was on the map. He held up the piece of paper. "This means a lot to me."

Tom got up to leave. As he reached the front door there was a sound of breaking glass at the back of the house. Royer shouted, "Goddamit, Suzy!" and rushed back.

Tom ran for the gate. As he closed it behind him Suzy came bounding around from the back of the house, eyes wild with hatred, fangs bare.

Tom knelt safely outside the fence, his face a few inches from the dog's insane anger. He held the pepper spray in front of Suzy's nose. "Nice doggie," he said, and gave her a squirt. With a howl of dismay, head shaking as if to rid herself of a swarm of bees, the dog retreated.

Glad to have escaped, Tom returned to his car. "The stuff works," he said to himself. At least he had a lead. Kilgore Smith. Lay-Z-Boy Ranch. Smelterville. Where was that?

46. Silver Valley

Tom Godot was not foolish enough to meet the kidnappers without letting someone know where he was. One hostage was too many. He didn't want to be the second.

He had to go to the motel registration desk to find a copy of the Spokane telephone book with the blue government pages. He found the FBI number, dialed it, but got a recorded message. They, too, wouldn't be open until Monday. So much for government agencies. Tom wondered if the Defense Department also fought only on a forty hour, five day week schedule.

The Comfort Inn was upscale enough to have some free stationery in the drawer, so he hurriedly scribbled a message for the FBI guy in case he came back to the motel. What was his name? Something like Old Faithful. Gaiser. "I had a meeting with the kidnappers and planted one of the transponders. I have a lead to who might have kidnapped Sylvia Hansen. Kilgore Smith, Lay-Z-Boy Ranch in Silver Valley." The RFD mail box number wasn't much help. There would be hundreds of such numbers spread out over the zip code area on country roads. Even if he had the right main road, the letter carrier might have to drive a couple of miles up some obscure lane to the ranch.

The sheepish clerk with the acne scarred face was still working the desk. Tom asked, "You knew that was someone from the FBI who came to see me, didn't you?"

The clerk nodded. "Yeh. We aren't supposed to tell anyone what room someone's in. Security. He showed me his badge and told me to keep quiet about it. I thought maybe you were a crook or something."

"He's helping me find my girl. If he shows up again, give him this envelope. Don't give it to anyone else."

"I go off duty in a couple of hours and I'm off tomorrow. I'll hand it over to the assistant manager when she comes in."

Not very good, Tom thought. Communications. Everything is communications. If this link fails, then what? He didn't know exactly how a transponder worked, what wave length the signal might be, and how one could pick it up. What good would the flashlight locator he had planted with Sylvia's things be if no one was listening?

The sun was down by the time Tom got a road map, passed a MacDonald's drive-up window for a big Mac and a diet Coke, asked direction at a gas station, and headed East on the Interstate 90 toward Smelterville.

The highway climbed east of Coeur d'Alene through woods and scrub timber over Fourth of July pass. Tom turned off at the exit that said Smelterville. The gas station was open. He went inside to ask directions.

The kid who manned the gas pumps didn't know anything, but an older mechanic slid out from under a battered pickup truck, wiped grease off his hands with an oily rag. "That's up Deadwood Gulch. Bad road. What you driving?" He gave the Tercel a skeptical look. "Might make it. Might not."

He'd have to backtrack to a hamlet called Page. As the dusk turned to darkness Tom wondered if he'd miss the ranch entirely. What if there were just a lane off and no sign? He drove slowly through the darkness, his body aching for sleep. The caffeine in the Coke wasn't keeping him awake.

The road narrowed and the paving deteriorated until the patched potholes gave way to washboard gravel. A single lane wound through a treacherous canyon then ended at a wooden arch. The sign over it said "Lay-Z-Boy Ranch. Three miles. Rough road." Hadn't what he was driving on been rough?

The track wound upward onto a sort of plateau. He came to a gate of weathered planks supported by twisted wire held tight by a rusty turnbuckle. Tom got out of the car, lifted the wire loop off the post that held the gate shut, shoved the gate open, drove in, and closed the gate behind him. He paused before getting back into the car.

At this altitude the air was cool and clear. This was big sky country. Far from the light pollution of the city, the canopy of stars was brilliant. What a universe! And here he was, an ant acting out this drama on a small planet orbiting a third rate star. No wonder people like Royer and his cronies wanted to be free of government interference. Anything that hindered their life in this glorious place must seem evil.

But he was not evil. He was just a tech writer who got lucky, fell in love with the boss's niece, and sold a book. Why couldn't life be simple?

The sign, "rough road" was an understatement. The only encouraging factor was the fresh tire tracks in the dust or in the wet edges of the mud holes. Someone had been back here and recently. If he had known what kind of roads he'd be on he'd have rented a four wheel drive.

Finally, as he came over a rise, he saw a distant light of a house. He drove slowly with the window down. Usually these places had dogs, and he wanted to hear. He didn't want any Suzy surprises. What he did hear as he neared the house was the sound of a generator and realized the ranch was off the power grid.

Someone inside had seen his headlights coming and switched on flood lights on the porch roof. The front door opened. A person was silhouetted briefly in the doorway, then stepped aside into the darkness.

There were two vehicles parked outside the house, a jeep and a station wagon. No pickup truck. Maybe this lead was a dead end. There was nothing for it, but to ask.

As he stepped out of the car he checked his pocket to make sure he still had his keys. As an afterthought he took the L.L. Bean bag and the copy of his book. Maybe, like Mr. Royer, Kilgore Smith was a fan.

47. Lay-Z-Boy Ranch

Whoever put up the flood lights had planned it well. Tom was blinded and in full view, a perfect target. The person on the porch called, "Who are you? Whaddaya want?"

Tom held up the book. "Tom Godot. Author of the best seller Conspiracy!"

"Funny time of night to be peddling books. We don't want any."

"I'm looking for Kilgore Smith. Otto Royer gave me this address. Said Mr. Smith might know where to find Sylvia Hansen."

"Smith isn't here."

"Is this his place? Will he be back?"

"Might, might not."

"Mind if I come in? I promise not to offer any encyclopedias or magazine subscriptions."

Tom was reluctantly admitted and noticed that a double-barreled shotgun was leaned just inside the door.

Though the outside of the ranch house was rustic and dilapidated, the inside was warm and pleasant. A stone fireplace dominated one wall. A pair of hunting rifles were hung over the fireplace. No doggy toys here. Through an open door Tom saw something out of character-- a computer monitor. It was on, a screen saver playing out random patterns of color.

Something about the living room was familiar. At first he couldn't decide what, then realized that, like Ted Brewer's office, this one had framed stock certificates. Tom studied one. A silver mine. "Ted Brewer has some of these in his office at Book World," Tom said. "You collect them, too?"

"Not mine," the man said. Now that he was in the light Tom saw that this was no cowboy, but a city type. Dockers slacks, expensive outfitters shoes, and a safari shirt with big pockets and an elegant cut. He looked like one of those yuppies who drove a sport utility vehicle but never took it anywhere but to the golf course or the grocery store. The jeep parked outside must be his. If this was an Aryan Nation household, there was nothing Aryan about the man's features. He might be Italian, Mediterranean, maybe even Jewish.

"You live here?" Tom asked.

"No. Just a guest. I'm a lawyer."

"The way things are going for me lately I could use one," Tom joked. Suddenly his stomach curdled. He stifled a belch. "Can I use your bathroom? I had a burger and a coke, not my usual fare. I don't think it agreed with me."

"Down the hall."

Tom passed the computer room, looked in an open bedroom door hoping to find a clue to Sylvia. No sign. He found the bath. He leaned over the sink and belched, afraid he was going to be sick. He wanted a look around the house, so he flushed the toilet, ran the water, washed his hands and returned to the living room.

"I didn't expect to see a computer at a ranch," he commented.

"Web surfers."

"Really? I'd like to try that some time. Mind if I look?"

The man blocked the way. "I'm sorry, but I can't tell you when Kilgore will be back. You say you're Tom something?

"Godot. Tom Godot." He had seen something in the computer room on the floor under the desk, a briefcase. It had a United Airlines carry-on tag on the handle. It was his briefcase. He was almost sure of it. "And you are?"

"Isadore Plotnik."

"The ACLU lawyer for the Aryan Nation! I saw your name in the News Chronicle." Then he had come to the right place. "Don't you have qualms about defending the rights of Nazis?

"Kilgore Smith isn't a Nazi. He has a constitutional right to his views. I don't have to agree with him, just to defend those rights. I'm not in the mood to argue politics with you, Mr. Godot. I'll tell Kilgore you were here. I'm sorry you drove all the way out for nothing."

"Whoever kidnapped my girl also stole my briefcase and my laptop computer. The briefcase in the computer room looks like mine. Mind if I examine it?"

"I don't know anything about any briefcase. I think it's time you left, Mr. Godot."

Tom changed the subject to the framed mining company shares. "Looks like these are collectibles," he said, trying to memorize the names. El Dorado, Bonanza, Lucky Lady. He was sure Ted Brewer had the same shares in his office. Ted Brewer had claimed his shop assistant had been handed the copy of Conspiracy! with the kidnappers' note inside. Tom didn't believe him. He was sure Brewer had a connection to this.

"If I can't sell you a copy of my book, the least I can do is give you one of my souvenir key fobs." Tom reached into the L.L. Bean bag and took one out. As he handed it to the lawyer he twisted the cap to activate it. "See? It's a flashlight. Very handy for finding keyholes in the dark."

Plotnik read the label, "Tom Godot, author of Conspiracy! Thanks," and put it in the pocket of his designer shirt. Staying between Tom and the shotgun leaning inside the front door, he let Tom out, then stood in the doorway waiting for Tom to get back in the Tercel.

"Tell Mr. Smith that I'm staying at the Comfort Inn in Coeur d'Alene. He can reach me there."

"I'll tell him. Remember to close the gate!" the lawyer called. "Smith's got cattle here. He's very particular about his gates. Don't want to let out any cows."

"I'll be careful," Tom said, started the engine, and turned the car around. His briefcase was at the Lay-Z-Boy ranch, but he was sure Sylvia wasn't. She was with Kilgore Smith. If his hunch was correct, an old silver mine would be a good place to hold a hostage, but which one was it? Lucky

Lady, El Dorado, or Bonanza? Or some other? There must be scores of abandoned mines in Silver Valley.

48.¶

Tom Godot had nearly fallen asleep at the wheel once he got back on the I-90. It was nearly midnight when he returned to the Comfort Inn in Coeur d'Alene. There was no one at the reception desk, but he could see that the envelope he had left for... what was his name? Something to do with Old Faithful? was still in the box. What good were communications if they never got through?

He fell into bed, taking off only his shoes. His mind was befuddled with the events of the last twenty-four hours. Sylvia kidnapped. Two flights across the country. The EPIRB wrist watch and the bugged key fob flashlights. Harold Stevenson dead. Who was using his name? Lady Agnes, the woman in the red dress? Peter, the blue-eyed man? The MacArthur Foundation had to have plenty of money to afford a Lear jet. Who were they? Conspiracy! indeed! It was all a conspiracy, one inside the other like a Chinese box.

His briefcase, records, and presumably his laptop computer were at the Lay-Z-Boy ranch somewhere in the hills above Smelterville. The PGP encryption manual was still in his suitcase, not that it would have made any difference. If they didn't have his pass phrase, the kidnappers couldn't crack the encrypted files, even if they were able to break into the system at MOM.

Pass phrase. That was a key to part of this. He remembered that the recognition signal he was given at the airport was "The wages of sin is death." That was Harold Stevenson's pass phrase for the encrypted files at MOM. His own, "How does your garden grow?" for messages encrypted with his public key and sent to him was not known to whoever was posing as Stevenson or to anyone else.

The last detail that boiled up in his memory was that on Monday... which was already today... he was supposed to do a reading at a bookstore in Spokane. Some book tour this was turning into! He would call Mary McGann in the morning and ask her to cancel it for him.

He dreamed of Sylvia, Sylvia hog tied in the back of a pickup truck, Sylvia frightened, helpless. Sylvia depending on him to somehow rescue her. He was no knight in shining armor, no action hero. He was just an ordinary guy with a desk job and a Visa credit card. Until he got the royalty check for Conspiracy! his bank balance was two paychecks short of oblivion. It was one of those anxiety dreams. He did not sleep well.

He'd forgotten to draw the curtain and the morning sun lit up the room like a searchlight pinning an escapee like a bug on a prison wall. Shielding his eyes, Tom pulled himself up on the bed. His mouth felt like he had been gagged with a wad of cotton and his shoulders still ached from the tension of mountain driving.

A shower would help, and a change of clothes. He looked at his new EPIRB watch, saw that the Nile office in New York would be open, and called Mary McGann.

"Hello? Mary McGann."

"It's Tom Godot in Coeur d'Alene, Idaho."

"Tom! Glad to hear from you. I was going through my faxes this morning and I'm missing your report from Book World. How did it go?"

Jesus! Did she have to micro manage every detail? How many copies had he sold? Twenty-one? It felt like a hundred years ago. "I have to cancel the Spokane reading. Sylvia Hansen's been kidnapped by white supremacists. I was flown to Washington and back in a private jet."

"Hold on, Tom, you're talking a mile a minute. Take a deep breath and start over."

Tom tried to gather his wits. "I found out something important. There is no Harold Stevenson. He's dead. I mean, the real Harold Stevenson is dead. My co-author's been using his name. It has to do with something called the MacArthur Foundation. What do you know about them?"

Mary McGann's voice was guarded. "You're not supposed to know about that."

"Well I do know. You gave me Harold Stevenson's number yourself. It rings at the MacArthur Foundation."

Mary McGann paused. She was obviously weighing her words carefully. "The foundation owns a piece of the book. They sometimes support certain authors, but it's strictly confidential."

"So they're the ones picking up the expenses for this book tour?"

She hedged. "Partly. I don't know all the details."

"I can't imagine you not knowing every detail. I'm sure they're connected somehow to NSA, the National Security Agency. I met the people who say they're from the MacArthur Foundation think tank, but the gadgets they've given me are more like CIA stuff."

Mary McGann cautioned him. "Don't tell me any more about that, not over the phone."

Right, Tom thought. Now she's got galloping paranoia.

"What about this kidnapping?"

"The Aryan Nation want something out of the drafts of my book. I suspect the NSA even put them on to it. Do you still have the original manuscript Harold, er, Stevenson or whoever he is and I submitted to Nile?"

"It's somewhere here."

"Shred it. Delete it from any computer files. Better yet, destroy it. A deleted file can be recovered. Do you have a program called `destroy'? It removes any trace of a file."

Mary McGann clearly didn't like to be given orders, not from him. She was good enough at giving them. "I'll see about it."

"Don't just see about it," Tom insisted peevishly. "Do it! They'll be coming after you next."

"What about the book tour?"

Now Tom was fully awake and angry. "Forget it! Call the store in Spokane and cancel today's reading. I don't remember the name of the place. It's in my briefcase, and that's been stolen. I'm sick of being the bait to draw the crazies out of the woodwork. Right now all I'm going to do is try to rescue Sylvia. Then I'm heading back to San Jose and the safety of my boring cubicle at MOM." He hung up.

He had one more call to make. Then maybe, if nothing else worked he would go to the county records office or the public library or wherever he could find out the location of those silver mines. Action was better than sitting around waiting for the phone when the kidnappers got stuck. The Sylvia password would get them past the CMOS, but not into his files at MOM. There were other gates to breach and the Grand Poohbah's firewall.

He called the MacArthur Foundation. This time the switchboard lady recognized his voice and put him through.

"Hello?"

Tom couldn't recognize the voice. "This is Tom Godot in Coeur d'Alene. Who have I got? I know it's not Harold Stevenson. Is this Peter?"

"No. He's not here. How was your flight back to Idaho?"

"Uneventful. The best kind. But I've made some progress here. Do those little flashlight things do what you claimed?"

"Yes."

"Well, if things worked out right, Sylvia Hansen has one of them. The ACLU lawyer for the Aryan Nation has another. My briefcase is up at a place called the Lay-Z-Boy ranch outside Smelterville. I have a hunch that Sylvia might be at some silver mine, but there are dozens of them up here. Can you locate Sylvia for me?"

"Peter's putting a team together. It'll take a few hours."

What kind of a team? Where? "What do I do in the meantime?"

"Wait."

"What do I tell the FBI? I got interviewed by an agent Gaiser from Spokane. He didn't believe my story. Says he's going to investigate me. A lot of good that's going to do."

"You have nothing to worry about, Mr. Godot. You're clean."

"Oh, yeh? Sylvia Hanson's `clean' too, but she's been kidnapped because of me, and I don't even know what the hell is going on."

"You're doing a good job, Tom. Leave the rest to us."

"The hell I will! I'm not going to just sit around this motel room waiting for a phone call. Shit!" Tom hung up.

Tom stripped off the clothes he'd slept in and got in the shower. The stream of hot water was refreshing. He reached for the soap and discovered Sylvia's shampoo. He had forgotten to pack it for her. Sylvia. He remembered how she trembled uncontrollably when he put his arms around her that night in front of her apartment. He thought of how she froze when he touched her in bed. She had been afraid of being touched. She had built up her confidence enough to be with him at the motel, but she was sure to be set back by this trauma. What if she was raped? His stomach turned at the thought of someone forcing her to have sex. She'd never get over it. How was she coping now? He turned the water temperature to cold to shock himself into an alert state.

He realized he wasn't thinking rationally, he was so upset. He'd never be able to find and check out all those silver mines. Maybe instead of wild goose chases around old mines he should try the Lay-Z-Boy ranch again. Where was that slip of paper with the address? Maybe he'd get through.

Tom hurriedly dried himself off and sat naked on the bed. He went through his pockets. Here it was. He spread out the crumpled information about the Lay-Z-Boy ranch and dialed the number.

This time someone answered. "Yeh?"

"This is Tom Godot. Is this Mr. Kilgore Smith? I was there last night and missed him."

"How'd you get this number?"

It was a bad connection. What did they have? A wireless phone? The sound kept fading in and out. "That's not important now. I saw that you have my briefcase there, so I assume you also have my laptop computer. It also occurs to me that having the CMOS password wouldn't do you a whole lot of good. Why don't I help you get whatever it is you want?"

"What's the catch, Mr. Godot?"

"No catch. I just want Sylvia Hansen released."

There was a silence. Obviously a discussion was taking place. This time a different voice came on. "You remember the east bound exit ramp off the I-90 for Smelterville?"

"Sure."

"Park your car off the ramp and wait. Someone will pick you up and take you to Sylvia Hansen. You'd better come alone."

"What time?"

"Noon." The connection was broken.

Noon. That didn't leave him much time. No one had picked up his note for the FBI agent but the Spokane office should be open.

Agent Gaiser was not surprised to hear from him. "I've talked with our man in Bismarck. He confirms your story about Mary Contrari."

"Great," Tom said, relieved. "So you won't have to investigate me before you get on with the real problem."

"I wouldn't say that, Mr. Godot. We're very interested in your connection with the National Security Agency. I've checked out your security clearance at MOM, but that's limited to their premises. Why don't you tell me what you're up to? I'm a good listener."

"This isn't about NSA. This is about Sylvia Hansen. I'm to be picked up at the off ramp for Smelterville at noon. I promised to help the kidnappers if they release her. They insist I come alone."

"Noon doesn't give us much time. You wouldn't by chance have a cellular phone?"

"Nope."

"Too bad. I thought all California boys had them."

Tom looked around the motel room, remembered his keys. "I've got one of those flashlight things on my keys. I'll activate the signal and you can follow it."

"That's a nice theory, Mr. Godot, providing the gadget works. You don't know the wave length or the effective range?"

"Not a clue. But I gave you one of them. Use it to test."

"I've already sent it to the lab."

"Oh, terrific. Where's that? Virginia? I hope you used express mail. Let's hope by the time you do track down my signal you won't just find a skeleton in the woods."

Tom hung up. He hoped the FBI weren't like the bail bondsman whose sign he had once seen in Los Angeles: "I'll get you out if it takes me twenty years."

The man at MacArthur said it would take time for Peter to get a team together, whatever that meant. The FBI didn't impress him with their effectiveness. He'd been advised not to contact the local police. He was on his own.

He had slipped away from the Sons of Freedom and talked his way out in Bismarck. Why not this time?

49. The Mine

A mountain fog filled the valley at Smelterville and after he parked at the ramp a fine mist blotted out the view through the windshield. He had arrived early enough to order a plate of spaghetti at a little cafe near the gas station where he had asked directions for the Lay-Z-Boy ranch.

The elderly waitress wore a dirty apron and an unexpected hair net that might satisfy the letter of the health code, but not the intent. She unceremoniously dumped a ladle of watery spaghetti on his plate where it lay in a puddle. The greasy meat sauce was out of a can, and the imitation Parmesan cheese was clogged in the shaker. So much for cuisine in Smelterville.

Since she appeared to be a local old timer, Tom asked, "Have you ever heard of the Lucky Lady, El Dorado, or Bonanza silver mine?"

"The Lucky Lady isn't far from here. It should have been called the Unlucky Lady. I don't know the others. Most around here have been closed for years."

Why the Unlucky Lady? Tom wondered. He could probably look it up someplace. Sounded like another one of those boom and bust stories of hope, exploitation, greed, and disappointment that was such a frequent pattern in mining country.

At the off ramp several cars passed. Up on the I-90 logging trucks carried away the wealth of the forest.

Someone knocked on the roof of the car. The face beyond the glass was indistinct. Tom rolled down the window. "Yeh?"

"You Tom Godot?"

"Yes."

"Got some ID?"

Tom showed his California driver's license.

"You're the first person I've seen whose license picture looks better than he does."

Tom rubbed his eye. "I got punched out. Are both eyes black now?"

"Could be worse," the man said. Tom had not seen him before. He was lanky and had English features, gaunt cheeks, the kind of heavy beard that always looks unshaven. He wore a shapeless Indiana Jones hat with a wide brim frosted with mist from the fog. "Leave your car here."

Tom took the L.L. Bean bag with the Conspiracy! flashlights and followed the man across the road to a heavy truck that might be US Army surplus or stolen from the National Guard. It had the original camouflage paint, but the machine gun rack over the canvas top was empty. It was a high step up into the dusty front seat. "Where are we going?"

"Up the road a piece. It's not far. It just feels like it."

The man was right. They drove into the mountain mist and were soon headed up a track that was carved out of the side of a ravine. The windshield wipers had pushed so much dirt in the past that they had scratched arcs in the glass. Beyond the scratched windshield Tom could make out boulders and timber, but the trail was so winding he never got a clear view ahead.

The truck lurched and the gears ground. "Got to double clutch this old deuce and a half," the man said and muttered curses as he fought the gear shift, clutch and steering wheel on the hairpin turns. They were still climbing.

They cleared the top of the fog bank and emerged into a breathtaking view of mountains like peninsulas and islands in a sea of cloud. If his mission weren't so urgent and stressful, Tom might have just stood to savor the view.

"Here we are."

It was a mine after all, as he had suspected. A battered sign was painted "Lucky Lady" in peeling letters. Under it someone had tacked a warning, "Danger. No trespassing." At the top of the road Tom recognized the black pickup truck with the camper box on the back. Beyond the parking space a narrow gauge track led to a boarded up entrance. The tailings had been thrown down the side of a ravine, damming up the stream below.

Tom was led to a weather beaten shack. The panes of window glass that weren't broken were opaque with years of dust. The door swung open as he and the driver approached and a voice called, "Mr. Godot. So glad you could come."

Inside three men sat around a table. They had a laptop computer open in front of them, wired into a cellular phone. He recognized one of the men at once. "Ted Brewer. I knew you had something to do with this. This what you call accommodating your customers? Does Book World also supply textbooks for kidnappers?"

Brewer had exchanged his dapper outfit for a set of khaki coveralls and military style boots. He gestured to the large man in cammies. "This is Kilgore Smith. You might have seen him on the podium at the park on Saturday."

Tom remembered the face now, the heavy eyebrows that met in the middle. "Last time I saw you you were wearing suspenders to keep up your pants."

The man smiled and made a fist. "How's that other eye?"

Ted Brewer didn't catch the reference to Tom's being knocked down in the park. "I think you've met our computer consultant before." He gestured to a younger man at the table. No coveralls or cammies for him. This one wore a short blue jean jacket and a baseball cap reversed.

Sure enough. Tom recognized the ring through the eyebrow. Odd how someone into body piercing would team up with the Aryan Nation. Maybe this kid was a skinhead, except he wasn't bald. A tuft of hair protruded through the band of the baseball cap he wore with the bill in the back. "You didn't waste any time," Tom said. "What is it? Rick? From Bismarck, isn't it? Had any luck with my laptop?"

"Some. You really should have bought one with bigger keys. It would save time if you just gave us what we want."

"Sure. But I want to see Sylvia first. Where is she?"

"Up at the mine." Ted Brewer turned to the man who had driven the army truck. "Show him. Here's the keys." Brewer tossed a bunch of keys. "Wait a minute, Godot. What's in the shoulder bag?

Tom opened it for him to inspect. "Some souvenir Conspiracy! key fob flashlights. See?"

Brewer inspected the bag and took one. "Pretty cute. You should have had these at the reading."

"Why don't you each take one? Good will gesture," Tom said, and handed one to each of the men, twisting each to the on position as he did. "Tell all your friends. Buy my book."

Ted Brewer was amused. "Always the salesman. I could use you in the store."

"I only do one night stands." Tom shouldered his L.L. Bean bag and followed the man in the fedora hat up the steep rocky slope to the entrance of the mine. It was closed by a stout wall of heavy timber. The wide wooden door had two padlocks, one high, one low. Whoever had mounted them knew that the weak link in many such arrangements was the hasp and its fastenings. These were heavy metal and bolted, not screwed to the door and the frame. The locks themselves were antique but formidable.

The mine inside the entrance was dark except for a Coleman lantern hissing about fifty feet back. "This must be the hard hat area," Tom quipped as he ducked his head. Where was Sylvia? Tom saw that the kidnappers had provided her with an old mattress, a filthy blanket, a Portapotti, and a jug of water. Tom was relieved to see that they had given her the overnight bag. He hoped the signal from the trick flashlight could be picked up through the solid rock of the mountain.

Sylvia Hansen emerged from the dark depths of the mine. For once her short stature was an advantage. She could stand straight. She was wearing the same clothes she had on at the parade, the blue Gore-Tex jacket, the Sorrel boots, the electric blue Lycra pants. "Tom! They've got you, too."

"No. I've come to get you out." He had expected to find her tied and gagged, but her captors apparently were satisfied that the heavy door would be enough to lock up a diminutive slip of a girl.

Tom put his arms around her and whispered into her ear.

"Did you find the flashlight in your bag? Keep it with you. I've got some pepper spray. I'll pretend to tie my shoe and leave it here. I don't know if they'll let us go when they get what they want. I've got a punch knife, though it's four of them against the two of us."

Sylvia turned her face to him and stopped his whispering with a kiss.

"These aren't Comfort Inn accommodations, but she's been well cared for, Mr. Godot. Now let's get down to business."

"She could use one of those flashlights herself," Tom said.

"I'll give it to her," the truck driver insisted. "No funny stuff from you. Godot. I don't what else you have in there." He fished out one of the trinkets and gave it to Sylvia, then hustled Tom back to the entrance.

Tom pretended to stumble. "My shoe!" As he crouched to fumble with his laces he hid the pepper spray under a rock. If one of the men tried to molest her at least she'd have a defense. She might even use it to escape. Then he was led out of the mine and watched as the heavy door was shut and the two padlocks secured.

"Is the mine safe?" Tom asked.

"There was an explosion years ago and a bunch of men were killed. The rest refused to go back to work. They said the mine was jinxed." The man with the fedora gave Tom a searching look. "My great grandfather was a miner in Cornwall, but you'd never get me to work in one of these pits."

Back in the Lucky Lady office Rick the computer hacker explained the setup. "There's no power or phone line up here, but I've patched your laptop into this cellular phone.

It's digital, the latest, so you can call MOM and log onto the system there."

"That's what you want?"

"We want all the encrypted drafts of your book, especially the first draft."

"That's what I don't understand," Tom said. He tried to remember the book as it had first been transmitted to him by Harold Stevenson, or whoever it was who claimed to be Stevenson. The writing was clumsy, didactic, more of a synopsis than a book. It was also far too technical, going into great detail in how the conspirators could cause communications satellites to malfunction. Only a technician or a sci-fi buff willing to immerse himself in quack theories would be interested in that degree of specificity. Readers didn't want to know how something was done. Readers wanted only enough so they could get on with the story, following the hero up to the obligatory confrontation scene. Tom had to cut much of Stevenson's first draft and rework the plot so there was a confrontation. Then the villain got his just desserts and the hero got the girl. That was how these things worked, and that's how he had revised it. "Why all this interest in early drafts? Nobody would want to read that."

"We would," Kilgore Smith insisted.

"How did you find out there were any drafts?"

Ted Brewer knew books. "All books have drafts. We got a tip that the drafts of Conspiracy! contain key information."

"A tip? From whom?" Then he remembered Mary Contrari. At two of his readings she had asked pointed questions about the drafts, and if she hadn't been assaulted might have pursued him from bookstore to bookstore, always bringing up the same topic. Why? After the first week of the book tour there was almost always someone in the audience who asked about drafts, creating an interest where there shouldn't be any.

Kilgore Smith gave him a smug, self-satisfied smirk. "We're a bit better organized than you think, Mr. Godot."

What would Smith and the Aryan Nation do with the drafts when they got them? "Even if you could disable communications satellites, which I doubt, the government would never pay the billion dollar blackmail my book describes. What do you expect?"

"We're tired of waiting, Godot. This is a Christian nation for whites only. We're going to send the blacks all back to Africa and the Jews to Israel."

"And you think the drafts of my book are going to make that possible? Pardon me if I think you're just a little bit nuts."

Kilgore Smith's smug smirk turned into an angry, cruel look that needed no words.

Tom backed away from that line of argument. "What if I can't get the drafts you want?"

Kilgore Smith had been sitting when Tom first saw him. Now when he stood up Tom could see the man wore a heavy belt with a holstered pistol on one hip and a sheathed hunting knife on the other. "You'll get them. Don't make us do anything violent, Mr. Godot, like breaking your girl friend's legs. Would you still marry her if she couldn't walk? Would she marry you if you, let's say, could no longer function as a man?" He tapped the hilt of his knife.

Tom spread his hands in a gesture of compliance. "Take it easy. Haven't I always cooperated?" If the drafts were as harmless as he thought they were, there was no harm in giving these Aryan nuts anything they wanted. "Let's get on with it."

He would try to stall them. The people from the MacArthur Foundation were on their way, they said. So was the FBI, maybe. Ted Brewer might be a weasel, but Kilgore Smith was dangerous. Tom hoped someone would show up before Smith ran ut of patience.¶

50. Missing!

So far as Tom could tell, the hookup to the cellular phone worked the same as when he plugged his modem in at the motel.

"I've reprogrammed your dial up routine for the cellular phone," Rick explained.

Sure enough. Though Tom worked with computers every day, he still marveled at the skills of hackers like Rick, even when he resented and feared their intrusion. For them, breaking into systems was a challenge, every firewall a new level of gaming, like Myst or Duke Nukem. Morality and ethics were foreign concepts.

Reset, the communications program automatically dialed the server number at MOM.

Rick watched carefully as Tom entered his password to access the files at Mom he and the alleged Harold Stevenson had access to. He deliberately made a keyboard error, knowing if he missed on the third try MOM would disconnect, but that if he tried twice and failed, the Poobah back at MOM would be alerted that someone not familiar with the system was trying to log in. Unless Rick was really slick and worked through a cutout server someplace, this call could be traced.

"There it is," Tom said. "Four drafts. The one my co-author submitted with his proposal to me to rewrite it, the first revision, the version our literary agent submitted to Nile publishing, and the final version that's in print. Why don't you just buy the book? Twenty five bucks. I have nearly a case in the trunk of my car. If you buy six copies I'll give you the regular bookstore discount. Mr. Brewer knows what that is. Free autographs. No charge for the souvenir key fobs."

Kilgore Smith wasn't amused. "Cut the crap, Godot. You're running off at the mouth."

"So blame me for being nervous. You would be, too, if someone threatened to castrate you."

Kilgore Smith couldn't be diverted. "The first draft. Let's have the first draft."

Tom called it up. It was gibberish. "It's encrypted."

"So decrypt it."

"I'm not very good at this," Tom said, stalling. "I've only used the PGP program a couple of times." He wanted to stay on the cellular line as long as possible. All those calls were logged and could be traced to the owner of the phone. He also knew the repeaters for the cellular phone service would identify the zone the call came from. The longer this took the better.

"Wait," Rick said. "Download the draft to a disk." He produced a small floppy disk and slid it into the slot. He smiled at Tom. "Just for insurance, in case someone tries to delete it."

"OK." It was a large file, and run through the internet and the digital cellular phone took about fifteen minutes.

While the four men concentrated on the elusive screen image of the laptop, Tom checked his watch. How did you activate the EPIRB? The first button he pushed turned it into a stop watch. Not that. Then he remembered the slide under the case. Now to see if anyone flying over would detect the distress signal.

The system had been invented by the Russians for locating downed aircraft. Every EPIRB had its own identifying code. Any aircraft that flew within range of the signal would pick it up, identify the sender, and note the location. Now the gadgets could be bought from any marine supply store. Hikers could use them, and mountain climbers, anyone who might need to be rescued. Let's hope they'd rescue him and Sylvia. Modern communications were a marvel-- when they worked.

"All right. It's downloaded. Now decrypt it."

"I'll have to log off first," Tom said. He wondered how long Rick had been fooling with the laptop. There was no phone line to the mine, and no electricity. The laptop batteries had been charged before he put it away, but there was no telling how much time was left.

Tom took the computer to the PGP program, but couldn't remember the code combination. He stalled, deliberately tried the wrong combinations.

"You've got that all wrong," Rick said, adjusting his baseball cap. "Hit the help key. Hell, let me do it."

Tom refused to let go of the computer. "You have to enter the pass phrase."

"What's the pass phrase?"

Whoever claimed to be Stevenson had told him not to write it down, yet had passed it on to the person who met him at the airport. Tom knew that when he entered it the letters would not appear on the screen. "The wages of sin is death," he said, and covered the keyboard so Rick would not notice that he held down the shift key for Death, capital D. Without the exact combination of upper and lowercase letters, the pass phrase would not work.

The computer didn't do anything. The cursor blinked.

"It's heavily encrypted," Tom explained. "It's a large file, a couple of hundred pages. This is going to take time."

The computer beeped and little window at the corner of the screen flashed on and off. Low battery.

"Shit!" Rick exclaimed.

Kilgore Smith, unable to see the screen, had leaned back in his kitchen chair. Now he was attentive. "What's the matter?"

"Low battery," Rick explained. "I've got to take this back to town. But we've got the draft on disk and I know the pass phrase. The rest will be easy." He got up to leave.

"I'll drive you," the man in the fedora hat offered. "I'm the only double clutcher who can drive that deuce and a half."

"What about him?" the driver said, pointing to Tom.

Ted Brewer's face was an insincere mask of sympathy and consideration. "So sorry, Tom. We'll have to hold you along with your girl friend until we know for sure that we have what we want."

Tom watched as the truck was jockeyed around and headed back down the mountain trail. The mist trapped between the mountain ridges was burning off, showing more of Idaho's breathtaking scenery. The terrain was rugged. What if he and Sylvia did somehow overpower these two and escape? Sylvia was a climber, but he wasn't. There were grizzly bears and mountain lions in those woods.

With two of the four men gone, the odds were better. There was no telling when or if anyone would pick up the EPIRB signal or if the FBI or people from MacArthur would show up at all.

Ted Brewer unlocked the two heavy padlocks and pulled open the massive door. Inside, the mine was pitch dark. Where was the lantern? Where was Sylvia?

"Go get the other lantern," the Kilgore Smith told Ted Brewer.

Tom shouted into the darkness. "Sylvia!"

"Shut up, Godot!"

With Brewer at the office, Tom had only one man to contend with, but where was Sylvia? Waiting in the shadows with a rock, he hoped. They could knock this guy out, tie him up, and deal with Brewer. Ted Brewer didn't look like much of an opponent.

Tom fingered the sheath of the punch knife tucked under his belt. He had never used it. The thought of cutting someone with that wicked, triangular blade made him sick to the stomach. It wasn't a killing weapon, but something for self defense that could inflict terrible wounds.

Before Tom could decide what to do, Brewer was back with a feeble kerosene lantern. It must be an antique, Tom thought. The chimney had not been cleaned, but as their eyes grew accustomed to the darkness they could pick their way in the yellow light.

Tom tried out the Conspiracy! flashlight on his key ring. It shot out a pencil of light. There was the mattress, the blanket, the water jug, portable toilet, Sylvia's overnight bag and, oddly, Sylvia's Sorrel boots, but no Sylvia.

"I thought mines just went down," Tom said as he stepped over broken rock.

"This is an adit, " Brewer explained. "There are shafts, stopes, and adits. Names for different kinds of tunnels."

"Maybe she's fallen down a shaft," Tom said.

"Could be. I told her to stay put."

The mine did not take a straight course, but apparently followed the original vein of silver. A few hundred feet farther on they came to a side tunnel totally blocked by debris. "That's where they had the accident," Brewer explained. "The bodies were left there and the mine closed."

The passageway turned and they saw a light ahead.

"It's her lantern." Tom shouted again, "Sylvia!"

He felt a rush of air across his face as they turned the corner. There must be an opening somewhere, something Brewer might not know about.

The lantern stood at the edge of a square-cut vertical shaft about six fee

t across. The Coleman lantern, designed for use on table tops, did not shine downward, but to the side. Brewer tilted it to look down into the shaft.

"How deep is it?" Tom asked.

Kilgore Smith suggested, "Why don't you jump in and see?"

Tom shone his pencil of light into the shaft, but it was too feeble. He tossed in a stone. It bounced, echoing hollowly and finally splashed somewhere down in the darkness.

"I see something," Brewer announced, holding the lantern at an angle.

Tom leaned over the edge. It was a long way down, but he thought he could make out something in the watery rubble at the bottom. It looked like blue cloth.

51. Air shaft

As soon as they had locked her up, Sylvia explored the mine as far as she dared. She did not want to get lost, and didn't know how much fuel was in the Coleman lantern. She reasoned that the best time to escape is before you've been held so long that lack of food and sleep make you too weak to try. She found some discarded tools back in the mine, and given time could probably batter down the door, but not without being noticed. Then they're surely tie her up, as they had with rope and duct tape when she was first grabbed. If she was going to escape, it had to be by stealth.

She had felt the air rushing through the mine. Was it like Carlsbad Caverns, which seemed to breathe like some huge, subterranean beast, exhaling at night as the outside air cooled, and inhaling in the heat of the day? Or was there another entrance?

She found the shaft that dropped to lower levels, then sniffed the air, licked her palm and felt the draft. It was upwards. Looking up she thought she saw a faint light. An air shaft! It was six foot square, so the corners would give her purchase. But free climbing that shaft in the dark was risky. The light from the lantern would take her up maybe twenty, thirty feet, but beyond that was darkness.

She returned to her overnight bag. What did she have that might help her get out? She wondered if Tom realized she'd brought her climbing shoes. To him they probably looked like slippers, but no slipper laced up so tightly or had such a stiff rubber sole. She'd hoped for a chance to climb while she was in Coeur d'Alene, but hadn't planned on this.

The little flashlight, the one Tom gave her and the other one she found down in her bag might just work. How long could their batteries last? Twenty minutes? Or were they those pink rabbit ones that kept going and going and going?

But she couldn't hold a flashlight and still climb that rocky shaft, not even if she held it in her teeth. She remembered her sun glasses... Sylvia had paid over a hundred dollars for them, an indulgence. Now she carefully pressed out the lenses, put them in her pocket with the pepper spray Tom had hidden for her. She removed the laces from her Sorrel boots and tightly lashed the little flashlights to the bows of the sunglass frame. An extra loop went around her neck so the glasses wouldn't fall off her face. With the flashlights on, the beams of light pointed wherever she turned her head. Yes!

They'd be looking for her, of course. How could she delay them? She had packed a blue sweater and had put it on under her jacket to keep warm in the chill of the mine. Now she took it off, stuffed it with her laundry and dropped it down the shaft. Maybe they would think she had fallen and waste time doing down to get her body while she was climbing up.

Sylvia placed the hissing lantern at the edge of the shaft, adjusted the sunglasses with the little flashlights and eased out over the edge, feeling for a handhold.

The first rock she tested was loose and dropped with a clatter, a bounce, and a distant splash. She shuddered. Took a deep breath. Tried again for a handhold. Once in the corner of the shaft she could press against the sides. How high would she have to climb? Would the opening at the top be blocked? Barred? or impossible without pitons and ropes?

She knew the tricks of the free climbers, how a pocketful of steel nuts with loops of string could allow you to wedge into a crack and get a grip on what looked like a sheer, smooth rock face, but she hadn't brought any.

Once she had climbed thirty feet she was beyond the light of the Coleman lamp. It was far below her now. She had only to concentrate on the next hand hold, the next toe hold, the light in front of her face, and keep climbing.

52.

"She's fallen down the shaft," Tom said, barely able to control himself. "My God. Are there any ropes around here? Cables or something? There have to be."

"If she's fallen down there, Godot, she's dead. Too bad." For once Smith sounded regretful.

"Dead or alive, we've got to get her out," Tom insisted. "You want me to cooperate, don't you?"

Kilgore Smith backed away from the edge of the pit. "Once Rick gets your computer recharged and the manuscript decrypted we won't need you. Maybe we'll just shove you down after her."

"The least we can do is lower a light on a rope so we can get a better look."

"All right. I've got a hundred feet of rope in the pickup. Come on." They started back toward the entrance. As they rounded a turn in the passageway they heard a clatter, a crash of rock falling and a heavy thud.

Tom jumped forward. "Is this place caving in?"

Kilgore Smith wasn't fazed. "Old mines are always settling. We get tremors here, small earthquakes. Goes with the territory. You think the Lucky Lady is haunted by the souls of the miners who are buried here?" He laughed.

Tom ran down the abandoned track to the parked pickup truck. Sure enough, there was a coil of quarter inch rope. He retrieved it and hurried back up to the mine. Inside, he tied one end to the handle of the Coleman lamp. While Ted Brewer held the old kerosene lantern, Tom lowered the lamp down the shaft to illuminate the blue shape at the bottom.

The lamp hung upon a rock, had to be swung past, bumped the side of the shaft. "Careful!" Brewer cautioned. "You'll break the glass."

"That's the end of the rope," Tom said. "As far as it gets."

Ted Brewer was on his knees now, looking down. "I see it. You're in luck, Godot. It's not your sweet Sylvia. It's some old clothes."

A noise above made them look up. A shower of pebbles and small stones came down out of the darkness. "Watch out!"

Tom pulled back, realized too late that he had let go of the rope. A crash down below announced the end of the lamp.

From high above there was a scream, almost like an animal. "Goddamit, she's climbing out!" Smith exclaimed.

By the poor light of the kerosene lamp Tom could see Smith fumbling with his holster. Kilgore Smith aimed it up into the darkness. In the confined space of the mine the sound of the shot was deafening.

"No!" Tom shouted, and pushed Kilgore Smith aside.

The heavy man turned on his heel and stepped back to recover.

To Tom it seemed like a childhood nightmare in slow motion, only this time he was not running away through deep mud to escape from some evil. He saw Kilgore Smith, arms flailing for his balance, the pistol falling away as the man teetered backwards, and then disappeared into darkness.

Another stone clattered down from above, bounding from one side of the shaft to the other.

Tom aimed his tiny flashlight up the air shaft, but it was suitable for finding a keyhole in the dark and little else. He shouted, "Sylvia!" but there was no answer.

"Let's get out of here," Tom said, trying to see by the pencil of light from his flashlight and he hurried toward the entrance. When he had the open door in sight he realized that now they were only two, he and Ted Brewer. Tom put his hand to his waist where the punch knife was hidden in its little sheath. Now the odds were in his favor.

53. Bats!

The air near the top of the shaft smelled different, not that dry, dead smell of old timbers. The reason she had shrieked was she came upon a cluster of bats clinging to the wall. When she disturbed them a couple fluttered close to her face and she almost lost her grip. She worked her way around and moved higher. She kept telling herself what her first instructor had said, "If you can walk you can climb."

How high had she come? There was no telling, but she had to be near the top. Looking up, she saw a ceiling of solid rock, but she could still feel the rush of air. She turned her head and the pencils of fading light picked out the exit. From here it should be easy.

She pulled herself onto the level floor of the passageway and sat up, catching her breath. The pistol shot had missed her, but the ricochet of the bullet made a nasty whine and chips of stone had struck her cheek. She had been afraid to answer when she heard Tom's call.

Her hand felt something soft and yielding that was not rock. She looked down and saw bits of fur, then fragments of bone. Something had died in here, some animal. How had it gotten in?

She picked up one of the bones and studied it. What was it? A thigh bone of something? A sheep? What were the marks?

These bones had been gnawed, she realized, but how long ago? Could be years. She could not stand up in this passage and crouched low, studying the uneven floor as she crept up the slope. She bumped her head and cried out, stopped to feel her forehead. Was she bleeding?

Then she heard a low, menacing growl. She looked up. The batteries in the little lights were fading, but she could make out the reflected glow of the eyes of... of what? They were widely spaced. What was it? A bobcat? Too big for that.

Bats were not the only animals that lived in the old mine. Sylvia realized that she had stumbled into the lair of a mountain lion. She couldn't go back. She had to get past it to escape.

54 Black helicopters

"There must be a map of this mine, something that shows the air shafts and other openings," Tom said when he and Brewer got back to the shack. Except for the battered table and odd collection of old kitchen chairs, there was a vandalized filing cabinet with broken, empty drawers. Souvenir hunters had plundered the Lucky Lady of anything of value and vandals had wrecked the rest. "It'll take a mountain rescue team or a bunch of spelunkers to find Sylvia and get her out of there."

Ted Brewer had changed his opinion of Tom Godot. Now his voice conveyed a sense of awe and fear. "You murdered Kilgore Smith."

"Is that what you're going to tell the FBI when they arrive?"

"FBI?"

"On the way," Tom said. He held up his key ring with the Conspiracy! flashlight. "This is really a transponder."

Ted Brewer understood. "Another version of those locators the government embeds in people so they can watch their every movement. That's what Timothy McVeigh was afraid of. He was right, wasn't he? You're part of the government conspiracy to control everyone, to watch their every movement."

"Don't get hysterical. That's bullshit," Tom said. "I'm just a tech writer who got lucky and sold a first novel."

"Then your co-author, Stevenson, is using you."

"There is no Harold Stevenson," Tom said. "He's dead. Died in prison. That's the story, anyway."

"Maybe that's the story you've been told, Godot, you chump. Don't you see? You think the Aryan Nation is a conspiracy. Not so. The real conspiracy is the government. They're taking away our civil rights, bit by bit. But we're fighting back any way we know how. The Aryan Nation is working in your own interests, Godot. Don't you realize that?"

Tom wasn't in the mood for polemics. "Look, there's no phone here, so we'll have to drive down and get help for Sylvia and retrieve Smith's body. You got the keys to the pickup?"

"No."

"Can you hot wire a car?"

"Never tried it."

"I guess I should have taken that auto mechanics class after all," Tom said. "Looks like we'll have to walk."

Overhead he heard the hammering of an engine. Tom stepped out of the shack and looked up. He took Brewer's arm. "See? What did I tell you? Here come the black helicopters."

Ted Brewer blanched. "It is all true, what Kilgore and the Aryan Nation have been saying all along."

"What?" Tom waved to the helicopter, which was circling like a great black war machine as the pilot looked for a suitable place to put down.

"The black helicopters!"

Tom laughed. "Hooray for talk radio. Thank you, Rush Limbaugh!" The helicopter was settling down in a great cloud of blown dust. Choking, Tom ran toward it and waved to the men in SWAT team uniforms that were already jumping out of it like figures in an action movie.

Then he stopped. Their assault rifles were pointed at him.

55. Pepper spray

Sylvia Hansen was afraid to move. She reasoned that the cougar was as surprised as she was and would hesitate before charging. She remembered the pepper spray in her jacket pocket and took it out. But she hadn't studied it to see which was the business end, and how it worked. What if she pressed the trigger and it squirted blinding pepper spray into her own eyes? She'd be helpless.

She turned her face to the pepper spray canister, lighting it up. How did it work? When she glanced up she saw that the cougar had crept closer, ready to charge.

Sylvia couldn't turn back, but she could move forward. She tried to imitate a snarling cat herself. The cougar paused, moved its powerful front paws into a stronger position for a leap.

Sylvia had no room to maneuver. The shaft was too low for her to stand up. Pepper spray was powerful, awful, choking stuff. If she fired the canister in the confined space of the mine tunnel, she'd be as blinded as the cougar was. She didn't dare squirt it twenty feet. Then she'd have to pass through the choking cloud herself. She'd have to wait until the animal was close, then not miss.

She shifted to her left, making room to roll to one side as the animal charged. She realized that it would go for her face, for the twin lights now growing dimmer by the minute. Reaching behind her neck with her free hand, she slipped the boot lace over her head and set the sunglasses down on the rocks in front of her. Then she moved carefully to the opposite side of the passageway.

More rapidly than she would have believed, the cougar charged and pounced on the sunglasses, then tried to stop, confused. It turned toward her, a silhouette that blocked the faint light. Its jaws were a foot from her face, and she could smell its awful breath. She gave it a full blast of the pepper spray in the eyes and mouth.

The cougar screamed in anguish, pain, and rage and rolled, confused, carried by its own weight down the slope.

Sylvia picked up the sunglasses with the lights, put them back on her face, and scrambled as quickly as she could toward the mine exit.

She didn't know if the cougar had fallen down the air shaft or would come back, but she would be out in the open, better able to defend herself.

56.

"Face down on the ground! Now!" the lead man from the helicopter commanded.

Tom did as he was told. He felt someone grab his wrists and bind them behind his back. Then he was picked up by the back of his shirt and stood up while someone frisked him. "Uh, huh," a voice said as he felt the punch knife taken from his belt.

"We've got to get Sylvia Hansen out of the mine," Tom tried to explain. "I'm Tom Godot. Did you get my signal?"

The face of the man who stood in front of him was blacked with camouflage paint. "What signal?"

"From the EPIRB in my watch."

"Your watch?"

Someone pulled up his sleeve, removed the watch. "This?"

"Right."

"It's er, all right. This is our man. Let him go."

Tom recognized the voice. Peter, pumpkin eater, the blue-eyed man. "You got here pretty fast."

Peter had changed from his three piece business suit to a black SWAT team uniform, but the blue eyes were as Tom remembered. "I was right behind you when you left National airport."

Someone snipped the plastic tie that held his wrists.

Ted Brewer had his hands raised and was frisked, too, his hands cuffed behind him. "He killed Kilgore Smith!" Brewer shouted, "pushed him down the mine shaft."

Peter turned toward the mine entrance. "Sylvia's in there?"

"Last I saw," Tom shouted. "She's trying to climb out an air shaft. She's a rock climber."

"We'll send a team in." Peter turned to a man who was wearing ear phones and holding some sort of radio with a directional antenna. "What have you got?"

"Several signals. There's one from inside, one from Godot, here, another from that guy over there, and one..." He swung the antenna. "Up there!" He pointed up the mountain side.

Moving among the trees Tom saw a figure in blue. "There she is! It's Sylvia!"

Sylvia picked her way between the trees and scrub undergrowth. Her Lycra pants were torn and she had blood on her forehead from where she'd bumped her head. Tom scrambled up the slope to meet her. "You made it."

"Thanks to your pepper spray. There was a cougar in there." She paused, remembering, then broke suddenly from his embrace, turned away, bent over and wretched. Then, wiping her face, she managed a smile. "They shot at me." She had held herself together during her ordeal, but now that it was over started to tremble. She was suddenly weak, barely able to stand. She started to cry.

Tom kept his arm around her and helped her down to the group of rescuers gathered away from the whirling propellers of the helicopter. Tom had to shout to be heard. "I want you to meet Peter. At least, that's what he says his name is. He's from the MacArthur Foundation in Virginia."

The helicopter engine shut off and the whirling stopped. The dust settled. Again they could hear the wind rustling the tops of the pines. Now there was the sound of a vehicle coming up the narrow road. A black Jeep Cherokee came over the rise, pulled to a stop and several men in suits stepped out.

Tom recognized one of them. Like Old Faithful. "Agent Gaiser!"

Agent Gaiser approached. "What's this all about, Godot?"

"Like I tried to tell you."

The man who called himself Peter approached the FBI agent. He took out his wallet and showed some ID. "Let's, er, talk about this in private." The men walked to the jeep for a conference.

Ted Brewer was still shouting at Tom, "Murderer! You're worse than all the rest."

Peter and the FBI agent had come to some sort of agreement. Agent Gaiser took charge of Ted Brewer and read him his rights from a plastic card.

Peter returned. "I dislike these interagency squabbles. Makes, er, for too many shouting matches. Let's get out of here."

Sylvia fetched her overnight bag and boots from the mine. Three of the SWAT team headed in with flashlights and ropes to get Kilgore Smith's body.

Smith's corpse was zipped into a black, plastic body bag and placed on the floor of the helicopter at their feet. Tom stared at it. He felt sick. He had never killed anybody. He told himself it was an accident. He had only meant to upset Smith's aim. Would he be charged with involuntary manslaughter? This wasn't one of those stories where James Bond has license to kill, where everybody dies but no one gets hurt. Smith must have a family. There would be an autopsy, an inquest and an obituary in the paper, a funeral, mourners and a coffin. Pictures of Tom Godot, trying to hide his face from the cameras as he was led from the courtroom in manacles. He could expect a trial and a maybe a prison sentence.

The helicopter engine roared and the ungainly machine lifted off.

Peter relieved Sylvia of the sunglasses. "I'll take those," and untied the little Conspiracy! flashlights. "Yours, too, Tom. Can't have your signal confusing the team."

"There are more," Tom shouted over the sound of the engine. "The ACLU lawyer has one. And Rick, the computer hacker, has my laptop and the encrypted first draft of the book."

"Let's hope we catch up with him before he does any damage," Peter replied.

It was too noisy for conversation. Tom looked out the window of the helicopter. He had never flown in one before. When they came over a ridge and he saw the interstate below he remembered the Toyota Tercel parked at the ramp in Smelterville. "Can you put us down at Smelterville? My car is there."

"All right. But I want you two to meet me at the airport. You'll have to come back to Washington. It's time you met the person you know as Harold Stevenson."

57. Stevenson

The same Lear jet that had flown him to Washington and back on Sunday now carried Tom, Sylvia, and Peter across the country. This time he had his luggage, even the partial case of books. He'd checked out of the Comfort Inn and dropped the rented Tercel. Though he hoped never to return to Coeur d'Alene he was certain that it wasn't over. Brewer would be charged with kidnapping and he'd be forced to return as a witness. He was too ashamed to consider returning for Kilgore Smith's funeral. He didn't to face the man's relatives and friends.

The more he thought about what Brewer had said, the more Tom suspected that Peter or the FBI or whoever was behind all this would cut a deal with Brewer in exchange for his cooperation as a witness against the members of the Aryan Nation and the Idaho Nazis.

The long flight would have given the man who called himself Peter plenty of time to explain what was going on, but he was back in his three piece suit and secretive mode. When Tom quipped that with so many cross country flights he must be picking up plenty of frequent flier points Peter flashed a brief attempt at a smile. He wasn't one to make small talk. Instead, Peter hunched in a seat near the front of the plane, making calls on his cellular phone with frequent glances toward Tom and Sylvia at the back.

Tom cradled Sylvia in his arms. She had recovered from the aftershock of her escape from the Lucky Lady mine. Though she was as close as a hug, her mind was elsewhere. She had turned in on herself.

"You did good, Sylvia," Tom said. "I could never have climbed out of that air shaft. You've got a helluva lot more guts than I have. I've had fear of heights ever since I got stuck on the roof as a kid."

She took his hand and held it in a motherly fashion. "You'll get over it."

She didn't return his embrace. There was something else on her mind. "Just what's this all about? Who are the MacArthur Foundation?"

"I think they're a front for the NSA," Tom speculated. He tried to get his rescuer's attention. "Peter! How did the MacArthur Foundation figure out what Stevenson was up to?"

"We didn't. We have to thank your boss, Ivar Hansen, for that. He was lurking in the system at MOM and recognized the codes mentioned in the first draft. It had to be someone who worked at MOM on the chips. It was a breach of security, so he notified NSA."

"I remember how he snooped when I was doing the memoir. He'd have access to all the files Poobah protects." To Sylvia, "I should have asked your uncle Ivar after all. I bet he knows who the real Harold Stevenson is."

Sylvia was still reliving the shock of the last two days and had drawn away from him. Looking back on their night of intimacy, on his initial embarrassment and failure, on her awakening, Tom realized that he was just a stepping stone. She had come to him because he was available, not a threat, someone to satisfy her curiosity about sex and to deal with her own anxieties and frustrations. He realized she had used him, but his affection for her overcame any resentment he felt upon that realization. We all use one another, he reasoned. As long as they were willing participants, both parties gained, but she had stumbled into the fearful intrigue. She obviously didn't want any part of it.

In the case of Conspiracy! he had been used, too, but he'd been unaware of the intentions of whoever masqueraded as Harold Stevenson. He had been conned.

Sylvia hadn't conned him. She had trusted him as a partner to help her solve whatever problems she had with her sexual inhibitions and he was more than willing. He cared about her more than ever, more, he realized, than she cared about him. He was no knight in shining armor, but he had become something else, not just your ordinary nice guy. Intentional or not, he had killed someone.

When the plane landed to refuel Peter didn't say where they were and wouldn't let Tom and Sylvia off the plane except for a quick pit stop at a hangar toilet. He didn't want them to be seen.

At Washington National airport it was the same routine as before, the chauffeured Lincoln town car with the dark, tinted windows, the same sterile apartment with no sign of habitation.

Peter apologized, "It's er, only one bedroom but I think the couch opens up. There are towels in the bathroom." To Sylvia, "I know you'll want to wash up. You've had an ordeal. It wasn't in the game plan. Sometimes things go wrong. Don't leave the apartment. I'll be back soon."

When the door shut behind Peter and they were alone Sylvia asked, "Tom, what's going on? I don't understand?"

Tom put his fingers to his lips and whispered, "Neither do I, but I'm sure whatever happens in here is recorded and filmed."

"You're starting to believe Mr. Brewer's tall tales."

"Whatever. If we're here long enough to stay overnight I'll sleep on the couch. I don't want us to be in any porno film."

"That's all right," Sylvia said, then corrected herself. "I mean, it's all right for you to sleep on the couch, not to be in a film. I hope there isn't a camera in the shower, because I'm going to take one."

While she showered, Tom found the remote for the television and channel surfed until he found the CNN evening news. They had not made the national news, no story of best selling author accused of murdering Aryan Nation Nazi, no dramatic rescue of kidnapped damsel in distress. They were not even a blip on the screen. Nothing out of the ordinary was happening, a storm, a shoot out, a scandal in Washington, a plane crash. What else was new?

Tom and Sylvia fairly jumped when they heard a key in the door and Peter came in. "What would you prefer? Dinner first? Or a visit to, er, your co-author."

Tom had waited too long already. "My co-author."

They crossed the Potomac and were driven back into Washington. The evening rush hour was over. Tom didn't know the city and had no idea where they were. Finally the Lincoln pulled up in front of a row house in an upscale neighborhood. There was no name on the door and no number.

Peter rang the doorbell and waited. After a long time the door opened.

What struck Tom first was the man's collar, a high foam padded affair worn by people who suffered whiplash or a neck injury. He was middle-aged and wore a bathrobe and slippers. He had not had a haircut in a long time. His hair, gray at the temples, was unruly. Tom concluded that this was a man who did not get out in public, a recluse, an eccentric. Tom guessed he would have a cat.

He did, a white Persian that rubbed against its owner's pajama cuffs. The man scooped up the cat and held it gently, stroking it, while he tried to collect himself. He was nervous, even fearful. His lower lip trembled. "Peter? What's wrong?"

"I've brought your co-author, Tom Godot."

Now the man smiled as if relieved. "Oh. Then it's over."

"No, it's not over," Peter said. "Can we come in?"

The man backed away from the door. "I wasn't expecting visitors."

It was an untidy apartment. Newspapers were stacked beside the couch. Books lay about, open, as if he would start to read one, then begin another, or read several at once in a state of distraction. No one had dusted in a long time, and there was an unmistakable smell of cat.

Peter noticed the chairs were full of cat hair and chose not to sit. "I think you already know this young lady."

There was no recognition at first.

Sylvia was puzzled. "No."

Like so many apartments, this one had a fake fireplace with a gas log. There were framed photos on the mantelpiece and Tom recognized the people in one of them though he had not seen the picture before. It was Ivar Hansen with his wife, his brother, Sylvia's mother, Ivar's sister and a man he did not know, but could guess. "Erik Streicher."

Peter had a look of sudden admiration. "Excellent! You're very good, Tom."

Sylvia grabbed Tom's arm for support. "Uncle Erik!"

Erik Streicher realized who she was. "Sylvia! How very grown up you are." He had a sad expression on his face and seemed suddenly to age. "It was a long time ago. I'm sorry."

Sylvia was searching her memory. Her expression changed from curiosity to understanding and finally to anger. "You! You son of a bitch!"

Erik Streicher did not look like a monster. He looked like a defeated, middle aged eccentric, a recluse who had no friends and whose only company was a cat. "I meant no harm. I couldn't help myself. They made me go through therapy. Behavior modification, they call it. Electric shock. I don't have those fantasies any more."

"Do you know what effect that can have on a child? Have you any idea?"

Now Erik's expression changed. "Do you have any idea what they did to me? The divorce? Banished. Shunned. When the family memoir was published I was left out of it entirely, as if I was not only dead but had never lived."

Tom tried to explain. "They wouldn't let me make any mention of Erik Streicher. I didn't know anything until Sylvia told me afterwards."

"You think I'd let your Uncle Ivar get away with it? Just erase me like some mistake on a blackboard?"

Tom began to understand. "So you said you were Harold Stevenson and asked me to co-author a book. But how would that get you even with Ivar Hansen? That doesn't make sense."

"It does if you know what I know," Erik Streicher said with a diabolical look on his face. "I helped program those MOM chips for the communications satellites. I knew the back door to the control system. I knew how to show whoever wanted to use the information how they could bring down the whole system, and then blame it on Ivar Hansen. That would bust his ego balloon, that self-serving egomaniac, handing out copies of his family history to everyone in sight and trying to pretend I never existed."

"Then it could work," Tom said, "that crazy plot in the first draft about blackmailing the government and threatening to shut down world communications if the money wasn't paid."

"It would have, but then Ivar Hansen snooped in the files. Remember what you wrote in the memoir about his father and the OSS? He's got clandestine operations in his blood. Ivar sicked Peter and his pals at NSA on me. They decided to use Conspiracy! for their own purposes. That's when they told me I'd either go to prison or, if I cooperated, simply suffer house arrest. You see this collar?" He pulled away the foam padding. Underneath the high foam was another collar, a thick, leather band. Ivar pulled gently at it and showed the skin under. It was chafed and red. "Cute, isn't it? Instead of an ankle tether like they do for prisoners under house arrest they made me this special one. It's armed. If I try to remove it it will blow my head off. If I go beyond the front steps it gives me an electric shock like a dog.

"But we rewrote the book," Tom said, trying to understand. "None of that information has gotten out. You haven't committed any crime."

Now Erik Streicher was laughing. He had to steady himself on the back of the couch, knocked a book onto the floor, picked it up. "You know so little, Tom. Have you ever heard of the Mills-McNaughton Act?"

Tom hadn't.

"It's an act providing for the preventive detention of subversives. All buzzwords to hide the truth. The Mills-McNaughton Act allows the government to track and imprison for an indefinite period anyone they think is a danger to the security of the United States. NSA considers me a danger."

"But preventive detention is illegal. You can't imprison someone because he might some day commit a crime, but hasn't yet."

Erik Streicher's eyes rolled. "Oh yes? Wait until they put one of these collars on you, Tom Godot."

Tom looked at Peter. "Is this true?"

Peter gave him a weak smile and the shadow of a shrug. "The world is a complicated, dangerous place. We have to be prepared."

So, Tom thought, Ted Brewer's fears were correct. The Sons of Liberty and the Aryan Nation were not entirely crazy after all. There was a conspiracy, and he was part of it, witting or not. These were powerful forces, people with hidden pools of government money, the ability to muster a SWAT team on short notice and to fly across the country in Lear jets. And the authority to arrest whoever they thought might be a danger to state security.

Tom should have felt trapped, but he turned to Erik Streicher and smiled. "You may have got your wish. A guy named Rick has my laptop and the first draft of the book. He may very well decrypt it. He knows the pass phrase."

"The wages of sin is Death. Capital D."

"Right."

Peter was still confident. "You said he has one of the transponders. We've traced his cell phone. He won't get far."

Tom was no programmer, but he had heard of trap doors, easy entrances that bypassed all the firewalls. "Rick is a pretty slick character, even if he does have a pierced eyebrow and wear a baseball cap backwards."

"We'd better go," Peter said. "I have to make sure our people have caught up with that hacker."

"Wait!" Erik Streicher pleaded. Again he was the mild, defeated recluse. "Sylvia. I'm sorry. I beg you. It was a long time ago. You were just a little tike. I was confused and couldn't understand my own emotions. Can you forgive me?"

Sylvia had recovered from her shock. "I forgive you. It's in the past. Let's forget it." She held out her hand toward the unkempt, shabby figure in the leather collar, the drooping bathrobe and slippers. Then she abruptly changed her mind and gave him a quick embrace."

Erik Streicher tried to put his arms around Sylvia but with a sudden shudder of revulsion she pulled back.

When they last saw Erik Streicher he was leaning against the couch, his face covered with his hands as he made stifled animal sounds.

Peter hustled them out of the row house and into the back seat of the waiting Lincoln. He whispered an urgent call on his cellular phone as they drove away. Then he turned around and faced them with a bland look as if nothing had happened. "I understand you like Italian food, Tom. Washington is a wonderful city for food. All those, er, government expense accounts. How do you like veal parmesan? It's time you had a dinner on me."

Epilogue

Jake Friedman finally got through on the third number.

"Mary McGann."

"Jake Friedman in Portland. I'm trying to catch up with Tom Godot."

"You're in luck. He's here in my office. I'll put him on the speaker phone."

Jake Friedman rocked back in his recycled office chair and swiveled so he could look out the window. It was raining in Portland, not a heavy rain, but one of those week long soakers that softened the hillsides and flooded the creeks. "Tom!"

"Yes."

"Saw you today on Good Morning America. Sally and I watched the show in the kitchen. You were terrific. That kidnapping story, and the escape from the gold mine..."

"It's a silver mine."

"No matter. I thought Sylvia Hansen would be on the show with you. What a love story."

Tom corrected him. "It's not a love story. She's gone back to the university. I'm not part of her long range plan." He sounded regretful.

"Too bad. The phone's been ringing off the hook and several faxes were waiting here when I got to the office. Looks like we have a movie deal for Conspiracy! What do you think? Could you write a screen play?"

Tom didn't answer at first. "Don't know the first thing about it. I seldom go to the movies. I don't even own a VCR."

"Too bad. How about another book?

"I've already started one," Tom said.

Jake Friedman could smell a movie sequel. Conspiracy II. "What's it about?"

"My book tour."

Mary McGann broke in. "How many movie offers have you had?"

Jake told her.

"Then it's time for an auction," McGann said. "I can see we'll have to print another hundred thousand copies."

"It all goes to show what hype can do if you have the right backers." Tom said. "But this time we'll put Erik Streicher's picture on the dust jacket along with his pseudonym. The man deserves to be remembered, no matter what he did."

Friedman had a copy of the Oregonian on his desk. The story of Tom Godot and the Aryan Nation was alluded to in a review of the book. Life imitating art, the reviewer wrote. "What's this reference to the National Security Agency?" Friedman asked.

Tom Godot's voice had a hesitant quality. He was choosing his words carefully. "Rumors."

"Sure someone doesn't have a gun to your head?"

"Or an exploding collar around my neck, like Sylvia's Uncle Erik?"

"It was too bad about that. Funny way for someone to commit suicide."

"That's what they're calling it," Tom said. "Personally I wouldn't be surprised if it was set off by remote control. Don't quote me on that. I don't want any hassles with the FBI. They're threatening me with a manslaughter charge unless I make some sort of a deal. I can't talk about that. At least they got my laptop back."

"Where was it?"

"Inside my briefcase in a dumpster along with a transponder someone gave me. The FBI tracked it down, but not the hacker. He's disappeared."

Mary McGann broke in. "About this auction. Why don't we set it up and you can fly to New York for the event?"

"Any time."

Tom had other news. "Jake, did you hear? I've got a fan club. It's linked to my web site."

"How did you manage that?"

"I have a fan in Washington, a remarkable lady who always wears red and is called Lady A. She's in charge of all the mailings."

A fan club for an author was a gimmick Jake Friedman hadn't thought of. He was a happy man. Being agent for Tom Godot and Conspiracy! had won him mention in Publisher's Weekly. The phone was ringing. Eager authors were pestering him to represent them. He had hardly begun and he was already looking for assistants.

In the afternoon, between CNN reports of the latest Washington scandal and genocide in Africa there was a flash about a communications satellite gone awry. The satellite used to relay signals for beepers and cell phones had started spinning out of control. No one knew the cause. The company that owned the satellite promised to shift the transmissions to rented space on another. It might take a few days.

The satellite failure reminded Jake Friedman of Godot's book. Could there really be a conspiracy to disrupt world-wide communication, or was it just a coincidence? This communications stuff was beyond Friedman's understanding or his interest. Technology didn't impress or intimidate him. As long as his toaster made toast, he was satisfied. If the fax machine croaked, he'd find another at some garage sale. If a communications satellite failed, someone would just send up another, wouldn't they?

The end?

About Harley L. Sachs:

Though born in Chicago and raised in Indiana, Harley L. Sachs considers himself an international, having lived in Germany, Sweden, Scotland, and Denmark. He earned a degree in English at Indiana University, then served in the US Army in Germany. After getting his Master's degree at I.U. he returned to Europe and worked under cover for several years. He met and married Ulla in Stockholm, Sweden and they spent a year's honeymoon in a Scottish castle. Returning to the USA, Sachs taught English briefly at Southern Illinois University then moved to Michigan Technological University in the Upper Peninsula where he and his wife raised three daughters. He took early retirement and now lives in Portland, Oregon.

Harley L. Sachs is the author of many novels, short stories, magazine articles and newspaper columns. His short stories have been broadcast on the BBC World Service short wave and on Oregon Public Radio's Golden Hours .

If you enjoyed *Conspiracy!* you may want to order *Betrayal*, the first in the Irwin Glass series. Here's a sample:

She came through the doors of the American Library in Moscow, a dark-haired, gorgeous woman in a long coat with her Slavic face framed by a fur collar. It was one of those first impressions that imprint on your mind and stay with you forever. Stunning, like being struck by lightning. I remember Dante is said to have seen Beatrice only once as a young girl, and she haunted him forever. It was like that with me and Svetlana. Standing with a tray of shots of sour mash American bourbon I took one look at her and was smitten. It was a look that has haunted me ever since like a blessing, an enigma, and a curse.

My interest in Russia began when I was only ten. I was just a kid, but what happens when we are ten years old can set the pattern for an entire life. As a ten year old I found an old shoe box of family pictures in the attic of our South Bend, Indiana home. There was a shoe box with a medal in it, a purple heart, and a picture of my dad in uniform, standing with a bunch of buddies in a tropical place I guessed was Vietnam. I knew my dad had been in Vietnam, but he never talked about it. I knew when he saw homeless vets begging on the street he always gave them a dollar. He didn't wear one of those baseball caps emblazoned with "Vietnam" or "veteran." He wanted to forget all about it, never talked about the war. I didn't even know where Vietnam was.

What struck me even more than my Dad's army photo was a cracked, yellowing portrait of a shabby-looking man posing uncomfortably in a studio. On the back of the photo was some printing I couldn't read, and the address of the studio, I guessed, and the city, Moscva. I showed the picture to my dad, who was irritated that I'd been going through the stuff in the attic. "That's your paternal great grandfather Isaac Melamed," he explained. "I think he fled Russia to escape conscription for twenty-five years among the Cossacks."

That's all he told me. There was also an old letter in the box of photos written in a foreign cursive text and small, so whoever wrote it could get the most on a single sheet of what must have been expensive, very thin paper. Someone had removed the stamp from the envelope and the postmark was illegible. I wanted to read the crabbed handwriting, and felt like if I couldn't read it—no one else in the family could— I was denying part of our ancestry. All I knew then was it was Russian. I didn't know if it was from Isaac Melamed or some other relative. It was a mystery.

I loved mysteries. I used to read kids' books, like the *Mystery of the Spanish Treasure* and stuff like that. This was a real mystery. What was that forgotten or hidden past? As a kid I did not know about family genealogy and my parents didn't care. Busy making a living and involved in their own day to day existence, my folks had no interest in family history.

I figured out that Moscva was Moscow and I found it in our atlas. I didn't know anyone who could translate Russian. Even if I did, I wanted to read the Russian letter myself. The South Bend library didn't have much about Russia, but what little I found intrigued me even more.

Having no other particular interest, when I went to Indiana University in Bloomington I majored in Russian Language and Literature. It turned out that I had a knack for foreign language. Other students just memorized vocabulary and grammar. I embraced it. After four years I could almost pass for a native speaker, except for lapses of an American accent. There are some things you can learn only in the country itself. It followed logically to get a Masters in International Relations.

My father taught high school social studies in South Bend, was forced by a shuffle of personnel and budget shortfalls to take early retirement and while I was away at grad school moved to a double wide in Ocala, Florida The irony was that after all that preparation the shoe box of family photos, dad's medal, the Moscow photograph and the letter in Russian, the original catalyst, were left behind in the South Bend attic for whoever moved into the house. I guess dad didn't care, was too busy, or didn't want to remember.

I took the Foreign Service exam. My Russian language skills got me the five point bonus and I passed even though I had to detect subtle nuances in editorials in *Pravda* and *Isvestia*. My Russian language fluency pointed me in the direction of the then Soviet Union

Though President Reagan and Gorbachev were talking about arms control, the cold war was still on. It's different today. Back then the American embassy in Moscow had been bombarded with microwave transmissions that forced them to cover all the windows with aluminum shutters. The transmissions hadn't been intended as an attack on the health of the personnel inside, but to activate the bugs planted in the walls, the furniture, and so on by the KGB snoops.

I was apolitical. I had not voted for Reagan. In grad school I had not bothered to register. But the State Department wasn't supposed to lean toward one party affiliation or another, so being neutral was a good thing.

As part of my studies I had read "Will the Soviet Union Survive until 1984?" That year had passed and the Soviet Union was still intact. Gorbachev seemed to be going strong with his Glasnoz, Openness, policy.

Getting to Russia was the fulfillment of a dream, the achievement I had worked for through six years of college. I wanted a posting to somewhere in the Soviet Union. The only job for which there was an opening was at the USIA library in Moscow and I took it, hoping to move up in the Foreign Service later. The main thing was to get into the system even though the job at the American library was not a perfect fit.

So here I was at last, in Moscow. Wow! It was a thrill for me to stand in Red Square, the site of all those displays of military might in the May Day parades. The Soviets were smart, making Lenin's tomb the platform for the reviewing dignitaries. Troops passing on parade were saluting both Lenin and the Soviet leaders, a powerful symbol.

But the Russia I found wasn't quite the world I had imagined when reading *Crime and Punishment*. That was nineteenth century czarist St. Petersburg. Dostoevsky's Russia was before the telephone, when to reach someone across town you sent a telegram which was then delivered by some poor functionary in a shabby uniform.

This was the Soviet world of palatial Metro stations, crowded busses, and Russians who looked at me with envy when I returned to my billet with groceries from the American commissary. Russia had food shortages, and the affluent capitalist Americans were both resented and envied. The xenophobic Soviets regarded all foreigners as spies. Well, I was not a spy, and when riding the busses hid my purchases out of shame for my relative affluence.

What the American library needed most was someone who knew contemporary American literature. In grad school I had been so busy with Russian and Soviet literature and International Studies that I was weak on American lit.

The library director, Susan Lutz, would have preferred someone else. I realized that, but did not take the incipient hostility seriously. I saw the library job, while not terribly prestigious in itself, as a stepping stone.

Until I got tripped by a beautiful woman and a glass of vodka.

Ironic how one night of indiscretion can ruin your life.

....

Betrayal is also bundled with the three volume sequel *Retribution.* and *Burnt Out.*

Here's a list of books by Harley L. Sachs:

MYSTERY NOVELS

The Mystery Club Series

THE MYSTERY CLUB SOLVES A MURDER

First and most popular of the Mystery Club series. Mary Higgins finds the body of Dora Reed on the roof of the Plaza retirement building, notifies the police, then tells the Mystery Club. They assume several suspects: the manager of the Plaza, Dora's son Donald, or a Plaza employee. Dora's husband, Ed Sutherland, is in Hawaii on board the yacht Miss Chief with an all girl crew. Carrying on their own investigation, the Mystery Club finally suspects Sutherland, though he seems to have a perfect alibi. If they can prove it to their satisfaction, will a court ever convict him-- if he can be found somewhere in the Pacific?

THE MYSTERY CLUB AND THE DEAD DOCTOR

Second in the Mystery Club series. The Mystery Club consists of five elderly women who live at the Rose Plaza and discuss mysteries written by women. The Mystery Club ladies have no idea of the consequences when Viola Cartwright, their blind member, asks them to go over her Medicare bills. That leads to suspicion about the identity of her personal assistant, Dorothy Anderson, who turns out to be using a stolen identity. Viola's doctor runs a phony clinic owned by a member of the Russian Mafia. Soon the investigation of Medicare bills leads to murder and tragedy, stopped only by the courage of Mary Higgins.

THE MYSTERY CLUB AND THE HIDDEN WITNESS

Third in the Mystery Club series. The ladies of the Mystery Club discover one of the residents is a crook under WITSEC, the witness protection program. He apparently keeps dipping into the employee gift fund. The Mystery Club bands together to track down the missing money, but what they discover is danger.

THE MYSTERY CLUB AND THE SERIAL WIDOW
Fourth in the Mystery Club series. Caroline Kostinsky, new resident at the Rose Plaza, is a widow four times over and she's looking for a fifth husband in retired General Hardcastle, but when drunk she says she killed all of her husbands. Except for her confession, there's no evidence. Now what?

DELIVER ME FROM EVIL
Responding to a posted invitation for new members for the Mystery Club, Judge Ira Kahane and Ursula Besette show up. Ursula, at a turning point in her life as a new Rose Plaza resident, is interested in Wicca and Kabala. Roberta Nelson believes one should not suffer a witch to live. Judge Kahane tries to lead Ursula on the right path, but there is conflict and tragedy coming.

WHITE SLAVE
Sequel to *The Mystery Club Solves a Murder*. The appearance of Ed Sutherland's gold bracelet in a Portland pawn shop revives retired detective Casey's interest in the cold case. He doesn't know that Sutherland has been picked up and is a slave on a Korean fishing boat. Sutherland, penniless, .without clothes or identification, is stranded in New Zealand. Can he find his way back to Portland and be somehow redeemed or face a death sentence for first degree murder?

The Irwin Glass Series

BETRAYAL
Prequel to *Retribution*.   Irwin Glass, BA in Russian, MA in International Relations, has a promising career in the Foreign Service in Moscow until he is snared in a classic "honey pot" seduction. He's young and naïve, honest, always wants to do the right thing, but at every turn he is betrayed.   The incident in

Moscow destroys his career. He is accused of being a paid Soviet agent and is pursued by the consequences of his encounter with the KGB twenty years later. Some enemies never let go

RETRIBUTION
Sequel to *Betrayal.* Newly married to Ivy Hartshorn, Irwin Glass gets a dunning letter from the IRS for taxes on interest at the Washington, DC account he didn't think he had. It's a joint account with his missing birth daughter and the balance is huge. Assuming it's money Katya's KGB father of record, Vladimir Putinsky (now Putin) deposited for her living expenses, Irwin moves it to force her to contact him. But Ivy warns him that he is laundering money and the people it belongs to will come after him. Irwin's complicated life is catching up with him, but this time he will find retribution.

BURNT OUT
Irwin Glass is approached by FBI Agent Wilkins who asks for Irwin's lists of foreign students. Not satisfied he wants more and is looking for potential terrorists among the Moslem students. Gradually Irwin is sucked into the role of FBI informant on the Michigan Institute of Technology's Muslim Students' Association and the results are tragic.

THE IRWIN GLASS TRILOGY
All three Irwin Glass books in one package deal. The Irwin Glass Trilogy combines all three of the Irwin Glass Mysteries: "Betrayal," "Retribution," and "Burnt Out," following the chaotic career of Irwin Glass who began, in "Betrayal," as a state department clerk in Moscow only to be caught in a classic honey pot seduction. Betrayed at every turn, he was sent back to the United States in disgrace to try to start a new life. No such luck. His teaching career is upturned by the revelation that the Moscow seduction had a consequence in the form of a beautiful student Katya who claims to be his daughter. In "Retribution," Irwin's KGB nemesis is in the United States seeking political asylum, but in fact is fleeing the Russian Mafia with Irwin as quarry. After "Retribution," Irwin thinks he is

home free of all that intrigue, but the local FBI agent has a hold on him and wants information about potential terrorists among Irwin's students at Michigan Institute of Technology. There are risks to being a reluctant FBI informant, and Irwin's reports may be misconstrued with tragic results. What Irwin and his wife really want is a normal life, but his mysterious Russian birth daughter Katya remains an enigma. Is she or isn't she?

Other Mysteries

MURDER BY MAIL

German exchange student Klaus Hitz is more interested in making money than in asking questions about his work assignment. He doesn't know that the industrialist father of his punk girl friend is using him in a terrorist conspiracy to kill everyone in the United States with a mass mailing of a scratch and sniff virus. The plot begins to unravel when a Polish nurse brings blood samples from Libya and alerts a CIA agent. While the CIA and FBI track down the terrorists, Klaus Hitz gradually figures it out. How can he avoid being murdered or imprisoned for being naive?

MURDER IN THE KEWEENAW

CIA agent recovering from Post traumatic Stress after failed missions in Finland and a divorce is fishing in Lake Superior when he snags a corpse. He thinks he has seen the girl before and his attempt to identify her leads him to a ring of deadly pornographers. It almost costs him his own life.

CONSPIRACY!

Technical writer Tom Godot can't believe his luck when CONSPIRACY!, the book he has co-written with the elusive Harold Stevenson, is a hit. The book details a plot to hijack communication satellites. As Tom crosses the country on his book tour, he is disturbed by people interested in early drafts and dogged by an NSA agent. Communicating by fax with his editor and by encrypted e-mail with the mysterious Stevenson, Tom reaches out in his loneliness to his California girl friend

Sylvia Hanson who turns out to be a pivotal figure.   There is another conspiracy, and Tom is part of it

THE GOLD CHROMOSOME

When Adam Rottman's childless Aunt Sadie Gold died, the eight cousins learned her estate was in an irrevocable trust, the proceeds going to Adam's sister Sarah while she lives.   After Sarah's death, the money would go to the last surviving cousin. It's a fatal tontine Adam's lawyer brother Harold set up. Would the cousins kill each other for one million dollars? Sarah's car is found in the river, but not Sarah.   That begins a series of mysterious deaths.   Coincidence? Or Murder? Who will be next? Adam and his psychologist wife Deborah must stop the chain before he, too, is eliminated.

BEN ZAKKAI'S COFFIN

Born of a Jewish father and a Catholic mother, Herman Bachrach insists he has no religion, but he is drawn by circumstance into a holocaust vendetta over gold stolen by a Swiss bank from Jewish depositors.   Seduced by a woman who calls herself Diana, no last name, Herman is suspected by detective Sheehan to be her murderer.   Someone else wants him dead.   His Jewish boss provides him with a lawyer, but sends him to Switzerland to finish the job "Diana" started. It's an assignment he can't refuse.   The result is an epiphany of identity that changes Herman's life forever.

THE LOLLIPOP MURDER

A warning for wannabe novelists! What happens when a stable of neurotic novelists who live in their pseudonyms and are bound by iron clad contracts are invited aboard their miserly Florida publisher's yacht for the Miami Book Fair only to find that they have no hope of ever earning a dime of royalties for their books? All this as Hurricane Gerta threatens to sink the yacht at the dock.   It's grounds for murder

NOVELS

SAM IN LOVE
A coming of age romance for mature young adults. U.S. Army life in Europe in the 1950's was an equivalent of the Grand Tour of the eighteenth century when young men traveled and sowed wild oats. Marty, roommate of Sam Logan, a PFC draftee serving in the US Army in Munich, Germany, says all Sam needs is to get laid. Sam is not a virgin, but has a Midwestern ethic and believes in love. He doesn't know quite what that is. No Casanova, Sam, through a series of tentative encounters, thinks he's found the love of his life.

STOPRAPE.COM
Kerstin Mikkola, a young TV reporter at KDUP in Marquette, Michigan has hopes of a better network job. Her interview with a marine victim or rape might be just the ticket. Her interview about the web site StopRape.com goes viral on U-tube and Kerstin finds herself in the thick of consequences she did not anticipate.

THE ACCIDENTAL COURIER
A romance, road trip, and mystery all in one. Charles Kosko, retired orchard owner from Oregon, decides to take a bus trip in Europe and finds himself involved in a whistle-blower's scheme to discredit an American cell phone company that uses rare earths mined by slaves in the Congo. Unable to speak any foreign language, and without his US passport, he is picked up by a beautiful Israeli woman who says she is his driver. But is he really her prisoner? They are pursued by an African mining engineer, who hopes to intercept the delivery of stolen rare earths,

SCI-FI AND FANTASY

NEVER TRUST A TALKING HORSE
The narrator of this dystopian novel escapes preventive detention into a world he discovers has gone mad. Hungry, he is told he can eat for free at Lachumba's supper club, only to discover that he might be the main dish. He rescues Iris I. Iris from the ovens and in a series of episodes explores the

insane world in search of a livelihood. He gradually realizes why he was incarcerated in the first place, but by then it is too late. His and Iris's roles have been reversed. Arrested, they are given a sadistic sentence which is their final challenge.

THE SEARCH FOR JESSE BRAM
Jesse Bram, the young hero of this metaphysical science fiction adventure, is unaware of his Jewish roots. An Eldre of mixed breed, he is marooned on the post apocalyptic shunned planet URth where technology and books have been destroyed. The URthlings variously view Jesse as a bringer of cargo for the half-breed prefect Hrod, as the reborn Savior by crypto-Christians, and as a link to the past by a remnant of Jews. The Galactic Federation suspects him of treason and he is pursued by an enigmatic Trinian policeman. If Jesse survives, will he be convicted? If acquitted, what next?

SHORT STORIES

THREADS OF THE COVENANT: THE JEWS OF RED JACKET
A collection of twenty-one short stories about Jewish life in small town America centering about two main characters, David Katz, the only Jewish boy in Red Jacket, and Richard Goldman, the only Jewish professor at Copper country Community College. Each story depicts another aspect of what it means to be a Jew in a small town as each character comes to realize his own identity.

MISPLACED PERSONS
Though set in different locales what these stories have in common is a central character who is out of his element, in the wrong place, coming to grips with cultural, generational, or physical displacement. In PROBLEM FOR THE TEACHER an expatriate fumbles for a living; in LIMBO an ex-G.I. is adrift in Copenhagen; in TRIUMPH OF THE WILL a nervous wreck seeks recuperation; in MISCALCULATION a

would be tax evader succumbs to his own fears; in THE LIE a drunk gets himself into difficulties, and in THE GIRLS OF FREDERIKSHAVN an old man is trapped by girls looking for action.

YOOPER TALES AND OTHER FUNNY STUFF

Extracted from the massive volume of Sachs's published Essays and Columns: 1992-2011, this collection of stories related to Michigan's Upper Peninsula, known as the UP, home of Yoopers, reveals the truth about snow fleas, ice worms, the humungous fungus (world's largest living thing) and the rigors of winters in the remote north woods. You can also learn how to catch and cook the Mosquito Giganticus and why visitors won't come. Sachs has several awards for his humor.

AHOY! QUARTERDECK!

Originally published as IRMA QUARTERDECK REPORTS but re-released with new illustrations and, in the paperback edition, with sea shanties, this funny book is a series of boating anecdotes about Irma and her bumbling husband Ralph ("I can't believe I lost the anchor") Quarterdeck in their many boating adventures and mishaps. One reviewer says the book is as informative as Chapman's famous manual, but more fun. Readers will find plenty of laughs in this book and at the same time learn a great deal of boating fundamentals.

ANNA-LENA'S TROLL AND OHER STORIES

Each of the three Sachs daughters has a story in this children's book. "Anna-Lena's Troll" explores the nature of trolls, which represent the dark side of human behavior as Anna-Lena's nasty letter to Santa is rewarded by the gift of a nasty troll. "The Return of Baby Suzy" is the true story of Cynthia's worn out doll and its resurrection. "The Stars for Christmas" is the remarkable surprise Belinda got along with her new eye glasses. Other family stories are Christmas related.

NON-FICTION

THE MISADVENTURES OF CPL. SACHS
Adrift through college at Indiana University, author Sachs was drafted at the end of the Korean War. Physically unfit for combat, he was sent to Queer Company for basic training, then by a fluke was shipped out to Germany instead of Korea. Thus began his own version of the traditional Grand Tour.

FREELANCE NONFICTION ARTICLES
This third edition of a monograph on freelance writing first published by the Society for Technical Communication is newly updated. This little manual provides tips for interviewing, article structure, article preparation and submission, photography, and business practice.

CHILLY-CHILLY-BANG—HOW WE FREELANCED THROUGH EUROPE'S COLDEST WINTER IN A VW WITH A KID
Companion piece to *Freelance Nonfiction Articles*. The former is a how to book. This is a "how we did it" memoir. The author knew nothing about Volkswagens when they set off, but as they worked from VW dealer to dealer getting the old Combi fixed, he learned! It's as much a book for VW enthusiasts as it is for writers.

Both FREELANCE NONFICTION ARTICLES and *Chilly-Chilly-BANG! How we Freelanced Through Europe's Coldest Winter in a VW with a Kid* are combined in a double volume, *The Writing Life*.

THE 1957 SACHS ARCTIC EXPEDITION
After military service in Germany the author took the GI Bill to Sweden. With no income in the summer, and not even sure there was a road to the far north, he set off hitchhiking to North Cape, the northernmost point in Europe in search of the midnight sun. Illustrated.

FROM TENT TO CASTLE: MEMOIR OF A YEAR LONG HONEYMOON

Setting off from Stockholm, Sweden on rebuilt one speed bicycles, Harley and Ulla embarked on an open-ended honeymoon with no fixed destination and equipped with a tent, a thin double sleeping bag, a tiny gasoline stove, and $3000. After arriving in Britain, Ulla discovered she was pregnant. Tired of unrelenting rain, they advertised for a cheap place to spend the winter. They were offered the gatehouse to Borthwick Castle outside Edinburgh, Scotland for $25 a month by British author Theo Lang.

"IS"

As Bill Clinton said, "It all depends on what the meaning of "is" is."

A problem we all have is distinguishing between what is real and what is not. This is in fact an age-old question. This volume switches between classical instances of the problem to the author and his psychiatrist and his wife. What is real? That all depends on the meaning of "real."

QUEER COMPANY

Not a gay novel, this is a fictionalized memoir of an experimental basic training unit at the end of the Korean War. All the draftees were physically unfit for combat but the army didn't want to discharge them. Instead they got modified training in a company unfortunately designated Q. In the Army phonetic alphabet Q is Queen, but Q company was called queer. A copy is in the US Army historical archives.